Scintillate

THE LIGHT KEY TRILOGY

Scintillate

THE LIGHT KEY TRILOGY

TRACY CLARK

Entangled Publishing, LLC
2614 South Timberline Road
Suite 109
Fort Collins, CO 80525
Visit our website at www.entangledpublishing.com.

Edited by Karen Grove and Kate Fall
Cover design by Pamela Sinclair

Ebook ISBN 978-1-62266-146-6
Print ISBN 978-1-62266-145-9

Manufactured in the United States of America

First Edition February 2014

ONE

I was kindling for the fire raging in my body. Whole one moment, but soon reduced to ash. And the world would forget I had ever existed when the wind scattered me to the stars.

It's possible that feeling like death made me morbidly poetic.

A hand touched my fevered brow, leaving behind a ghostly imprint, as if I'd been branded with ice. I floated in a haze of voices and images. Sensations pricked at me from the world, but I had one foot out that door, frustrated that no one would let me go through it. My blood flowed searing and thick through my veins, and my mind took to conjuring relief, dreaming I floated on sheets of water beneath an icy moon, though my body burned under its cool gaze.

Every ounce of strength had been wrung out of me. Janelle found me on my hands and knees on the bedroom floor, trying to crawl to the toilet. She had to help me to the bathroom, even pull down my undies for me, which might have mortified me if I'd had the energy. Right then, I decided I could maybe love my stepmom.

"I think we should take her to the ER," I heard my father say before I threw up again. Another racking spasm of heaving and spitting, my body turning inside out.

"I'll go start the car," Janelle said. Her frantic vibe scared me more than my father's thinking I was sick enough to warrant a hospital visit. I heard the rattling of keys, the slam of the kitchen door to the garage. Disjointed, frantic whisperings faded in and out. Then it was really quiet for a long time. Or a minute.

In the ER, white walls and strange faces rushed by in a blur.

Blood pressure.

Blood tests.

Foreign latex hands on my barbed skin.

"Her temperature is 106.2," the doctor said. "It's dangerously high. Because of the vomiting, I'm going to administer a rectal suppository so it will stay in her system long enough to start working on her fever."

"Great," I groaned.

My father smoothed my hair. "Sorry. I think it's necessary, sweetheart."

I nodded. They could stick that medicine in every orifice I had if it would make me better.

"We'll give her something for the nausea and an IV. She's likely very dehydrated."

I dry-heaved again to punctuate the doctor's comment, then I drifted off into a strange half sleep with no peace. My flimsy awareness was like a pesky mosquito I couldn't swat. My body ballooned and shrank, in my mind, to strange and disproportionate sizes. I was sure if I opened my eyes, my hands would be big, helium-filled, Macy's Thanksgiving Day Parade versions of themselves while my head would be as small as a tennis ball.

Pain pricked the soft inside of my elbow. In my bleary daze, I could swear my father was drawing my blood into smooth little vials that clinked together when he dropped them into his breast pocket.

"Could this have anything to do with her mother?" Janelle

whispered.

I fought to stay alert, needing to hear his answer.

He responded with silence. Janelle's voice lowered. "What if Cora's got it?"

My already erratic heartbeat stumbled.

Dad didn't answer her. He did that—left questions lying on the ground like dirty socks.

I fought against the oblivion blanketing me. I wanted to ask him why *he* was taking my blood. I wanted to ask what Janelle meant about my mother. I wanted to ask him so many things, but sleep dragged me under to where there were no answers.

Sometime later, a few pairs of hands lifted me off one bed and onto another much colder one. Freezing, actually. My back arched with the shock of it against my bare skin. Like lying on one of those gel ice packs Janelle insisted on putting in my lunch bag.

"It's c-c-cold."

An unfamiliar voice answered, "I know, sweetie. It's a refrigerated bed. We need to keep your body temperature down, get the fever under control."

Every nerve in my body came alive, making my sensitive skin feel like an angry army of sharp new hairs were pushing to break through. My teeth chattered, and I tasted the sharp tang of blood from biting my tongue. "This—this is inhumane. C-can I have a blanket?"

"Sorry, Ms. Sandoval. The point is to cool you down, not warm you up. No blanket. You can have this sheet, though." She draped scratchy fabric across my legs, too insignificant to count as covering. My shivering started almost immediately, a deep shaking that rumbled from my chest outward.

Eventually, I slept, though fitfully due to a creepy light that appeared whenever I closed my eyes. It began as a far-off point but advanced—bit by bit—toward me. My stomach clenched with fear. The light moved deliberately, as if nothing on earth could stop it. As if it were time itself stalking me. A lucid shred of my mind knew this must be delirium from the fever, but it didn't make it any less scary.

I wished Dad were with me. He'd hold my hand and talk until I fell asleep to the soothing timbre of his voice in the Chilean accent everyone said he had but I couldn't hear. When he talked, I only heard…my dad.

I was a child of accents I couldn't hear: Dad's Chilean one, inaudible because I was used to it, and my mother's Irish accent that had faded from my memory because she didn't bother to stick around.

All I inherited from my mother was my fair Irish complexion. My curvy figure was pure Chileno, as was my hair: deep brown, almost black, and wild as if it had been wound around thick tree branches every night.

My awareness drifted below the waves and bobbed back up to the surface now and then, especially when people came into the room. It was like my body registered their presence before my brain did. I wrestled one eye open and saw the outline of a tall, gangling man standing in the doorway. The glaring lights of the corridor behind him were so bright, the man himself was shadow. He stood absolutely still, watching me. I wondered if there had been a shift change with the nurses and, if so, why wasn't he, you know, *nursing me* instead of standing there, staring?

Chills assaulted me again, a rolling tremor that made my skin hurt and my chest ache. "Please…," I mumbled, though I didn't know what I was asking for.

The man glided into the room, bringing the bright, white light with him so that the hall behind him darkened as he walked toward me. With every step he took, my heart picked up speed, churning to life like an accelerating train. An icy wind blew through me, taking my breath with it.

He stopped just out of arm's reach and continued to stare at me with dark eyes. They had a crazy look to them, the kind of eyes you see in pictures of serial killers, deranged and remote. This man didn't belong here. I knew he didn't. *What do you want?* my brain screamed. I opened my mouth but couldn't form words, could barely keep my eyes open. I struggled for air.

The light reached into me. I was being pulled out of my body. Evaporating. I crossed my arms over my chest, trying to hold me in. The man took a step back. A flicker of frustration passed over his face. He backed out of my room, his light retreating with him. From the doorway, he gave me one final look, a chilling smirk.

"A mighty flame follows a tiny spark."

"What time is it?" I asked in a scratchy voice when the nurse came in for the umpteenth time to check my temperature.

"Almost morning. The doctor will come see you in a while."

I swallowed past the burning in my throat. "Is my dad here?"

"I think he's the gentleman sacked out on our waiting-room couch. Devoted guy, your father."

I half smiled. "He is." After my mother's disappearing act when I was five, it seemed like he tried to love me twice as much so I wouldn't feel the sting. It still stung. What he didn't realize was that twice as much love was like wearing twice as many seat belts. His love was starting to feel like a five-point harness.

"Knock, knock." My father stood in the doorway. His pants were a wrinkled mess, as was his shirt. His tie was gone, and one sleeve was rolled up to his elbow; the other flopped around his wrist. It was alarming to see his meticulousness so spoiled. He ran his fingers through his salty black hair and walked to my bedside, nodding politely to the nurse as she left. "How're you feeling?"

"Tired. I swear they checked my temperature every hour last

night. As if anyone could sleep on this icebox anyway." I fixated on the slow drip of IV fluid streaming into my arm. "And you were here, right? You took blood samples from me." My eyes flickered up to meet his. "Why?"

"I did," he admitted, grudgingly. Were all scientists trained to be vague in case they couldn't prove their hypotheses?

"But you study *outer* space, not inner."

He smiled, wry and sparing. "They're not as different as you think, kiddo." He ran his hand over my forehead, a temperature check concealed in a gesture of affection. "I wanted to run some tests of my own. You've been very sick, honey."

His answer gave as much satisfaction as chewing on air. "Tests of your own?" I pressed. "And why did Janelle ask if my sickness had anything to do with my mom?"

"Janelle was worried, grasping. This has *nothing* to do with Grace." He sighed as if her name was heavy coming off his tongue. "There have been some mysterious deaths, not anything the general public needs to know about yet, but I'm on a team that's working to find out what might be the cause. Keep that between us, okay? I took your blood as a precaution." He shrugged like, *can you blame me? I'm your father.* "Your hospital tests aren't back yet. They still don't know what's wrong with you. There was one point when they weren't sure—" Dad's voice cut out before continuing. "Losing you, Cora— I'm not sure I could've dealt with it. Not you."

We stared into each other's eyes, saying all the words we never said aloud about loss, about fear for the other's safety. About love. It was an old, silent conversation we'd shared at different times over the years. Though lately, our real conversations had become a little more combative since I realized we were on opposite sides in a war of independence.

Dad broke the silence, his eyes glassy. "Thank heavens you're a fighter."

Strange that Dad would call me a fighter. *Me?* The quiet, introspective book lover. No one had ever called me a fighter before. I barely remembered the last twelve hours. I had been in another place, floating in and out of consciousness.

What part of me did the fighting?

Dad bent over and placed a gentle kiss on my head. As he straightened, a fuzz of light formed around his head, undulating like heat waves on pavement, as though he were going to slowly rise up into the ceiling.

I recalled the strange man from last night. A chill passed over me. I didn't exactly have a handle on the past few hours, but I remembered being scared down to my soul. Did I have what people called a near-death experience? If so, there was anything but love and peace in the white light.

I reached for my dad. "My eyes are funny."

He squeezed my hand. "You're tired. As soon as the doctor is done with us, I'll make sure they let you sleep for a good chunk, okay? I'll go find her now."

I nodded and blinked, but still the distortion around my dad persisted. Even as he walked to the door to look for the doctor, the hazy light followed him, seemed part of him. He was mountain and he was mist. I closed my eyes. I was just tired.

Janelle made a drive-by visit, a Tasmanian devil with control issues and impeccable nails, dropping off folders of schoolwork, neatly grouped by color and stacked by due date. She had already arranged a makeup date for my missed math test. She exhausted me, but I appreciated her efforts. I was happy when Dad had finally remarried five years ago. He deserved to have a life, and I had hoped it'd take his focus off me so I could have one, too. That hadn't exactly panned out.

Just when I began to sink back into my pillows, the door swung open again, and I couldn't have been more surprised by who entered. Of course, I knew of Finn Doyle. The whole school knew of the intriguing new student from Ireland. Despite the fact that he was from the place of my birth, and that I'd cultivated a robust obsession with Ireland since my dad moved us to the States when I was little, I'd never tried to get to know him.

Finn Doyle had unfortunate taste in friends.

He was one of *them*. The banal, popular crowd I found so irritating. I nicknamed them the VIPs. (Vapid. Irritating. Populars.)

I gaped at Finn in his striped volunteer apron as he neared my bed, while trying to ignore the cloud of colors surrounding him. It wasn't unpleasant, though. Kind of like the sun was setting over his shoulders.

"A *guy* candy striper?"

"That's surprisingly discriminatory. The family friend I'm staying with, who since birth has been *male*, works here as a lab tech. And I do believe your doctor is a woman. I'm willing to bet the world's ready to accept a guy candy striper," Finn said in his thick Irish accent. He followed through with a wide, teasing smile.

There was something so focused about him as he spoke to me, it was unsettling. I scowled, getting on my own nerves for allowing Finn Doyle to make me self-conscious. I did my best to avoid the VIPs at all times. They were like soul sandpaper. Some of my humanity rubbed off with each interaction.

It didn't matter that Finn had been in the States as a foreign-exchange student for only a couple months. They'd snatched him up and adopted him the minute he landed. Gorgeous guy from Ireland with impossibly adorable accent equaled immediate *in* with the VIPs.

"I'll have you know a guy can deliver flowers as well as a girl can," Finn continued. "Perhaps better." He gave a slight bow and whipped a bouquet of daisies from behind his back. My dad always gave me daisies. "More flourish and technique."

An insufferably amused smile curled the corners of his full lips. I noted a dimple on his left cheek and added it to the list of his irksome qualities. I looked away from him, out the window, anywhere else.

"I've seen you around school before," he said thoughtfully. "You seem different somehow, up close."

Did he have to point it out? "I've been *sick.*" I was sure he heard the word "moron" at the end of my sentence, even if I didn't say it.

"Right. Well, I imagine being in the hospital would make anyone cross. Or is this your normal disposition?" he asked, setting the flowers on the bedside table and arranging a few stems to his liking.

I glanced sideways at him. "Yes."

Finn leaned in and adjusted my pillow. He was so close I could see the faintest hint of a tattoo reaching up from his chest to his neck. I had an intense, irrational desire to know what the tattoo was, and it was all I could do to fight the forceful urge to pull his T-shirt collar down for a better look.

Finn smiled a pirate's smile, rogue and full of mischief. His gaze flitted from my hand back to my eyes, and I realized I *had* grabbed Finn's T-shirt and still had it wound tightly in my fist.

Startled and flushing, I released him. The impulse had been powerful, overwhelming, but how could it make me act without any awareness or control? It was disturbing. I drew the sheet up to my chin, wishing I could sink into myself and disappear like a TV fading to black.

Clearly, the fever had fried a few brain cells, but still I recognized his tattoo—three interconnected spirals spreading like the traces of fingertips over the left side of Finn's chest, teasing up to his collarbone.

I'd seen the triple spiral before. It was a symbol carved into the megalithic stones of Newgrange, one of the world's oldest prehistoric sites atop a grassy hill in Ireland—older even than Stonehenge or the Great Pyramids. Though the symbol of the three spirals had been hijacked by Celts, Wiccans, and even Christianity over time, no one had a clue as to the original meaning of the carving. I had a picture of it in my Ireland scrapbook.

I longed to ask him about it, to feed my hunger for all things Irish, but I couldn't hoist myself over the wall of pride I'd already erected. Not to mention swimming through the moat of embarrassment after grabbing his shirt like an idiot. "Sorry," I murmured.

"Cross is okay," Finn said, low and husky in a way that underscored his words. "There's not a sailor on the planet who doesn't love the challenge of a good storm." I could see the smile in his eyes and how he fought to keep it from his lips.

We eyed each other. A deeper gaze than anyone besides my father had ever dared to hold with me. It was unnerving, but I was determined not to be the first to break it. The VIPs could *smell* weakness. I might be the quiet type, but I was not in the mood to be toyed with.

Finn studied me a moment more. "Your eyes remind me of home," he finally said, and walked out.

Two

As quickly as the illness came, it disappeared. Well, almost. An MRI, a neurologist, and an eye doctor could find no medical reason for the visual "anomaly." They even tested to rule out a stroke. I was finally discharged and sent home, which would've been a relief if my eyes weren't still funkadelic, projecting ghostly colors around everyone.

I begged Dad to take the scenic route home from the hospital, winding on West Cliff Drive, past the Santa Cruz boardwalk and beach. I gazed out the window at the blue-gray Pacific. It always struck me there was a whole universe under that live expanse of water, so much more than hinted at by the surface.

Kind of like people.

I steadied the vase of daisies between my knees as we rounded another curve. "Thanks for the flowers, Dad."

His brow scrunched up into a series of thin lines. "I didn't send flowers."

"Oh," I said, thinking suddenly of the boy who delivered them. I pushed the thought of Finn Doyle out of my head. "Probably Janelle,"

I speculated aloud, but found myself fantasizing that my real mother had sent them. It was a secret game I'd always played with myself. She was somewhere close by, watching over me. She knew when I was sick. When I was little, she had watched me at the park as Dad pushed me on the swings. Did her legs twitch to run to me when I fell? Did her fingers ache to wipe my tears when I cried? My mother was a constant spectral presence—and not just for me. I could see Dad's hyperawareness when we were out in public, glancing around a little too much, always looking over his shoulder.

Maybe he played the same game.

Before I could censor it, the question fell from my lips. "Do you think Mom could be nearby?"

Dad squeezed the steering wheel a bit harder. "No. She's nowhere nearby."

His certainty irritated me. "How do you know? Do you know where she is?" The words dropped from my lips like petals. Fragile. Easily crushed. I held my breath.

His eyes met mine. Couldn't he see the hope there? But his next words were cold, hard. And final. Petals crushed under his heel.

"I know she's gone."

A lump formed in my throat and wouldn't go away no matter how many times I swallowed. We were quiet the rest of the way home.

"Don't you find it disturbing they can declare me healthy when I'm seeing all these weird colors around people?" I asked Dad as we got out of the car. He supported my arm as we walked from the driveway to the house. I didn't need it but let him help me anyway.

"You had a very high fever, Cora. A fever like that can have serious repercussions, but you've been cleared by your doctor. I'm sure it'll resolve in short order."

I snatched my arm away. "Nice, dismissive way to talk about my possible *brain damage*."

"Let's see how it goes. If you're still…seeing things after a few days, then we can take you to another specialist."

"But, Dad, it seems like it's getting worse, not better."

He halted on the brick walkway. "Stop being melodramatic, Cora. You're fine!"

It was so uncharacteristic of my father to speak that way, I almost laughed. But his anger was startling, made even more so by the muddy red color that erupted from him like a solar flare. I watched it, mesmerized, then pointed at him. "Red."

Dad flung open the front door. "You'd better go to your room and lie down."

I stepped past him and walked inside to the squeal of "Welcome home!" from Janelle. I marched under a homemade banner and clouds of balloons and went straight to my room, slamming the door. Hot anger flowed through my body in a rapid current, heating me uncomfortably. I wiped my sweaty palms on my pants.

Some people were intent on acting like lower life forms devoid of sensitivity. I was in eleventh grade. I got that every day in school. What I didn't understand was why my own dad was doing it. He completely dismissed me, treated my concern like a trivial performance. I wouldn't lie about something like this. I was scared something was truly wrong with me, permanently damaged. Who was I supposed to talk to about it, if not him?

I rolled onto my bed and stared out the window, watching the blue sky turn milky in the fading daylight. When the room grew too dark, I flipped on the lamp next to the bed. As I pulled my hand back, a streamer of light followed behind like the afterglow of a sparkler.

I held my hand up and stared. A bright silver hand-shaped halo pulsed around my skin as if it were fiery, splintering metal. When I moved my hand, the light moved with it. Wiggling my fingers did not make it disappear. Swooshing it from side to side only made the streamer effect stronger. Awe and worry crashed inside me.

There was a light knock at the door. I stuffed my hand under my leg as Janelle burst in with a bed tray. "Dinner! I thought you might like some real food after that hospital stuff. You don't even want to *know* the things they've found in hospital food. I saw this documentary once, on *60 Minutes*. They found like eight different kinds of hair—"

"Thanks, Janelle," I muttered, completely losing my appetite.

She touched my forehead, her expression concerned. "Some homecoming, huh?" Her head bobbed as if it would incite me to agree. "Your dad is just tense. He was *so* worried about you! I've never seen him that distressed. You'll both be right as rain in the morning."

What if I'm not right as rain? What if my brain is permanently fried? What if I still see the jagged, forest-green color stretching out of your perfectly coiffed head?

"I'm sure we will be," I said. "Thanks for the dinner. I'll eat a bit before I go to sleep. I think I'll go to bed early so I'm rested for school."

"Oh, Cora. I don't think you ought to jump right into school tomorrow. Why don't you give it a couple of days? I've already contacted your teachers. You were practically at death's door."

"You didn't need to do that. Really, I'm fine. It's the last month of school, and I already missed one test." I attempted a smile, but it fell flat on my lips. "With finals coming up, I don't want to get any more behind than I already am." I wanted life to get back to normal, but as I looked at my hand again—pulsing with brilliant silver—I knew in my gut my train had jumped the tracks.

THREE

My stomach fluttered nervously as I got dressed for school and saw how pronounced the silver light was around my entire body. With or without clothes, I glowed. I sparked. I looked freaking flammable. The shiny light was a part of me, moved with me, flared out from my torso when my anxiety erupted.

Something was definitely wrong with me, and I wanted to know what. The fever had to have affected my brain, and it was getting worse.

Exhibit A: the patrons in the busy Starbucks all had bodies shrouded in misty blankets of color. I stood in line before school and tried to gawk inconspicuously. Not an easy thing to do. I was sure that anyone who really looked at me would know I was an agitated mess. Good thing people don't *really* look at each other.

I fixated on the woman in front of me who, if you counted the misty blue-white fog around her, had a personal space boundary of about three feet, nearly touching my abdomen. I took a tiny step back.

It would be one thing if my eyes projected the light consistently, but no two people glowed exactly the same. I shifted from one leg to the other, eager to order my coffee and wait outside for my cousin, Mari. Preferably at a table where I could close my eyes for a couple of minutes and turn this off. I had to get my wits about me before school. Janelle might have had a point about not rushing it.

The room suddenly grew cold.

Icy air spread across my back.

My eyes blinked heavily as my energy plunged. People faded in and out of focus, and I swayed on my feet, my legs rubbery. A heaviness spread through me, as though an iron anchor had been cast inside my body. I rolled my gaze over my shoulder, that simple movement causing my stomach to lurch. Behind me, the same dark eyes that had stared coldly in the hospital stared at me again. The man, who was shrouded in a solid cloak of white light, stood a few feet away, and an invisible rope of taut energy stretched between us. It was as though he were tugging on it, pulling me out of myself. I felt the same weightlessness, the same sense of bleeding invisibly as I had in the hospital. But when I opened my mouth to cry out, I was unable to make any sound. Feeling a snap of release, I pitched forward, and the man walked out of the building into the bright morning.

My heart thumped as I waved off people's offers to call someone for me and stumbled out into the morning sun. I looked up and down the street for the man before collapsing into a metal patio chair. Breathing deeply, I willed myself to calm down and think rationally. What in the hell was that? I had thought, maybe, the hospital incident had been a delusion brought on by fever, delirium. But that was the same man, affecting me in the same terrifying way. I was sure of it. The same man who had frightened me by whispering about fire and sparks.

He never touched me. So why did I feel as if I'd been severely violated?

Mari smiled as she marched toward me, her pace exact, like she had gone through boot camp as a toddler. I watched shimmering gold light dance off her olive shoulders and wondered if it was the screwy vision thing or her shiny shirt reflecting in the sun. Mari had a sequin addiction. All attempts at intervention were unsuccessful.

She looked at me from behind the curtain of her short black bob. "Why are you staring at me with crazy eyes?"

I blinked. "Uh, because only you could pull off combat boots with a sequined tank."

"Thanks. Seriously though, your mouth is talking fashion," Mari said, leveling her gaze at me, "but you look like you were just visited by a clown carrying a doll, with slasher music playing."

"*Shhhh*, it's only seven a.m., and I've already had more bizarre than I can handle," I answered in a quivering voice.

"Okay, let's get our caffeine, and you can tell me all about it while we walk to school. Dun's waiting for us. Are you okay to go to school? You look like hammered crap."

"Thanks." Part of me wanted to go home and crawl in bed. But aside from seeing colors around everyone and the abrupt blanket of fatigue covering me since I saw that man, my body was fine. My psyche was a mess. Maybe school would be a good distraction. I was spooked, and didn't want to be alone.

We sipped our lattes while walking. Mari's lips tipped up in an amused grin when I told her about meeting Finn in the hospital. "Finn Doyle delivered flowers to you? That's almost worth getting deathly ill for."

"I know, right?" I inwardly cringed at the thought of seeing him at school. I was baffled by my behavior. Mostly, the part where I had lost all control of my faculties and clutched his shirt like a thug in a dark alley. The only thing worse than doing that was not knowing why. It had been uncontrollable.

"So, how you doin'?" Mari asked.

"Better. But they ran more tests because my vision is…fuzzy."

"Well, your fever was so high, you probably nuked your brain. I bet there's a mushroom cloud of intelligence around your head."

"That's the problem, though. There seems to be a mushroom cloud around *everyone's* head." In fact, the light surrounding Mari's entire upper body appeared to expand and contract when she breathed. I rubbed my eyes again and sighed.

"You'll be okay, *prima*. Not to change the subject, but I'm changing the subject. School's almost over. You think your dad will finally let you come to Chile with me this summer? Plans are in the works already."

"Yeah, right. I think we're lucky he lets me go to public school with you. If he had his way, I'd still be homeschooled, I'd never leave the house, and if I did, I'd be bound in Bubble Wrap and have an armed escort."

"To need an escort, you'd have to actually *go* places."

I glared at her. "I go places."

"Uh-huh." Mari linked her arm through mine, and we walked around to the front of the school where our best friend, Dun, sat on the retaining wall in front of the flower beds. The ends of his long black hair lifted with the light breeze, as though invisible fingers caressed the silky threads.

"No guy should be allowed to have prettier hair than chicks," Mari said, waving him over. She could always be counted on to speak her mind, and she usually said what I was thinking but was too shy to say. Nobody seemed to get offended when she threw her curveballs of truth at them. Maybe it was all in the pitch.

In the last year, the Good-Looks Fairy had paid Dun a visit and granted him another foot of height so he towered over us at six feet, with broad shoulders and a fierce Apache-warrior look. He didn't seem to realize he had changed, which only made him cuter.

The day Dun became my friend, I was thirteen and I'd discovered him crying into his knees against a tree outside my house. He was bloody and bruised from being beaten up by Mike Hahmer, then just a mini-VIP. Mike had tried to cut off Dun's long black braid.

It sucks to say it, but Dun was ripe for picking on back then. Raggedy clothes that were always too small and smelled faintly of old lunch meat. He was Native American, and the boy had actually worn moccasins. Some people are not enlightened enough to deal with moccasins.

I remembered Dun sniffling pitifully and saying, "He said he was 'scalping' me." Mike hadn't finished the job. The braid dangled like a broken tail, cut halfway through. I convinced Dun to come in. Mari showed up, and the three of us powwowed about the half-shorn braid. We declared that he should obviously have a Mohawk because he was Apache and because it was very badass. From that day forward, Dun walked a bit taller. And nobody messed with him. Not that anyone would mess with Dun with Mari around. People could sense the undertow of danger in her. She was the only girl in a family with four brothers—that was practically prep school to be a lethal female assassin.

"Oh, and brace yourself," Mari whispered to me. "Dun's gonna grill you about Chile, too. He's serious about going. His grandma said if he can pay for it, he can go. I'm donating airline miles to the cause."

"You want him to go *that* badly?"

"Obviously." Mari gave me a sideways glance. "I want you to come that badly, too. But money's not your problem."

It was so wrong that Dun might get to meet my own grandmother before I did, but there was no point in griping, yet again, about my dad's militant overprotectiveness. I'd never get to go to Chile *or* Ireland, no matter how many times I asked. My chains didn't reach that far.

Dun kissed my cheek, then Mari's. "How are my girls?"

I swear I inhaled a palpable hit of happy when Dun touched me. I would also swear he was glowing a bright, sunny yellow. My mouth dropped open in astonishment that the color matched the bright mood. "I was worried about you. Mari says you're seeing double or something. Am I doubly handsome this morning?" He grinned.

I glanced around at the throng of students passing in all directions, swirls of colors trailing after them like their own personal clouds. The colors had substance, too, like fabric. There were endless variations, prismatic and ever-changing. I felt light-headed.

Dun eyed me with concern. "You okay?"

"I-I don't know. Don't make fun of me, but I'm seeing colors around everyone. It's overwhelming, like walking through a kaleidoscope." I looked down at my shoes. "Strange things are happening… It's scary," I admitted in a microscopic voice. "I think something is seriously wrong with me, and my dad is totally blowing it off."

And something about my mother. What happened to my mother?

"Well," Mari said, her brown eyes taking a thoughtful skyward slant that meant she was thinking, which could be dangerous. "Let's whomp on this with some research."

I eyed her skeptically. "No offense, but if the doctors don't have a clue, how are *we* supposed to come up with the answer?"

"Aren't there a ton of sites, like, what-the-hell-is-wrong-with-me dot com?" Dun asked.

Mari smacked him in the back of the head.

"My dad made me swear I wouldn't look it up online. He says misinformation will only make me paranoid, that I should deal only in facts."

"Your dad never said *I* couldn't look it up," Mari pointed out. "Hey! We should e-mail Grandma. Mami Tulke's the authority on all things bizarre."

"Great," I said, with absolutely zero confidence that my little Chilean grandmother was going to be able to diagnose this strange ailment. "She'll probably advise me to sleep with a lizard skin under my pillow or something."

Mari knocked Dun's shoulder and motioned to me with her head.

"Speaking of Mami Tulke, guilt trip. Now."

"Oh, yes." Dun held up one finger and cleared his throat. "Rule number one of the Articles of Friendship states we do all things of a fun and adventurous nature together. Rule number two states that if you cannot adhere to rule number one, you'd better have a damn good reason."

"I love how many rules we have, yet there never seem to be more than two," I said.

"Mission statement. We are a non-club club with rules that are not rules," Mari said as if that cleared everything up.

"I think you two are forgetting that I don't have any decision-making clout here. My dad will never let me go. It'll kill me to watch you guys fly off into the sunset without me."

Mari elbowed me hard in the ribs. "Yo, Finn Doyle is staring at you, hard."

"No, he's not," I said, forcing myself to keep looking straight ahead. "Why would he be?"

Dun leaned in to Mari. "I think something *is* wrong with her eyes," he murmured. "Cora, you don't see what everyone else sees."

I dared a glance in Finn's direction, and our eyes met and held. The air around him pulsed with a subtle golden-pink glow that radiated from him in smooth waves. I blinked and tore my eyes from Finn's. Dun spoke the truth, all right. I was definitely seeing things differently than everyone else.

FOUR

All morning long I had floundered in my classes, distracted by the subtle haze surrounding my classmates and teachers and the gradations of the colors around them. At the end of each class, I couldn't remember what had been reviewed for finals.

It was like I could *see* people's needs and desires, their frantic plays for attention, their sadness, their longing to make other people feel what they were feeling. Though maybe I attached meaning to the colors to try to make order out of the chaos. It was confusing, and rather than forging a connection to people, it made me feel more different and alone than ever. Especially because the only color I ever saw radiating from myself was bright silver. It never varied.

Not once did I see another person with a silver shadow like mine.

Desperate to avoid the colorful mob of kids, I slipped into the Agriculture Center's greenhouse at lunchtime. It was my favorite place on campus. Warm, humid air settled on my skin as soon as I walked in. I could practically sense my curls springing up and my skin drinking in the moisture. I exhaled happily, letting peace wash over me.

Janelle had packed a typical pyramid-worthy lunch. Every food group was represented, except for the oft-neglected and woefully misunderstood top—the sugar group. When life got a bit heavy, sweets were my drug of choice. Janelle had left me without a fix.

"I'm so glad you're back, dear." Mrs. Boroff, the agriculture teacher, flashed me a warm smile. Her white hair was piled atop her head in feral ringlets like an aged Greek goddess. Her gardening apron stretched across her plump little body. I was always amazed at the amount of stuff she kept in the pockets of her apron. Mrs. Boroff went back to misting her beloved orchids. "I'll go out on a limb"—she chuckled at her own pun—"and say *they* missed you, too." Her fleshy arms gestured to the plants. "You've got the greenest thumb I've ever seen."

"Next to you, of course."

Mrs. Boroff sent a light spray of mist toward my nose. "Of course."

I watched, mesmerized, as the droplets floated down. Through them shone the clearest light I'd seen around someone so far. Mrs. Boroff's physical edges were blurred by soft green light tinted with gold. I couldn't see where her body ended and the light began, as though the light was a part of her.

I ran my fingers over my eyelids. It had been like this all morning, colors popping up and flowing around people, then disappearing. "If it's okay with you, I thought I'd have lunch in here today."

Mrs. Boroff peered above her bifocals. "You know it's fine with me. Are you hiding from anyone in particular?"

"Not hiding. I need quiet." Colors could be loud.

Looking through the glass windows, I noticed the VIPs frolicking in their exclusive little circle, backs to everyone. They always banded together in a wagon ring, emulating the pioneer strategy: keep the *savages* out.

I watched two girls who called each other best friends. They joked and giggled, but the reddish light around them was anything but friendly. It competed for space in angry jabs. It made me think of all the times my body tensed around the VIPs even though they were smiling to my face. Were invisible energies always there, always telling the truth, if only we knew how to decode them?

Finn Doyle laughed with Serena Tate, who had her hand on the arm of his striped shirt. I could see the outline of a white tank underneath it. His short dark hair was a bit wild, spiked and crested down the middle. He looked like a rock-star poet, all the dark temptation of a rebel mixed with a sweetness, like maybe his biggest secret was the teddy bear under his pillow. He laughed at something one of the girls said. When he turned on the full flare of his smile, he was undeniably stunning.

Finn looked up and spotted me watching. I had an absurd urge to duck but squared my shoulders and turned away.

"Enjoy your quiet," Mrs. Boroff said, heading out the door.

The door swung open again a couple of seconds later. "Forget something?" I called out to her.

"Yes. I forgot to properly introduce myself the other day."

My head jerked up. I liked the question in Finn's tawny eyes, to balance out his confident smile. I also liked the soft colors that blanketed him. He looked…warm.

"I know who you are." A barb of pain stung my finger when I carelessly pricked it on the needle of a cactus. "Damn," I whispered.

Finn stood beside me. "All right there?" He pulled my hand toward him to look. The crackle of energy between us flustered me, so I stared down at our hands together instead of looking at his face. Vapors of golden-orange danced from his skin. He wore a double strand of beads on his wrist and behind them, a leather bracelet with silver studs. The beads were gleaming and faceted, surprisingly delicate. *A gift maybe? From a girl back home?*

"Yes," Finn said.

"Yes, what?"

"You asked if these were a gift from a girl."

I slipped my hand from his grasp. "I did? No I didn't."

Perhaps I should've gone to the nurse. There was seriously something wrong with me. First, I fist his shirt like a deranged mental patient, and now I couldn't trust my mouth not to blurt out fluttering thoughts.

"My mother gave them to me. Before I came to the States."

"Oh? It's sweet that you wear them."

He smiled but crinkled his brows together. "Why wouldn't I?"

"They're very feminine," I answered, more bluntly than I meant. Coy and flirtatious were obviously not in my repertoire.

"In actual fact, she made me promise to not take them off." He fingered them lightly, causing the beads to sparkle in the diffused sunlight of the greenhouse. "So, are you saying you think I'm feminine?" he asked with a tilted smile. He leaned toward me a fraction closer. Intermittent hints of red hairs mixed with the dark whiskers on his jaw below his curved lips. I wondered what his bottom lip would feel like under the pad of my thumb.

I stepped backward, stuffing my rising hand into my pocket. Oh, hell no. There was *nothing* feminine about him. He was all male. It radiated off of him like fumes. But not in the testosterone-soaked way of most of the guys at school. He wore his masculinity like a light scent that made me want to get a bigger whiff.

Finn looked around the greenhouse. The sun-drenched room illuminated the flecks of honey in his eyes. "I've walked past this place a hundred times, but I've never been in here before."

I followed his gaze upward to the ceiling. The translucent panes of glass were of varying ages and colors. Some crystal clear, others a faint yellow and deep amber. It felt like being inside a prism, a weathered crystal hanging in the sun, casting slanted shafts of golden light on the emerald plants inside and heating Finn's distinctive colors.

"This place is a miracle. I don't blame you for hiding in here."

My gaze snapped to meet his. I looked into his eyes, which alternated between shy and knowing. "I'm not—I—I *am* hiding." I looked away, shocked at my admission. I plucked the spent stems off a geranium. "It's just that I can breathe in here." I sighed deeply, feeling decidedly short of breath since Finn had come in. How did he manage to suck all of the oxygen out of a place full of plants?

He cocked his head toward the window. "You can't breathe out there?"

I looked again at the wall of kids preening and posing outside, the overwhelming clouds of color rising and falling around them. "No."

"You're different from them."

Story of my life. I'd always been different, never fit in, but he had no idea how different I felt lately. "That's probably not a compliment, but I'll take it as one."

Finn tickled my nose with the tip of a fern. "I meant it as one."

I swatted it away. "Why are you in here? Really. Did one of *them* dare you to do this?"

He grinned, amused. "A skeptic, huh? If I was dared, it'd be something along the lines of 'I dare you to approach the beautiful girl with the large Do Not Disturb sign on her chest.'"

I stared at him. The light swirls of faint red and pale yellow radiated from him in tranquil drifts. Maybe it was the brilliance of the light in the greenhouse making me uncertain whether the light was his, but the strange thing was, I couldn't just see it, I could *feel* it. Strongly. Finn had gravity, pulling me toward him.

My hand was suddenly on his chest, quickly registering the hard heat of his heart under my fingers. I pulled it away as if I had been burned. Embarrassment mixed with confusion, warming my cheeks while giving me chills. "Go away," I whispered. "You're too…potent."

He bit his bottom lip and gave me a lingering stare. "I'll take that as a compliment. Until next time, Cora," he said with a slight bow of his head before walking out.

My body hummed, a warm aftereffect from Finn's visit, as I meandered through the greenhouse, examining the botanical prints and pictures Mrs. Boroff had tacked to the narrow wooden slats between the glass panes. Most looked like they came out of an ancient Latin field guide. There were a few contemporary prints of rare or extraordinary flowers. But one in particular caught my eye.

My heart quickened. Someone captured on camera what I had been seeing around people since I got sick. It was a picture of a maple leaf, but it looked like an X-ray. The intricate vein patterns were highlighted in brilliant white as if lit from behind. The leaf glowed with shades of purple, pink, and indigo. A luminous white light outlined the entire leaf. Starry points of it dotted the veins. There was an entire universe contained in one leaf.

"Can you tell me about this picture?" I asked Mrs. Boroff when she returned.

She pushed her bifocals up her nose and waddled over. "That, my dear, is a leaf."

"Clearly, but—"

"Beautiful, isn't it? It's Kirlian photography of the leaf's aura."

"Its *aura*?" I'd heard that word before but had assigned it to the realm of all things woo-woo, categorized with reincarnation, chakras, and past lives, a word belonging to the hippie types who made up such a big part of Santa Cruz. I couldn't believe the possibility hadn't occurred to me before that moment. "You believe in auras?"

"Oh yes, dear. Every living thing has an aura. It's the energy field around us. The *essence* of who we are." She leaned in and whispered excitedly, "Our dense little bodies can't contain *all* that we *really* are. We spill out around the edges."

With my thumbnail in my mouth, I asked, "Can people see auras?"

Mrs. Boroff winked. "Only the truly special ones. If you're interested, there's a bookshop called Say Chi's on Edgewood, near

Fourth Street." She scribbled the name and address on the back of a pansy seed packet and handed it to me. "That's where I found this picture. The store has an entire section devoted to Kirlian photography."

"Thanks, maybe I'll check it out."

Damn straight I would. As soon as possible.

FIVE

After school, I yanked my hair into a ponytail, wrapped my favorite green scarf around my neck, and went to the garage for my bicycle. I pulled the seed packet with the bookstore address from my pocket.

"Where are you off to?"

I startled. I hadn't noticed my dad sitting in his parked car in the dim light of the garage. He was home unusually early. I'd hoped to get to Say Chi's and back before he got home from work. "Why are you sitting there like a stalker, Dad?"

He climbed out of the car. "I didn't want to miss the end of the news segment on NPR."

He narrowed his eyes as if I were dodging his question. "Where did you say you were going?"

"I didn't."

"Right. That's the problem."

"Well, if you *must* know, I'm off to Say Chi's bookstore. The doctors are useless. I'm going to figure things out on my own." I rang the bike bell and pushed off.

"Hold on!" I stopped mid-pedal but didn't turn around. The

sound of his shoes shuffling toward me on the pavement played on my nerves. "You can't diagnose yourself. And Say Chi's isn't exactly a supplier of quality medical reference books." He held the seat of my bike, which made me want to jam on the pedals and rip it from his grasp. "Is your vision still blurry?"

"It's not blurry, Dad. It's clear. In fact, I feel like I'm seeing clearly for the first time in my life. I don't think there is anything wrong with my eyes. I think I'm seeing *auras*."

A phlegmy yellow pulsed from his chest like a festering sore, bringing to mind the phrase *yellow-bellied coward*. He swallowed with effort, his face now pale. "Auras?"

His fear sent ripples of dread through my body, concentrating in my chest. Hopefully, I was reading him wrong. "I think so. That's why I need to go to the bookstore. I'll explain it to you later." I expected further argument, but Dad let go of my seat and stared as if I were a ghost. As if he could see *my* colors rising from my skin into the clouds. It had been years since he had looked so sad. It struck an old, helpless chord inside my chest, so much so that I almost didn't leave. If he had continued to stare, troubled and haunted, I might have stayed. But he turned and walked slowly toward the house.

Instead of a bell, when I opened the door of Say Chi's, I heard a recorded female voice say, "Peace be with you." The scent of incense assailed me. At least it wasn't patchouli. That kind of stink was like dirty, weedy tar.

I scanned the large, airy space. Above the door was a round window with tiny circular windows inside it, like bubbles trapped within a bubble. It gave the store a bright infusion of dotted light. Exotic jewelry and scarves from foreign countries, Tibetan prayer flags, wind chimes, and tarot cards surrounded me. An enormous circular table was laden with various types of glimmering crystals.

There were books, of course, mostly New Age topics. I recognized one author, Edmund Nustber. When Dad couldn't sleep, he liked to watch his late-night show on TV, where the wild-haired Mr. Nustber raved about paranormal wonders, aliens, and crop circles. Janelle called him Edmund Nutbar.

"Hello, young lady." My head snapped up, and I met the direct gaze of a statuesque black woman with the most impressive head of dreads I'd ever seen.

"Your hair is art," I said.

The woman chuckled and rounded the table, grasping my hand in her own. "I'm Faye, proprietor of Say Chi's. What are you seeking today?"

Suddenly, I was beset with questions. Underneath all of them, what I sought most was to know what was happening to me and why I was different. "I think I'm seeing auras," I blurted, though I realized with relief that I hadn't seen any colors at all coming off her. It was a heavenly break.

Faye's hand slipped away. She took a few steps backward, and I wondered if I weirded her out. Then she said, "Do you, child? Can you see mine?"

I was being tested. Or doubted. Neither of which sat well with me. I didn't look directly at Faye, but just beyond her. Slight waves, like a mirage, shimmered off her head then faded. I concentrated. I thought I saw a deep blue flash, but then it quickly disappeared. "This is stupid." I turned to go.

"Wait!" Faye called. "What did you see?"

My shoulders slumped forward. A dead end. There were no answers here. The doctors were right. My father was right. It was all in my head. "Nothing. I saw nothing," I admitted.

Faye then slipped a shimmering crystal from around her neck. "Now?"

I blinked. Immediately, Faye's colors jumped into focus. Brilliant blue, like a morning glory, and the golden light of a candle on a dark night; both were most pronounced around her neck and head. "Beautiful," I whispered. This woman's aura was clear and defined, which was why the sudden infusion of black around her lower abdomen became so apparent. The black seeped into the light like spilled ink. I stared.

"You can see it," Faye said in a shocked murmur.

I nodded, dumbfounded. "Is something wrong with you?"

"Cancer. Caught it early, thank the Lord. I've told no one," Faye said, while draping the necklace back over her head. The light vanished.

I felt ashamed. Like a Peeping Tom. Did I have any right to see these private things? I impulsively hugged her, surprising myself. "I'm so sorry."

She laughed wryly and patted my back. "Sorry? No, dear. Don't be sorry. It's like being sorry your ears can hear Mozart or the wings of a hummingbird." Faye pushed me back at arm's length. "You look scared. I gather this is new, and you need to understand it."

Faye led me through the bookstore, past shelves of books on everything from occult practices to diets for your zodiac type. I watched as her thick finger trailed their spines. "Ah," she said, landing on one in particular. She tilted it out and passed it to me. *Beyond Form—How to See and Read Auras.*

"That ought to get you started. And this," Faye said, handing me a laminated sheet. "It's a color chart. It will help you recognize the meanings of the colors you see. But don't take it as gospel. Sometimes, the seer's own perceptions are more important. Pink is often described as a loving color, but if green is the epitome of love to *you*, trust it."

She offered a plate of cookies and looked intensely into my eyes. "You have a gift."

"It doesn't feel like a gift," I said with a sigh, taking a cookie. "How many people can do this?"

Faye smiled. "Not many, I suspect. Lots of charlatans claim to. I think you're the real deal."

"Is your necklace some kind of protection?"

She waved her hand and chuckled. "Ooooh, I sure hope so, from the energy vampires of the world."

I shivered, thinking of the man in the hospital and how I felt like my life was being sucked from me when he was near.

"Don't look so frightened. It's simply a figure of speech. Haven't you ever been around someone whose mere presence wore you out? They could be as nice as cool lemonade in summer, but instead of feeling refreshed, you feel just plain sapped?"

"I can think of lots of people who make me feel that way, especially at school."

"Ha! That's because teenagers are exploding with new energy." Her arms waved in the air. "Y'all are a bunch of out-of-control aura-bombs discharging around each other." She laughed. I liked the sound of it—spicy and soaked with joy.

I asked to see the display of Kirlian photography. We walked to the back corner of the store where there was a large gallery with dozens of pictures of plants and people, their auras captured beautifully on film. The sight of all those people, all those colors, was amazing confirmation of what I'd been seeing.

"There's something missing here," I ventured, the sense of unease about myself becoming a familiar gnaw. "None of these pictures show an aura like my own."

"Indeed? What does *your* aura look like?"

"I don't have any of these colors, not even white. My aura is nothing but silver."

Faye glanced away from me for a moment, thoughtful. Her eyes had the faraway look of reaching for a memory. She gazed back at me with an intensity that made me flinch.

"Tell me."

"In this business you hear many tales over the years, scraps of legends and myths. Many attributed to places in the British Isles, like Ireland and Wales, some from civilizations much older even than the Druids or Celts. But if you're right and your aura is pure silver…" She riffled through her bookshelves. The chaotic way she did it—pulling out one book, setting it on the floor, running to a different shelf, fanning quickly through the pages of another book, disappearing into the back of the store—made my skin prickle.

"What are you looking for?" I asked, standing over her as she sat on the floor, her skirt in a puddle around her, with two books open on her lap.

Faye looked up at me. "Something's playing hide-and-seek in my memory. If I could find it—"

My voice shook. "You're kind of freaking me out. Find what?"

She stood and fingered a long gray dread like a pet snake. "What they *call* people like you." She covered her lips with two fingers, then her eyes darted back to me. "I've read about it, or heard about it. I can't remember which. But I do remember this—silver ones are *very* rare. Almost mythological. So rare they're thought to be wiped from the earth."

Wiped? I didn't like the sound of that.

She paused a moment, possibly weighing whether to continue, and then spoke softly. "I feel a strong impulse to tell you this, so I'm going to follow it. If I'm right, well then, honey, don't go telling folks about your silver aura. It's a risk you shouldn't take, no matter how much you trust someone. Evil wears many masks, and there are those who want nothing more than to find someone like you."

SIX

After tossing around in my bed all night, I finally dragged myself up and got dressed in the half light of sunrise with nagging questions plaguing me. I had gone to Say Chi's for answers but left with more questions.

People wanting nothing more than to find someone like me?

Why would anyone care if my aura was silver? Yet again, I was reminded of the man and his strange words at the hospital as he faded from view. *A mighty flame follows a tiny spark.*

I was the spark.

That much I could see with my own eyes.

But who was he?

Bumps sprang up on my arms. Fear and uneasiness had become a coat I couldn't remove. I rode my bike home so fast last night, I nearly got hit by a car. I was unable to sleep through my worry, knowing everything in my life had changed but not why.

After scanning the book about seeing and reading auras and finding nothing on silver people, I sat at my desk and fired up my computer. For the first time I could remember, I outright disobeyed my father by getting online and searching "seeing colors around people" and "auras." Silver was rarely mentioned in color charts. When it was, the description of seeing some silver in a person's aura was pretty benign. No, I didn't have a lot of money. No, I wasn't pregnant. God. I yawned and scoured the pages with weary eyes for any reference to the ominous stories Faye mentioned about people with silver auras but found nothing.

Maybe I was the only one, the last of a mysterious tribe of freaks.

Maybe we *had* been wiped from the earth.

Chills rolled over me, raising the hairs on my arms. I bit my lip and decided to forge ahead and put my query in a public forum on a site where people had online discussions about seeing auras. Perhaps they knew about scary people with all-white auras, too. I didn't see the harm in simply asking about colors. Maybe someone else out there had seen someone silver like me or *was* someone silver like me.

Maybe I wasn't alone.

Halfway through typing my question, my bedroom door swung open. My dad's eyes went to the computer screen before they landed accusingly on me as he crossed the room. His face darkened when he read what I'd typed. "What are you doing? You know how I feel about this, Cora," he said, stabbing at the power button on the computer. My question on the screen blipped to blackness.

"What are you afraid of, Dad? How can looking up information about auras possibly harm me?"

"It's not information, honey. It's *mis*information."

"Says the man who watches Edmund Nustber on TV."

He sighed in frustration, causing his aura to expand to dirty brown overlaid on yellow. "For entertainment," he said. "Not for facts."

I folded my arms. "Well, this is *my* entertainment." He started to shake his head no, to open his mouth and toss another prohibitive statement at me, but I'd had enough. I glared at him. "The more you tell me not to open a box, the more I want to."

Later, swerving through the halls at school, I told Mari and Dun what had happened at Say Chi's. "I'm convinced I'm seeing auras."

"Can you see your own?" Dun asked.

"Yeah. But mine is completely different than everyone else's. I've only got one color. Mine is silver." A quick jolt of worry coursed through me. Faye had said not to tell anyone about my aura. Mari shot me a dubious look. "Truly, I look like a giant sparkler. It flares out really far from my body, too. And there's nothing online about it."

Mari looked interested albeit skeptical. Though, skepticism was a regular look for her. "Still, isn't it cool to be able to see people like that?" she asked.

"No. It's disturbing, like watching everyone walk around naked."

Dun snickered. "I could get with that."

Mari yanked at the sleeve of my hoodie and hooked her arm in mine. "You're going to have lunch with us today," she informed me. When I gave her "the eyebrow," she said, "Well, you hid out in the secret garden yesterday. Time to practice your social skills."

"Hid? Why does everyone keep saying that?"

"Everyone?"

"Never mind. I like the greenhouse. This is not breaking news."

Dun leaned close. "In breaking news, I may or may not have spotted someone who may or may not have resembled Mr. McIrish in the greenhouse yesterday."

"Nuh-uh!" Mari squealed, mouth agape. "Finn went in there to see you?"

I scowled. "Why is that so unbelievable?"

"Insecure much?"

"Repeat after me," Dun said. "Whale. Oil. Beef. Hooked."

Mari and I stared at him.

"C'mon. Do it."

We rolled our eyes and said the words.

"Say it again. Faster."

We did. Repeatedly. "*Whaleoilbeefhooked.*"

I laughed, finally hearing the joke.

"Now I've taught you how to talk Irish," he said with a stupid grin. I liked Dun's aura, which was almost always a happy gold/white color, like the edge of a cloud with the sun behind it. Mari's outline was a bit more complex. She also radiated a happy blush, but she was mercurial, ever changing.

Though there was a beautiful familiarity to the colors around the people I cared about, they didn't understand that my world wasn't the same since this had started. No one could hide their true colors from me.

And they didn't know I was now terrified of something—or someone—I couldn't name.

After school, I slung my messenger bag across my shoulders and walked toward the Santa Cruz Parks and Rec Center, where I volunteered at the Boys & Girls Club. Rain threatened. For the millionth time, I wished my dad would let me get my driver's license. But apparently, the world gets bigger with wheels underneath you, and Dad liked my world nice and small. He'd kill me and Mari both if he knew that on Tuesdays—her day to get the car that she shared with her brothers—she'd been secretly teaching me how to drive.

Each palm tree lining the street rustled like crisp paper in the wind. Overhead, the slate sky growled, and I felt a drop peck my cheek, followed by five more in quick succession. I walked faster.

My neck bristled with the sensation of eyes on my back. I looked over my shoulder and spotted a tall man about a block away walking briskly behind me. He wore a black woolen cap and a gray leather jacket. Longish blond hair stuck out in tufts from under the cap. There was something familiar about his lanky build, about the way he stared.

That's when I recalled the chilling sensation of falling out of myself in his presence. Like being sucked into a tornado and spit back out.

For every step I took, he seemed to take three. The gap between us narrowed, and his aura—pure white—flared between us. Internal alarms I didn't know I possessed blared at me. My quick steps beat in time with my heart.

The rain intensified, splattering the contents of my bag as I dug out my umbrella. I wouldn't open it. I wanted a weapon, and the umbrella was more useful closed. The man drew even closer. I ran.

Next to me, a car honked. I jumped, pointing the umbrella defensively at a classic powder-blue Mustang. Finn leaned across the passenger seat and rolled down his window. "Do you want a ride?"

I glanced back. The man now walked in the opposite direction, having abruptly switched course. I resented the fear pulsing through my body. When I most wanted to break free from the sheltering of my childhood, someone made me want to run to the safety of my father's arms. I felt exposed and vulnerable. Had he followed me from school? I looked back at the handsome boy in the car, opened the door, and slid in. "Thanks," I said. "You have good timing. Honestly, I'm pretty sure I was being followed."

Finn looked through the back window streaked with rain. "I don't see anyone back there, but I don't like the sound of that." I liked the way his lips pursed together in worry.

"Sorry, I, uh, I'm getting your car all wet."

Finn pointed at himself. "Irish. Rain doesn't faze me much, but I prefer to enjoy it from inside." He looked me over. "The rain is lovely on you. Though you might try *opening* that umbrella next time."

"I thought it'd be more valuable as a spear."

His eyes roamed from my face to my hair, which must've resembled the twisted strands of a mop. We did that thing again, where we looked in each other's eyes a fraction longer than was considered comfortable in polite society. Or maybe it wasn't that the look was longer. It was deeper. His greedy stare settled on my wet lips, and I finally looked away.

"I'm Irish, too," I told him in an unnaturally high voice as he pulled into traffic.

"Yeah? Seems everyone has a bit-o-the-Irish in 'em here. Maybe it's because we tend to leave when things go really wrong on our island."

"No. I mean my mother was from Ireland."

"No *shite*?"

"Truly. Lock, stock, and shamrock. I was born there."

Finn gave me a surprised look, which kind of pleased me. "Were you now? I believe ya. You're quite fair. From what county?"

"Kildare. I don't remember it. I was five when we left."

"My family is from County Meath, north of Kildare," he said with a twinge of excitement. "But there is something else about you." He reached up and gently teased a wet strand of my black hair through his fingers. "Something…striking. A little bit exotic." He looked at me again below his dark lashes, sending bubbles streaming through my body.

"South American. My father was born in Chile."

"Why did your family leave Ireland?"

My jaw went rigid. "Things went really wrong."

Finn didn't press, which I appreciated. I pointed the way to the rec center. He slowed in the empty parking lot, and I opened the door before the car fully stopped, my foot hovering over the asphalt whizzing by. "Thanks for the lift."

"I thought you were going to stop the car like a superhero," Finn teased, then cut the engine. He gestured to the rec center. "What are you about in there?"

I rubbed my hands together to warm them and maybe dispel a bit of jittery energy. "I volunteer. We help out the kids who are kind of on their own."

His eyebrows rose. "You mean they have no family? Orphans?"

"No. Most of them have at least one parent. I empathize with the kids who are looking for the whole sandwich and only get the crust, you know?"

"Do you mind if I tag along? I'd like to see what you do."

"No, you wouldn't," I said with a dismissive wave.

"Yes," he said, opening his car door. "I would."

I got out and crossed my arms. "Why? What is *up* with you?"

"What kind of foreign policy is it not to show a visitor your customs and culture?" Finn laughed, which sparked some irritation in me. I wanted to walk away, but his gravity pulled me out of my own tight orbit.

He raked his hands through his wild hair, the kind of hair that wanted to be messed. Why was I suddenly imagining leaving rows in it with my fingers? My hands clenched. I turned and began to walk toward the building.

"Cora."

I paused. My name falling from his lips was exquisite, but sad, too. It sparked a rogue memory of my mother's Irish accent calling to me.

"Is it so hard to believe someone would be curious about you? Want to spend a little bit of time with you?"

Yes.

I turned around. "No. It's hard to believe that *you* do."

Quickly, Finn closed the gap between us. His breath formed small clouds of steam in the rain. The warmth of it touched my face.

"You're in my personal space," I said weakly.

We fell into each other's gazes again. A drop of rain landed on my head. His cheekbone. My nose. His beautiful mouth. He wasn't touching me, but it felt like he was. Every nerve responded to him. His spiced scent. His colors. They reached out and *caressed* me.

"Let me be around you, Cora. It's all I seem to want since we spoke in the hospital, so let me." Despite the determined set of his jaw, his eyes looked lost, bewildered. As if he didn't understand himself what he was doing standing there in the rain with me.

I blew out an exasperated puff and tramped toward the building. "Suit yourself. But," I called over my shoulder, "for every hour you spend with me, you have to answer a question about Ireland."

The double doors opened to a gymnasium full of children. Tennis shoes squeaked on the glossy wooden floor. The center had the dank smell of used equipment, kid sweat, and something vaguely food related. I could feel Finn's smile on my back. He slid onto a bench, watching me while I signed in.

Little arms attacked me from behind. I patted the familiar hands on my belly. Of all the kids I came here for, little Max was the one I wanted to take home. I had a serious soft spot for this curly-haired little boy with the sad, observant eyes. I turned to give Max a hug. What I wasn't prepared for was the monochrome of him. For days I'd seen a vivid array of colors around people. Even if Max's eyes held a little sunshine from seeing me, the light around him was devoid of it. In fact, it couldn't exactly be called light, but a gray, chalky smudge.

He had a sad shadow.

I blinked and knelt down as if seeing him for the first time. "How you doing, Max?"

He tried to turn away from me, uncomfortable with my scrutiny. He clearly wasn't used to people *really* looking at him. I swallowed hard, hoping the gray around him would go away and thinking that my vision might walk a fine line between a gift and a curse.

"Pardon me," Finn said from behind us. "This here looks like a bloke that could do with a real Irish tale. Am I right?" Max eyed him with suspicion rimmed in curiosity. "If you guess the ending," Finn said, reaching into a pocket of his shirt, "I'll play you a tune on my harmonica."

I sat on the bench, and Max cozied up next to me to hear Finn's story. I couldn't help but stare, grateful for the opportunity to study

Finn up close. How he moved his hands a lot when he talked. The way his lips curled around some words with that accent. How his dimple teased as he spoke. He locked on Max as if he were the most important person in the world. The colors around Finn reached out to the boy. If compassion had a shade, that's what was coming off Finn right then, comforting shades of blue and gold. Max opened like a shy flower under Finn's attention.

I couldn't deny that it touched me. *He* touched me. Finn scared me, but stirred me, too. Like I'd been half-asleep my whole life and was suddenly wide-awake.

"The harmonica?" I asked as we walked through the parking lot later that evening. "Not exactly a traditional Irish instrument, is it?"

"What? You'd prefer I do a little Riverdance?"

That image made me laugh. "I'd pay cold, hard cash to see you Riverdance." I peered at him sideways. "You owe me." He cocked his eyebrow and waited for my question. "Are there really a hundred shades of green in Ireland?"

"Aye," he said softly. "But not as many shades of green as in your eyes." A sweet heartbeat of time passed. Then we both chuckled at his corniness. Finn's cheeks reddened, but maybe it was the chill of the rainy night. "My charming Irish banter'll be needing some work, I reckon."

"It's okay. Charming banter is a fine art, one I definitely haven't mastered. We can practice on each other."

"How will I know if I'm improving?" he asked.

"I don't know… I'll swoon, maybe?"

"Okay, but do I have to swoon when you get it right? I don't know if it's manly to swoon."

Easy laughter bubbled up from us again.

My dad's car idled up ahead. "Oh, there's my dad. See you

Monday."

Instead of walking to his own car, Finn kept pace beside me. Before I could give an introduction, he stuck his hand through the open driver's side window and introduced himself to my father. His confidence and manners were charming. My neck warmed.

"You're Irish," my dad said, more an awkward accusation than a question.

I threw my bag in the backseat and got in. "Thanks for the ride."

"You bet. Cheers." He began to walk away but turned back. "Sir, would it be all right with you if I asked Cora to the movies tomorrow?"

Holy…

"Sorry, no."

There was an excruciating blink of surprise from Finn. I stared at his hand, which squeezed the window frame tighter while he stared at my father, both of us waiting uncomfortably for an explanation. When it became clear that one wouldn't come, Finn forced cheer into his voice. "Some other time, then."

Dad drove out of the parking lot. His hands clenched the wheel at ten and two.

"What was that?" I asked.

"That boy is Irish."

"I know, Dad. Last I checked, that's not a crime." I couldn't believe he had pulled a boy-block on me like that.

After a few tense moments, he let out a breath and smiled weakly. "We haven't had to talk about dating before. But I think it's time to establish some rules."

"Oh God. No, Dad. It's not *time*, okay? Finn gave me a ride because…" I nearly told my father about the man who'd been following me. Maybe then he'd see it was safer to finally let me drive. Then again, he'd have a whole new reason to be paranoid and overprotective. "…because it was raining and you won't let me get my driver's license. It's no big deal."

"I would be an irresponsible father if I didn't lay down the ground rules before the need arises."

I huffed and rolled my eyes. "What's rule number one? No dating until I'm twenty?"

"Objection. Conjecture." He tried to sound light. I watched his jaw clench. "Eighteen."

"Eighteen?" My heart rate matched the *click-click* of the turn signal. Eighteen was a year away. "'Cause I can't possibly be trusted to make good judgments about who to go to the movies with? When are you going to have some confidence in me? You never let me have any freedom. You won't let me drive. You totally blew me off when I tried to tell you something is definitely not right with my eyes. You're being irrational about the aura thing. You never tell me *anything* about my own mother, even when I ask you direct questions. In the hospital, Janelle said—"

"She's gone. That's it. There is nothing more to say about your mother."

"You know, the more you say that, the less I believe you. Why don't you trust me?"

He parked in the driveway and turned toward me. "I *do* trust you."

"No, Dad." I shook my head. "Not real trust. It's easy to say you trust a bird in a cage."

SEVEN

The next day, I woke with solid intent. I had to go back to Say Chi's and ask Faye how I could arrange for a Kirlian photograph of my silver aura. I needed evidence of what I was seeing. Also, if having a silver aura was so rare and evil people were looking for someone like me, Faye might have a crystal like hers that could block people from seeing it.

My body buzzed with nervous anticipation, and my mind hungered for more information. Unfortunately, my dad and Janelle had also awoken with an intention—to keep me as busy as possible with inane chores.

I finished vacuuming well after lunch, all the while my insides churned and my patience strained. Since I had bookended the previous day with fights with my dad, the lie about going to work at the Boys & Girls Club fell easily from my lips. Janelle smiled conspiratorially at me, and I knew my father had told her about Finn asking for a date. She assumed I was going to meet him, but after my father's rudeness, I wondered if Finn would even talk to me again. It seemed strange after having just a few encounters, but if there were no more, it'd feel like I lost something.

I returned to the old downtown section of Santa Cruz. The afternoon sun slanted over the roofs of the stores, casting long shadows on the narrow street. I bought one of my favorite treats—a cinnamon roll—and tried to shove my anxiety down as I walked past the eclectic stores, the sculptures of dogs made from river rock, and groups of teens who sat with their backs against the storefronts playing guitars for spare change.

I locked my bike in front of Say Chi's and pushed at the door, expecting to be given my peaceful benediction, but it was locked. The sign on the window said CLOSED. Odd for a downtown store to be closed on a Saturday afternoon. I peeked through the glass and yelped when Faye's face suddenly appeared on the other side.

She unlocked the door. I went to step inside, but she blocked my way. "I'm closed today." Her expression was strained. Her eyes glanced worriedly behind me and up and down the block. Her gorgeous candle-like aura morphed into the sickly, fear-tinged yellow I'd seen coming from my father.

My fingernails dug into my palms. "What's wrong? What happened?"

"I stayed late after you left, trying to find information on your…unique situation." Her voice descended to a whisper. "There was a particular volume I tried to locate that I thought might have something about"—her voice lowered even more—"*silver*. I came in the next morning and the shop had been broken into. They stole my hard drive and left this stuck to my monitor." She handed me a blue sticky note.

Be very careful the tales you tell. You won't like the ending.

My nerves tingled. From my peripheral vision, I watched shots of silver flare from my body.

Faye looked apologetic but resolute. "Whoever did this was sending a message, and I got it loud and clear. I'm off the case, honey."

My gut clenched. "I don't understand. Why would—?"

"Someone doesn't want people looking into this. This note is about *you*. Look, I wish I could help, but I'm a single mom with cancer and a special needs kid. I can't afford to have anything happen to me or to this shop. You might want to keep this quiet. Perhaps there's a reason people like you are so rare. I'm very sorry. Take good care of yourself. And please," she said, her dark eyes imploring, "don't come here again."

Faye shut the door in my face.

A cannonball of dread dropped into the pit of my soul with a thud. It pulled my heart down with it. *People like you.* Rejection was a sour pit I swallowed whole. I'd been turned away because of what I was. Blamed for something I didn't even understand. Faye was the only person who seemed to know anything about why I was different, and she wanted nothing to do with me.

I bent to unlock my bike and head straight home, frightened by the thought that someone knew about my search for answers and had threatened Faye because of it.

A riff of guitar music close by caught my attention. Ignoring it, I slipped the key in the bike lock, but the music stopped me again. It wound around me like wind, whispering, summoning. I shivered.

Despite my fear, I was drawn to the music. Abandoning my bike and my instinct to hurry home, I wandered a couple doors down, the melody beckoning like a finger, pulling me toward it.

The song wafted from the open doorway of a brick building on the corner, as did the warm, toasted smell of freshly ground coffee. I poked my head in the door. The weathered brick walls with crumbling mortar were covered with old posters of musicians. Aluminum pendant lights hung over the tables, casting a disk of yellow over each one. I spotted the source of the music at the front of the room. Dark jeans, black shirt with folded short sleeves exposing defined arms. And another tattoo.

Those eyes connected with mine, and every atom in the room crackled with delight.

Finn stopped playing his guitar and scooted off the stool.

"Cora! What a perfect surprise. Get in here!" he said, jogging over. "You're peeking in the doorway like you might not come in." He squeezed my hand and tugged.

"Well—"

"I'm so glad you came."

"What do you mean?"

"I got hold of your address from your mate, the serious girl who's always sparkling," he said with a teasing grin. I blinked in shock before I realized he meant Mari's sequins.

"Mari. She's my cousin."

"I stuck a message on your front door this morning. Didn't you get it?" When I shook my head, he said, "Brilliant. It's serendipity, then. Please stay." The look he delivered was pure smolder. My resistance burned to ash. It was both infuriating and completely delicious. "I'm warming up now. I start in thirty minutes."

He led me to a table next to a window near where he'd set up. "I—but—I—" But before I could utter a single pronouncement about how I didn't mean to come, how I had simply followed the music, how it had led me here, *to him,* Finn bent down and kissed my cheek.

"You smell like cinnamon. Yum," he whispered with a slight bite to his bottom lip. He held me with a look. "Don't run away, Cora."

I told myself this would be good, for just a little while, instead of going home and ruminating in spooked-out feelings about Faye and who might have broken into her store. Trepidation flared anew. Who would be threatened by someone looking into silver auras? Earlier, I had felt like I was in some kind of danger. Today, Faye had insinuated that *I* was the dangerous one.

People filed in and filled up the tables and the booths along the walls. I noticed Queen Bee Serena Tate, surrounded by her drones, eyeing me from their VIP perch in the front row. Serena's eyes scanned me derisively. This surprised me. The Queen Bee usually flies too high to take notice of the little people far below her. I could only assume her sudden hostile vibe had to do with Finn.

I knew I looked like a gigantic idiot for being there by myself. My teeth scraped against one another, and I contemplated bolting. Instead, I called in backup.

While I waited for Mari and Dun, Serena eyed Finn with a predatory glint, following his gaze to where I sat. She sauntered over to where he was set up, leaned in boob-grazingly close, and whispered something in his ear. He smiled but his eyes were locked on me. I distracted myself by pulling out and studying the aura color chart from Say Chi's.

I already knew the chart didn't mention my silver aura, but I wanted to learn and memorize what the various colors meant. If this wasn't going to go away, I'd better figure out how to use it.

White was supposedly the most transcendent and supreme of all colors. Purity. It was described on the chart as the color of a spiritual master. The chart clearly said that no one was ever pure white, which didn't explain the man who'd been following me.

I took a pen from my bag and wrote *Silver?* And along the bottom, Faye's warning to me: *There are those who want nothing more than to find someone like you.*

"What are you doing here?" cooed Serena's candy-coated-poison voice from over my shoulder. I was struck by the scattered orange-red-green of her aura. She was…inconsistent.

"Same thing you are, I suppose."

She leveled a challenging stare at me. "I doubt that. Finn invited *me*." She glanced down at the chart. "Peculiar reading material. Let me guess, you believe in past lives, too. Might as well," she said before I could retort. "Since you have no life, you can always fantasize about how fabulous your other lives might have been."

I stuffed the chart into my bag. "Mind your own business."

"Oh, hey," Mari said, appearing with perfect timing. She squared her shoulders at Serena. "I'm so glad I ran into you, Serena." I gaped suspiciously at Mari's agreeable tone. "I've been meaning to ask you a question."

"Yes," Serena said with a bored look. "What is it?"

"What grade did you get in Bitch 101?"

"Silly Mari," Dun singsonged with a smile. "Serena graduated from that class *years* ago. Isn't that right, Serena? You're what? In the Master Bitch class now? Jedi Bitch?"

"PhD in bitchology," I said, though my heart raced uncomfortably to be so forward.

An aggressive, dirty brown–red color flowed from Mari's torso toward Serena. Serena actually leaned back a hair. When she stalked off, Dun whispered, "Hey, didn't you tell us on the phone that Mr. Lucky Charms invited *you* here?"

I sat back and crossed my arms. "Apparently I'm one of many invitees." I didn't want to compete for a boy's attention. It was futile, anyway. I was a plain girl in a decorated society, and I wasn't about to change who I was to hold Finn Doyle's interest.

Dun and Mari slid chairs out and sat. They talked with the intimate familiarity of best friends: eye contact, hand movements, light touches. Yet it was more than their normal body language. A pinkish cloud extended from the middle of Mari's body toward Dun. It merged slightly with his own, infusing his yellow with a sunset glow.

I felt like I was watching a secret kiss.

Was this a new development? I cleared my throat. "I hope you guys behave yourselves," I warned.

"Afraid we'll scare away Dreamy McDublin?" Dun said.

Mari kicked him. "Why do you keep doing that—making up stupid names for him?"

Dun shrugged. "Heads up. Sir Shamrock approacheth."

"Howya," Finn said in greeting. He shook hands with both Mari and Dun as I introduced them. "Thanks for coming. I'll be starting now." His eyes flicked to me, and he winked. "Hope you enjoy."

Dun waggled his brows at me. "Well now—"

"Shut up," I said.

"Shutting up."

Finn began to play. Voices descended into a respectful hush. Soft strums of the guitar lifted and fell on shafts of daylight from the windows. A small patch of sun warmed my exposed neck as I listened. The orange beads of his bracelet flashed as he plucked the strings with slender fingers. His head hung over the guitar in reverent concentration.

His playing was amazing, sweet and peaceful. For a while I let go of how bizarre my life had become. I was entranced long before Finn closed his eyes and opened his mouth to sing. His voice was rich, smooth suede, perfectly suited for the blues: soulful and vulnerable. The kind of voice that reaches inside and squeezes what's tender.

When he sang an Irish bar song called "The Wild Rover," he got the entire crowd to join in on the chorus. A couple of times during his performance, his gaze fell on me and lingered as if he sang directly to me. I rested my chin on my hand, hiding my smile behind my fingers. The last song was in a language I didn't understand, but my soul spoke that language. Deep inside, something cracked open so that a bit of my truest self could peek out. His music was bluesy and mournful, eerily familiar, and it opened my heart in locked places. A tear landed on my wrist.

When the final chord of the last song reverberated through the coffeehouse, the audience jumped to its feet and applauded wildly. The force of energy from the crowd knocked the breath out of me, making me dizzy. I dared a look at the people in the room. The colors were unbelievable! Such power. It rolled toward Finn in a wave, a tsunami in slow motion. I had the impulse to leap in front of him, to protect him from it.

My body jerked in response to the thought, and I squeezed the sides of the wooden chair, willing myself to sit still. I couldn't trust myself and the strong urge to protect him. But from what? The big, bad colors I could see but that were invisible to everyone else? He'd think I was crazy.

Maybe I was.

A chill spidered up my spine. The man with the crazy eyes and pure white aura leaned against the brick wall a couple feet away, staring intently at me. Icy fear spiked through me, making my fingers tingle and my breath come in quick bursts. The sounds of the room fell away. My heart sped and my aura sparked as I saw the roiling ball of the crowd's energy pass over the man and collide with Finn. But rather than crush him, the energy crashed and blended with his own bright aura, making it grow and pulse fiercely. He seemed to absorb the light until the room grew dim to my eyes.

Untouched by the energy, the strange man moved closer and closer to me. I called out to Dun, but he couldn't hear me over the shouts and clapping. I was so small in my chair amid the standing crowd. The man and his dark eyes were all I could see. I tried to leap up to run, to grab Dun's arm, to call for help, but my chest jerked toward the stranger as if I'd been punched in the spine. I couldn't draw breath, couldn't move through the thick ice of my draining energy and rising panic. I was hit in the face with a blast of air. Then, a sudden flash of white.

The world tilted sideways, and I slid off.

EIGHT

Sounds funneled in before my eyes opened.

"Is she okay?" Dun's voice broadcasted alarm.

"Should we call an ambulance?"

"Freak." That was Serena Tate. Bitch.

I opened my eyes. Finn leaned over me, concern on his handsome face. He smiled when I focused on him. "I've never made a girl faint before. I must've really blown you away."

I was blown away all right. I craned my head around, looking for the white aura, the dark eyes that had stared hungrily into mine, but he was gone. "That man…"

Finn touched my cheek with the back of his fingers. "Man?"

"This is embarrassing," I whispered. "Help me up?" I held my hand out but Finn's arm slipped under my neck. He lifted my head and pulled my body to his. Suddenly, my feet left the ground, and he snaked through the crowd, carrying me against his chest toward the door. Mari and Dun followed. Many pairs of eyes watched us pass, but none of them belonged to the man who'd stalked me.

"You sure you don't need help getting her out of here? She's pretty hefty," Serena called out. "Corbin can take her feet."

Finn stopped. "Shut your gob, you thundering bitch."

I heard Mari verbally assault Serena as well with the threat of an upgrade to physical assault, followed by Dun's voice urging Mari out of the building.

This was beyond mortifying. I threw my arm around Finn's neck and buried my face in his pale skin, warm from the performance. His soft stubble tickled my temple. I could smell the faint odor of cloves. Taste his tattoo. My lips parted. Oh God.

"Okay, you can put me down now," I gasped in a near-panic, afraid my tongue would snake out for a little taste without my permission. It wouldn't be the first time my body acted of its own accord around Finn.

Finn kept walking.

"I'm good now. Honest. You can put me down."

He stopped in the parking lot. I expected him to lower me to my feet, but he held me close. "That's the thing," he whispered into my hair, "I don't want to."

I didn't want him to, either. I felt safe in his arms. We were warm together, and I knew I'd feel cold when he let me go.

Finn groaned, a sort of frustrated sound, and gently set my feet on the ground. I wobbled a bit and put my hand on his shoulder to steady myself. He slipped an errant curl behind my ear and bent to look in my downturned face. "Are you okay, Cora? Maybe you're not quite well yet. Has anything like that ever happened before?"

I shook my head no, but that wasn't the truth.

"What's this about a man?"

"The man who followed me the other day...he was here."

A deep crease of worry wrinkled Finn's nose. "Did he say anything to you, do anything?"

"No. He never touched me." *He didn't have to.*

Mari was still in an uproar about Serena Tate when they caught up to us. "Thundering bitch?" She laughed. "I'm liking you more and more," Mari told Finn with a pop of her gum. She touched my elbow. "Ready to go?"

"I'll take her home," Finn said. "She'll be okay with me."

Mari's eyes glinted. "I'm sure she's in good hands." She threw me a teasing smile and kissed my cheek, whispering, "I'll call you later, girl."

I leaned against the cold metal of Finn's car, not knowing what to say. He was going to think I was mental, if he didn't already. It wasn't just the man with his leering eyes and the painful wrenching from my body when he was near that had me frightened to my core. It was the ominous note at Say Chi's, and the palpable, ferocious energy of that room after Finn played. It was this difference in me that separated me from everyone else.

Finn leaned forward, his hand resting on the roof of the car next to my shoulder, fingers strumming invisible chords on the blue paint. "You look scared," he whispered, mere inches from my face. There was a teasing quality to his observation, as though he knew that his body pressing gently against mine and his lips hovering mere inches away were having an effect on me. I swallowed freakishly loud. Then his right hand wiggled next to my hip, and I heard a click as he lifted the door latch.

"Get in," he said, opening the car door. I let out the breath that danced behind my lips.

"I can't get in your car. I—I need my bag," I protested, standing a bit straighter even though I still felt weak and nervous.

He bent, retrieved my bag from the ground, and handed it to me. "Mari brought it out."

"My bike?"

"I'll get it for you later when I pick up my guitar and equipment. You just passed out, Cora. I'm not letting you ride your bike home," he said with a determined set of his jaw.

I bit my lip. "I'm scared," I whispered. The truest thing I could admit.

"Of?"

That man. Seeing auras. Being silver. Of you. "Of everything I can't control."

Finn smiled. "Aww, luv, too much is out of our control. Your best bet is to control the fear." He pressed lightly on the small of my back, guiding me toward the open door.

I slid in, setting my purse on my lap, and reached inside it for a Hot Tamale. When he got in the car, I offered him the box of candy. He dropped a few into his hand and tossed them in his mouth. "Man, that was something in there. I feel superhuman." He raked both hands over his scalp and leaned back, exhaling. "Jesus, I could use a pint. America is seriously lacking in pubs."

"Is it true that there's a pub for every five people in Ireland?"

Finn laughed. "Probably."

He still hadn't started the car. I looked out my window at the pink blossoms of the cherry trees falling onto the dark pavement. Admittedly, I also looked for the man to peek out from behind a tree, but saw nothing. I locked the door. "I liked watching you play. You're very talented. I was surprised—"

"Thanks a heap."

I laughed and cuffed his thigh with the back of my hand. "I was going to say I was surprised you were playing the blues."

"Oh, that. I've always loved American blues." His colors warmed. I pushed away the vision of his aura growing so huge at the coffee shop. It had seemed like a living entity. Hungry. "Your blues sings to the ghosts the way some Irish music does."

Intriguing. He didn't talk like anybody else. I rested my cheek on the leather seat. "Sings to the ghosts?"

He smoothed his scruff with his long, tapered fingers. "Ireland is littered with ghosts. Music is how we speak to them. But it also sings to the ghosts inside you." So, he *was* a rock-star poet.

When he caught me looking intently at him, he slid his fingers closer to mine and added, "We all have ghosts, Cora. Secret hurts. I do. You do. I can see it in your eyes."

"That's because you're really looking. So few people do."

"I adore your eyes."

Your eyes remind me of home. I loved how he'd said that in the hospital. He *saw* me. *Truly* saw me. But it was more than fanciful compliments. Every interaction between us rang of fate. Like we were destined to sit in this car tonight. Destined to share a story.

He ran his fingers through his hair. "It's not just the color of your eyes—though, damn, that emerald green against your black hair slays me. It's what's in them. I feel like I know everything…and nothing, when I look in your eyes." He glanced away, suddenly shy.

"Questions and answers," I whispered. He looked at me in a penetrating way, almost pained. "That's what I see in your eyes, too," I confessed. God, I never knew the desire to kiss someone could be so intense. He was right in front of me, searching my face, smelling of melted cinnamon, his gaze falling to my lips, lingering there.

He wants to kiss me.

His hand cupped my face. "You know how badly I want to kiss you?"

"Yes."

A surprised laugh. "How?"

"You keep watching my mouth," I whispered. "It makes my lips tingle."

How could I tell him that his aura had already kissed me?

He blew out a huge puff of air and turned abruptly away from me, then started the car. "Damn it! I've never wanted to taste something so badly in my life."

I stared at him, confused. Wouldn't this normally be the part where he *did* kiss me? Whatever his reasons, I decided to let him off the hook. "I can't date you, Finn." Saying it, I felt like a bee stinging itself.

"I can't date you, either." He chuckled and slipped my hand in his. Warmth wound through our fingers. His voice softened. "So, will you go out on a date with me?"

Finn insisted on walking me to my front door, just to make sure I was okay. To ensure I'd die of heart palpitations, my father intercepted us on the porch. I scooped up my bag and thanked Finn, but my dad invited him into the living room.

"What happened?" my father asked, his voice and face stony. "When you didn't come home, I went to look for you at the rec center, but it wasn't open. You lied to me? Didn't you notice how many times I've called your cell phone?"

Damn. I hadn't heard it over the music. "I ran into Finn downtown, and then I fainted."

Dad's eyes grew alarmed and a bit incredulous.

"Finn insisted on driving me home. He didn't think I should ride my bike after what happened."

"Is that so?"

"It is, sir," Finn answered.

"Then I'm sure I must thank you," my father said, not covering the ice in his voice.

Finn smiled. "No thanks needed." He looked around curiously. "You collect treasure boxes?" he asked, gesturing to my dad's impressive collection of various sizes and shapes of boxes around the room.

"Yes," I said when Dad was slow to reply. "He always picks them up on his business travels."

"That's a lot of travels. Do you keep things in them?" Finn asked, fingering one. I refrained from telling him that Janelle's latest stroke of brilliance was to put one in the bathroom filled with maxi-pads and tampons.

"No."

"No treasure?" he asked, friendly. Trying so hard. My heart went out to him.

"Cora's the only treasure I have left."

We all stood there, awkwardly.

"So, how long are you planning to be in America?"

I slipped my arm in Finn's. "Smooth, Dad. *Nice to meet you. When are you leaving?*" Both Finn and my dad laughed uneasily. I kissed Dad's cheek and pulled Finn out the door to say good-bye.

"Sorry about that. My dad's a scientist. Right now, he's experimenting with new ways to heighten awkward feelings in people."

"You never did give me an answer about our"—he inclined his head and whispered—"date."

"Is tomorrow too soon to go?"

NINE

At my request, Finn and I agreed to meet at Full Belly Deli at the base of Felton Highway. I questioned my brilliant idea of putting a dab of maple extract behind my ears—I didn't own perfume—when a man on the bus looked at me like he hadn't had pancakes in years. I scooted closer to the window.

Finn was already at the deli when I arrived, waiting for me at a booth in the corner. He sipped a soda and looked distractedly out the window. I paused a moment, my nerve faltering at the sight of him, unbearably handsome with his full lips and classical nose. But it was the rough of him, the unpolished bits, that made my blood run hot. That messy blue-black hair, the scruff of beard, the spiral tattoo peeking out of his collar that teased me with mysteries carved in stones in the fog-drenched moss of Ireland.

His hand relaxed on the aluminum table, long fingers splayed out on the shiny surface. I could see the reflection of it underneath, like two hands resting together. I wished it were my palm pressed flat against his.

I willed myself to move forward. "Hope you haven't been waiting long."

Finn's head jerked up. A smile tugged at the corner of one side of his mouth, making his dimple show. He stood and ran his hands down the back of my arms, sending warmth through my body, then motioned for me to sit. "Are you hungry?"

"No, thanks. I brought some snacks for us," I said, hoping it'd be a nice surprise. "There's something I want to show you."

We walked outside to the blue Mustang. The top was down. It was a great day for a convertible. The morning mist had burned off, leaving a brilliant and clear late May afternoon. I got in and stretched my arms over my head.

Finn flashed his charismatic smile at my pleasure. "What?" I asked, leaning my head back and looking at the limitless sky. "I've never been in a convertible before. And it's perfect for where we're going."

He started the car. "I'm intrigued."

I directed him up the winding canyon. Sun gave way to shade as a canopy of trees arched over our heads. With the top down, it was easy to smell the shift from the grit of the city streets to the dank, earthy richness of the forest.

Finn's hand tickled the back of my neck. "I love it when your hair is up like that. You have a beautiful neck."

Okay, wow. "Not bad on the swoon-o-meter." I wanted to resist the bait, yet I longed to turn my cheek into the warmth of his palm.

"Turn here," I instructed when we reached Henry Cowell Redwoods State Park. We drove past the wide green meadow of the redwood park entrance. I bubbled with excitement at showing Finn something most people would never see in their lifetime.

We walked side by side to the trailhead. "This," I said, gesturing to the path that wound through the redwood grove, "is one of my favorite places in the universe."

He craned his neck back and gaped at the towering sentinels

above us. "They're bloody enormous. I never imagined trees so large. How often do you come here?"

"A couple times a month. But I usually come alone."

He reached tentatively for my hand so that just our fingertips touched. The small contact sent a delicious thrill through me. "And you brought me. I'm flattered." He pulled my hand all the way into his. I wondered if he felt the tickling pulse of energy like a soft feather pressed between our palms.

I led him from tree to tree, watching him marvel at their majesty, enjoying his observations of the clay-earth color of the bark, the prehistoric appearance of the branches and foliage, how each trunk looked like enormous beasts had used them for sharpening their claws. Finn stopped to read each and every placard along the trail.

We ducked inside an enormous redwood trunk scarred with a gaping black hole from an ancient lightning strike. In this enclosed space, my senses were heightened. I was aware of the warmth Finn emitted when he stood behind me, the way our auras took up more space than our bodies did. My skin warmed when he gently touched my waist to follow me back out into the light.

"These trees are magical. But there's a secret in these woods that most people don't know about. Do you want to see?" I asked, unable to contain my smile.

Finn stopped in the path, a slant of sunshine illuminating his face. The same warmth shone across my nose and cheek as though there was a spotlight trained on us against the backdrop of the forest's muted greens, reds, and browns. "These trees aren't the only thing magical about this place." Finn cocked his head to the side. "What *is* it about you, Cora Sandoval?"

"Are you being rhetorical?" I worried he somehow knew how different I was. But there was something about him as well. It radiated from him, intense and luminous. His golden-pink aura pulsed and vibrated into an ever-widening and intensifying pool of light. I couldn't doubt what I could see with my own eyes. Finn was beautiful.

Physically, yes. But it was like I could see his soul. Who he *really* was. He was easygoing and gentle, soft ripples instead of roaring waves. I couldn't see the undercurrents beneath his smooth surface, but the danger of his riptide pulled me in. I saw he had fear as well, concentrated in a ball of yellow near his stomach, like it was protecting something inside. I wondered if that's what a secret looked like in someone's aura. I couldn't judge him if it was. Everyone had things they were afraid to reveal. I was keeping a huge secret, and the reason was pure fear.

Finn was strong, too. It showed in the intensity and depth of his colors. I'd seen this blend of colors coming off him before but hadn't known what it meant. I knew now. He was attracted to me. I didn't have to guess at it, I could read it. I could feel it with every beat of my heart in my chest.

His colors enveloped me as he drew closer, his eyes never leaving mine except to stray to my mouth and back again. Everything in me ached to have him touch me, to kiss me here in this hushed palace of ancient trees. Both hands reached for me, cradling my face. His fingers curved onto my cheekbones, behind my ears, into my hair. His thumbs ran gently across the surface of my lips to their outer edges.

I opened my mouth to him even before his lips were on mine. When he crushed me with his kiss, it was with an intensity of passion contained for years, not days—it was like we'd waited centuries, lifetimes, to feel each other's lips.

The unleashed force of connection rushed out of my body toward him.

Finn gasped against my lips and kissed me deeper. Hungrier.

My body responded to his fire by sparking to life. This want was loud, crashing against my skin, burning me from the inside out. Shockingly assertive thoughts swam through my mind. I wanted to pin him against the trunk of a tree, run my tongue along the curve of his upper lip, taste him.

Rough bark scratched my knuckles. I opened my eyes. Finn's were wide open and wild. I had done exactly as I was thinking. I had him pressed, captive, against the tree. His fingers dug into my hips. My silver aura flared from my hand against his neck, blending with the heat from his skin. A mystical merging of our colors.

I pulled away, breathless, sure my face was as flushed as his, my lips as pink and slightly swollen. "Is that how—how it's supposed to be?"

Finn smirked. I spun and tramped down the path, feeling noticeably colder with every step away from him. I heard his footsteps jog up behind me. "Cora, wait." His words bubbled with laughter. He slipped his arm around my waist.

"You're laughing at me!" I tried to slip from his grasp, though I didn't actually want to.

"No. No, I'm not laughing at you." His face turned serious and his voice soft. "If that's how it's supposed to be, Cora, then I've never had a true kiss before today."

I peered into his eyes, seeking the lie, but found only sincerity.

"This is strange for me, to be so drawn to someone." His brown eyes looked startled when he said that. "You affect me, warm me." His fingers touched my cheek. "I don't know of anyone who could feel this and not want more of it."

I sighed, agreeing completely. It *was* strange to be so drawn to each other. The sudden intensity of our attraction and connection was inexplicable, but I couldn't deny it was there. I'd be the last to demand that everything make perfect sense. So much of my life, lately, didn't. "You're only here temporarily, right? Are we stupid to get involved, knowing that?"

"Choices, luv. We either regret the experiences we have, or the ones we were too scared to have."

How could I argue with that? My entire life had been ruled by stop signs. My father didn't trust me to make my own decisions about dating, but wasn't it time I trusted myself?

My fingers wound over his warm hand on my cheek. He kissed my forehead and sealed an internal truce within me. I'd choose the experience. I'd allow myself to have this, which I thought was a colossal act of bravery on my part.

Finn was the first thing I'd ever done just for me.

"C'mon," I murmured, ducking under the split-rail fence intended to keep people from treading on the delicate ecosystem of the redwood forest. "We're out of bounds, so be careful and step exactly where I do, okay?"

"Out of bounds? Are you a closet rebel, Cora?"

I looked back at him conspiratorially. "I got permission from the park to break this one rule. I told them I was doing a story for school." I led him through the forest undergrowth, around large sword ferns, wild ginger, and redwood sorrel that looked like clover on steroids. "But my dad has lots of rules. No dating is the new one on his list."

Finn gave me a deep, inquiring look.

"My dad is overprotective. That's the short answer."

"And the longer, more interesting story is?"

I nudged his rib. "My mother abandoned us when I was five. I think it made him scared I'd disappear on him, too. Sometimes I want to be mad at him because he doesn't trust me. Won't give me the freedom to, I don't know, even *try* to blow it. But mostly I feel bad for him because he lives so fearfully. I don't want to go through life being so afraid of losing things that I never allow myself to enjoy them."

"So, there's your fear again."

"Yes. I guess. But look how great I am at ignoring my fear today." I bit my lip, quelling the unexpected emotions. I hadn't realized how heavily my father's sheltering weighed on me. It was like he trained me to be afraid.

"We have something in common," Finn said. "When I said I

couldn't date you, it wasn't some load of tripe. My parents are bloody overprotective as well. Makes no sense to me, but there you have it. Sometimes, I wish I had some brothers or sisters just to take the focus off me, you know?"

"I do know. I'm an only child, too. It's unnatural to be the sun that your parents revolve around. Well, parent." I couldn't believe how easy it was to open up to him.

"What was it you wanted to show me? I can't wait to see why we're fence-hopping in a state park."

A few feet away, sprouting from the base of a redwood, was the awesome secret I wanted to share with him. "It's an albino redwood." I pointed to a pure white tree in front of us. "It's extremely special and rare. Some people say there are fewer than thirty albinos in the entire world."

Finn reached toward it, but I stopped his hand. "They call them 'the ghosts of the forest.' I wanted to show you because you spoke about the ghosts inside us."

"What makes them this way?" he asked, staring at the milky-white stems and needles. Surrounded by the world of green, the plant looked like a phantom. Eerie and beautiful. A cloud at eye level.

"Albinos are offshoots of the larger tree, the same in their essential genetics, but no one knows why they're pure white," I answered.

Just like I don't know why I'm different.

I wondered: were some people made with pure white auras the way I was made pure silver? A mutation from what's normal? I suddenly wanted very badly to talk about it. I even opened my mouth to begin, but I couldn't admit how abnormal I was. I didn't want to scare away the most sweet, the most normal thing in my life.

Faye had said, *It's a risk you shouldn't take. No matter how much you trust them...*

We reached the fence and ducked back under, walking out of the grove hand in hand, both of us lost in thought. It was quiet, with only the sounds of birds, the gentle hum of insects, and the occasional plod of a runner jogging past.

Above the San Lorenzo River, we ate the sandwiches I brought while I told Finn how I liked to come here during rainstorms because I had the park to myself. My own private Eden. He told me about his Eden—the eastern coast of Ireland—and I listened raptly. He loved to sail and talked about his boat like it was a lover. I learned his father was an army medic and gone most of the time. His mother, also a doctor, worked in a large hospital in Dublin. He planned to attend Trinity College in the fall. His parents expected him to go into medicine. "It's the family occupation, but I want no part of it," he confessed. "Music is my passion. To them, it's just a hobby. To me, it's air."

We stopped talking and sat side by side, our shoulders touching, and watched the sun set through the giant trees. I gave him a chocolate-dipped strawberry. He gave me a kiss that tasted like spring.

TEN

What on earth was a caper? It didn't even sound like food. I wheeled my cart through the grocery store, searching. How can one mystery ingredient be so vital? The answer: it's a vital ingredient when Janelle is cooking Dad's favorite empanadas and a Chilean summer stew to make up after their fight about me when I returned from the state park. She insisted if he continued to smother me, I was likely to rebel. He insisted he'd been taking care of me fine all these years without anyone's help and would protect me as he saw fit.

It was uncomfortably quiet in the house after that, so I offered to get the groceries. Tired of wandering the aisles, I decided to cut to the chase and ask old Mrs. Oberman where I might find the mysterious ingredient. If they sold it, she'd direct me to it.

Mrs. Oberman shuffled toward me as I neared. Her movements were sluggish, but her smile wasn't. "Cora, honey! How are you?" Her body looked so feeble, I worried I'd see something off about her colors, then found myself wondering if old people's auras differed from ours, like a light on a dimmer switch, or do they stay bold and bright until the day we die?

Her aura blared at full blast, her light brilliant as a baby's, tinged with the soft blue, green, and pink glow of an early morning in the forest. I sighed, relieved. We exchanged pleasantries, and she directed me to the elusive caper. When I passed her again a few minutes later, I started to call out to thank her, but my words caught in my throat. The man who made me feel cold, like my blood pooled at my feet when he was near, was casually talking to her. I hid behind the end cap of the aisle. One part of my brain, the one that obviously controlled adrenaline, screamed at me to run. Another part encouraged me to hide and watch to see if I could learn anything about him, and to see how other, non-silver people's auras responded to him.

I peeked around the corner.

Mrs. Oberman peered up at him like a frightened child. There was something chilling about the way her hand grasped his arm, as if for stability. His satisfied smile sent shivers down my neck.

Her colors, which had been so bright moments before, were now diffused. No longer a blue sky, but one with the dreary gray cast of a squall. In contrast, the man's energy was brilliant and pure white. No other colors at all. His aura was a massive white cloud, swallowing her storm.

Nothing in my investigations explained this. White was only ever described as the color of great spiritual masters. A cleansing light. Angelic light. I struggled for a rational explanation. Perhaps Mrs. Oberman knew him. Maybe he was giving her bad news and that was why she looked so stricken.

His gaze flickered my way, and I quickly pulled my head back, praying he hadn't seen me. I glanced up at the tilted mirrors on the edge of the ceiling and cursed myself. All he'd have to do is look up, and he'd see me in the mirror as well. But my heart dropped when I saw in the reflection that Mrs. Oberman now stood alone. He wasn't there.

Instead, he towered in front of me.

I gripped the handle of my shopping basket, adrenaline surging. "Leave me alone," I said through a clenched jaw. My silver aura flared out from my body.

The man inhaled pleasurably like he could smell it, leaned in close to my ear, and said, "If I could have *you*, she wouldn't have to die."

ELEVEN

The man strolled away—casual, normal—as if he hadn't whispered menacing words about death in my ear. I was shaking violently when I tried to pull out my phone to call my dad, and it slipped from my trembling hand. Seconds later I heard a sound like a sack of potatoes dropped on the ground. Someone gasped.

Mrs. Oberman lay still on the polished floor.

I ran over, sliding onto my knees next to her.

I wrapped my hand around her papery arm and called her name. Her eyes were fixed open. The man with the white aura did this, I knew it. But how? I recalled her distressed expression, her dimmed aura, his glaring pure white one, his simpering smile in the face of her fear. *If I could have you, she wouldn't have to die.* Fear slipped an icy hand around my spine, shaking me.

Someone called an ambulance. I stayed with Mrs. Oberman until the paramedics came and they rolled her away on the gurney. Her body looked so small under the blanket, like without her soul she took up less space.

After I called my dad, he rushed into the store and gathered me up to go home. In the car, I warred with myself about how much to tell him. To any observer, the man had simply spoken briefly to Mrs. Oberman, spoken to me, and left. Who would believe my theory that he was somehow responsible for her death? My dad didn't even believe I saw auras. He was quiet and distant as we drove. I crossed my arms; his indifference ignited a fire of antagonism inside me. I wanted him to react.

"Someone *died* right in front of my eyes, and you're a million miles away! What? Is it your precious work? Are the mysteries of the universe more important than your own daughter's emotionally scarring experience?"

Dad tilted his head and gave me a strained look. "No, of course not. There's nothing in this world more important to me than you." He set his hand briefly over mine, his tone softening. "Maybe if you believed that, you'd be a bit more understanding about the things I do to protect you, including my work."

I wanted to believe him. He'd taken a sample of my blood because he was investigating mysterious deaths. Mrs. Oberman's death was certainly mysterious. Were they related? I was about to question him, press him to explain how his work was protecting me, when he loosened his tie and said, "Tell me everything that happened back there. But slow down this time." His eyes shone with sincerity. "I want to know every detail."

"Okay." I sighed, reassured by his interest. "But I'm warning you, if you dismiss what I'm about to tell you because it involves seeing auras, I won't say another word."

At home, Janelle made me chocolate-hazelnut tea and biscotti and coddled me as though Mrs. Oberman were a relative. It was the first time I let myself relax into a hug with Janelle without pulling away. It felt good to be hugged. There was something honeyed about mom hugs, even if she wasn't my real mother.

The whole event left me out of sorts, cold, and scared. I was beginning to regret telling my father the story after seeing the effect it had on him. His eyes were spooked as he stuttered through placating responses. Then he remained quiet for the rest of the ride home. I'd be lucky if he ever let me leave the house again. I purposely didn't mention the man had been following me or what he had said. Between my father's fear, Faye's ominous warnings, and Mrs. Oberman, the world was conspiring to make me a prisoner in my own home.

I dipped biscotti into my tea and settled back against my pillow with my Ireland scrapbook. Ireland was my *someday* obsession, the only connection I had with my mother. Finn had ratcheted up my interest, and I needed something to divert me from the memory of that man whispering in my ear. I shuddered again and scooted deeper into the pillows.

Pulling out the pocket map of Ireland, I traced my fingers over County Kildare, where I'd been born. I had a recurring fantasy that someday I'd go back to Ireland, to some quaint town with cobblestone streets and rock walls around thatched cottages. I would turn a corner and come face-to-face with my mother. In my fantasies, I'd recognize her, even though there was no way I could. Dad claimed all pictures of her were lost. But in my fantasy, she and I would stop. Stare. She wouldn't know me because I was grown, but she'd give me a long, searching look, like I was a secret the wind whispered in her ear. One of her ghosts.

I glanced at County Meath—Finn's home—and smiled. I flipped through pages of pictures I'd collected over the years of impossibly green meadows, seaside port villages, the imposing Cliffs of Moher, and the ancient megalithic site, Newgrange.

For years, I had been putting my name into the annual lottery to visit the burial chamber at Newgrange on the winter solstice. Tens of thousands of people put their name in each year just to see that event.

The mysterious, unknown, ancient people who built the site were sophisticated enough to construct the chamber in such a way that on one magical day, the winter solstice, the sun would sear through an opening above the entryway and shine its light deep into the burial chamber. If I won, I reasoned, it would be a once-in-a-lifetime opportunity. Dad would *have* to let me go. Next to the picture of the tomb, I came across a black-and-white photo: the carving of the triple spiral. Finn's tattoo did look like it had been traced from the three spirals. I'd forgotten to ask him about it.

My bedroom door flung open, and Mari blew in with only the top of her head visible above all the clothes she carried. I'd forgotten she was coming over with a pile of her own clothes to tutor me on fashion. Apparently, it takes serious effort and planning to look casually, accidentally adorable. "The key is to look stylish while still looking like you," she proclaimed, tossing the mound of fabric on top of me.

I unburied myself and gave her *the eye.* "I totally forgot about you coming over after—"

"Yeah, Janelle filled me in. That's totally macabre. I say we need to shake you out of this funk. Get up. It's fashion-show time. It'll be a good distraction."

"I don't think it's a good time."

She put her hands on her hips. "You almost died in the hospital. Someone died right in front of you today. You gonna lie there and act like you're dead, too, or live your life like you're glad to have it?"

She was so damn pushy! And she was right. I stuffed my scrapbook under my pillow and climbed out of bed, agreeing to try on a couple of options she'd assembled for me, things I never would have thought to put together. I slipped off one pair of her jeans that made my thighs look like kielbasa and then put on my favorite capris as an act of defeat. "I just ran out of give a crap."

"Those capris do nothing for your ass. And girl, really, you have a nice ass."

"You're assessing my ass?"

"Yes. Grading on the curve." Mari cracked herself up. "Seriously though, yours is a fully realized butt."

I tossed a shirt at her. "Speaking of curvy Latin butts, I'm hungry."

"Me, too," she said, judging her own backside in the mirror. "Think we can rip off a couple of empanadas? They smell insane."

We went on empanada recon, stealthily making our way to the kitchen like we used to when we were little and wanted midnight cookies, because Mari convinced me that if you ate a sweet at midnight, it would give you sweet dreams. My father caught us as he was coming out of his office, looking serious and grave. No longer empanada ninjas, we continued to the kitchen, each grabbing one from the cooling rack on the counter and wrapping them in napkins.

"We should call Dun and tell him to come over. You know how much he loves these," Mari said, nibbling the corner of the pastry. Steam coiled out with the pungent aroma of beef and garlic. "And he always cheers you up better than me."

"I'm on it," I said, but my cell phone was about dead after calling my dad from the supermarket. I set it on the charger and went to grab the phone in Dad's office. The phone was still warm from my father's hand. As soon as I touched it, my vision went black. Flashes of images and sounds assaulted my mind.

I *saw* my father speaking on this phone, his voice a panicked whisper. "*It's happened. Ever since she got sick, she's been different. Changed.*"

My grandmother's gristly voice scraped across the miles. "*She is her mother's daughter, Benito. We knew this could happen.*"

"*Yes, but for years, you held it at bay. Until I can further analyze her blood for a possible answer, you have to help her. They might have found us. Strange things are happening. I think we're not safe here anymore. If they see, if anyone figures out the truth about her…*"

I swayed slightly on my feet, the world around me invisible but for the vision of my father on the phone and their hushed voices inside my head. "*No, mijo,*" my grandmother said. "*I've tried. I don't think I can help her anymore.*" Despair. I could *feel* the utter despair coating my father, especially when Mami Tulke added softly, "*She is what she is. You cannot save her from this, just as you could not save Grace.*"

The flashes abruptly stopped, and the office whirled into focus. The phone burned in my grip, and I flung it across the floor, my heart thumping wildly, sweat beading on my forehead. My hand stung where I had held the phone, like I had been bitten on the finger by a small animal. I glanced down and gasped. A delicate inky line of black clovers wreathed my ring finger.

I stared in awe. The image had burned into my skin. I licked my finger and touched the tender area to see if it would rub off. The clover ring prickled when I swiped it, but it would not go away. I'd somehow been tattooed, marked by a memory.

"I take it Dun can't come?" Mari said from the doorway, motioning to the phone on the floor.

I willed myself to stop shaking.

"You buggin' out?" she asked, concern creasing her forehead into tight grooves.

I couldn't answer. How could I tell her I had just had a major hallucination that left me marked in some way? It was too weird. Too abnormal. Like the cloak separating fantasy and reality had been worn thin, and I didn't know what was real.

"I'm not feeling well," I choked out, and it was so true.

I mentally scrolled through all of my interactions with my father in the last couple of weeks. The hazy memory of him drawing my blood while Janelle asked if my illness could have anything to do with my mother. And he'd been so scared when I first told him I thought I was seeing auras. I could *see* his fear, especially after Mrs. Oberman's death.

"I need to talk to my father. Right now."

TWELVE

Dad entered his office with a perplexed and wary expression. One hand rattled a few loose coins in his pocket. My newly marred hand was tucked away in the sleeve of my hoodie. Mari and Janelle stood in the doorway with expectant, inquisitive looks on their faces.

"I need to talk privately with my dad. Can you give us a minute?" I said with more grit than I knew I had. The double doors shut us in the office together. I registered the sound of a fly beating itself senseless against the window to get to something he could see but not reach.

Truth could be like that.

"Dad…" Tears gathered in the back of my throat. "You spoke to Mami Tulke."

The statement versus question tactic worked. I could see from his shocked expression that it was true.

"Have you been eavesdropping?" His face contorted from alarm to stern reproach.

"If I had been, how would I also know what she said?" His office had a separate line. No other phones in the house connected to it.

He stood in shocked silence. His aura flared erratically, changing from a greenish-yellow to a mustard one that I'd come to associate with fear. "There is no sane way to explain this, so I'm just going to say it. I came in here to call Dun, and when I picked up the phone, I *heard* the whole conversation. Like a replay. I felt what you were feeling. I know what Mami Tulke said to you!" My voice rose successively higher, my own disbelief still coursing through me.

"I don't know what you're going on about, Cora. What you're telling me is impossible."

"I don't care how impossible it sounds! I am my mother's daughter. So tell me what that *means*! Tell me what you meant when you said 'if anyone figures out the truth about her.' Tell me what it is that you can't save me from, because freaky things are happening to me, Dad, and I don't know how to save myself. You're supposed to protect me."

His mouth hung open, his face drawn. He spoke slowly and softly, as if I were mentally challenged. "I never said that, sweetheart. You must have imagined it."

His words came out in a puff of black smoke. The gray-black hovered over his mouth a moment, curled around his lips and throat, then slowly dissipated.

His lie was a cannon shot in the mist.

It struck me in the gut. A condensed ball of yellow rolled from him—like I'd seen in Finn's aura in the forest, only much larger—floating like a polyp, an enormous cystic secret. He was lying to protect that secret.

I pulled my hand out and shoved the marking in his face. "Am I imagining this?"

He gasped. "You got a tattoo of your mother's wedding ring? How did you know what it looked like?" Even if I hadn't been able to see his aura, I could read the conflict in his eyes and the threat of tears in their rims.

My own eyes filled with tears. My mother's wedding ring? Fresh pain of missing her stabbed at my heart. I'd gone twelve years without knowing the touch of my mother, and now I had to wear an image of her wedding ring on my finger?

"This conversation is over. We will not speak of it again." My father turned and left me standing alone in the office, beating myself against the glass between us.

THIRTEEN

I watched my father eat his breakfast the next morning in the way a scientist observes the mating ritual of sloths. Suddenly, everything he did and how he did it was slow, irritating, and suspicious. I was consumed with questions about myself, about my mother, and now knew that my father, the one person I had trusted above all others, was hiding the answers from me. His idea of keeping me safe was to render me ignorant.

I'd have to find the answers myself.

The clock taunted me. I wanted him to leave so I could have the house to myself and search for clues. School could wait. It was just yearbook day, anyway. "Cora," Janelle's voice rang out as I rinsed my plate. "Are you going to let the water run forever? Do you know what a group of villagers in a third-world country would do for a gallon of our water?"

I smacked the faucet handle and dried my hands on my jeans. I watched her and my dad leave for work with the squinty-eyed scrutiny of a CIA operative. I was alone, and I had some sleuthing to do.

I locked the front door, hoping it would alert me if someone came home early. I searched my mother's name online. Nothing. No people-finding sites had any information on her. Increasingly desperate, I contacted the Missing Persons Bureau within Ireland's National Police Service. A man answered, and my heart stumbled over itself at the sound of his Irish accent. I'd written out what I wanted to say, which turned out to be a good move because I wondered if I'd be able to speak through my nerves.

"Hello. I'd like to know how I might obtain any information you have on a missing person from twelve years ago. Do you keep files that long? And if so, can I get a copy? The woman was my mother."

"All right. Let's take your questions one by one, dear," the man responded. "We do indeed keep the records on all missing persons. I'll need the name."

"Her name was—is—Grace. Grace Sandoval."

The clicking of his keyboard joined with static from the connection. I took a few deep breaths. Why should I feel so nervous? I was entitled to the information. I wasn't doing anything wrong. The man grunted. Maybe she had been murdered, and my dad never wanted to tell me. I almost hung up, but brought the phone back to my ear.

"I have no record of a missing person by that name."

That lent support to Dad's story that she abandoned us. She didn't care a whit about my father, about her baby. Me. But it didn't jibe with Mami Tulke's phantom voice speaking about not being able to "save" her. If my mother had died, why wouldn't Dad have said so all along? I mumbled my thanks and hung up.

I went to my dad's bedroom to look for something, anything. An hour's search turned up nothing, no mysterious cigar boxes in the closet, no secret wall safes behind paintings, nothing. Knowing him, he'd keep anything important at his office or in a safe-deposit box somewhere. Somewhere away from me.

I looked around the entire house, in every drawer, in every

cabinet, even bins in the garage. Finally, I stood in the living room, my hands on my hips, staring at the built-in shelves surrounding our fireplace. I realized I had been looking for something hidden in a dark corner but overlooking the things that had been right in front of me my whole life.

When I wanted to hide something private, like my Ireland scrapbook, I hid it with yearbooks, novels, and the old albums I liked to collect. Hidden. But in plain sight.

Dad's treasure boxes were scattered throughout the house. I flipped one open. Empty. The next one held guitar picks from when he used to play. Another held a pile of glass "jewels" I got at Disneyland. Every treasure box in the house was either empty or filled with frivolous objects. Except for one in the spare bedroom. It was empty, but when I tossed it onto the bed in frustration, I spotted a tiny key taped to the underside.

I ran back to the living room. Up on the highest shelf sat one last box. I'd skipped it in my search because it would require a ladder to reach it. Now I noticed it had a tiny lock on its brass clasp.

I dragged the ladder from the garage and propped it against the wall. It wobbled a bit as I climbed. The treasure box was made of dark wood and hand-painted with vines and tiny flowers. Its edges were scalloped with golden metal and dotted with studs. I took the key from my teeth, stuck it in the lock, and turned. It clicked and sprang open.

When I lifted the lid, I saw it was filled with items. Careful not to drop it, I took the box from its place and climbed down. I squirreled the box in my room and darted back to the living room to put the ladder away in case Dad or Janelle came home. They might not notice the box was missing right away, but they'd sure as heck notice a twelve-foot ladder perched up to the empty space. Every cell in my body was on high alert and pumping with adrenaline as I carried the ladder back to the garage. Then I ran back to my room to find out what treasure Dad had locked away.

Sitting cross-legged on my bed, I lifted the first item from the box: a photograph. I gasped, my body recognizing who it was even though my conscious memory didn't. The woman's face was obscured, half-buried in the wild black curls of the little girl on her lap, but I could tell she was laughing. Her arms wrapped protectively...lovingly... around the little girl. One hand rested over the middle of the girl's chest, right over her heart.

My heart.

It was me in the picture, without a doubt. The same wild hair, the same big green eyes and spider lashes. I remembered getting in huge trouble for cutting them one day because a boy at the park told me they looked like spider's legs.

I could've stared at that picture all day, but I had to see what else was in the box. I unearthed a leather portfolio bound with a cord. I unraveled it and opened the pouch. Two passports fluttered out alongside a birth certificate.

My birth certificate? The birth date was right, but the name was wrong. I struggled to stay calm, to keep my hands steady as I read.

Daisy Josephina Sandoval

Josephina was Mami Tulke's first name. But I was born as *Daisy*? My mind flashed back to every birthday, every special occasion when my father gave me daisies. It was my father honoring my real name.

But who sent the bouquet Finn delivered in the hospital?

I flipped open one of the passports—an Irish one. My little-kid face smiled back at me. There was only one stamp, from Ireland to the United States, to San Francisco. The second passport was for me as well, this time under the name Cora, with a picture of me from about two years ago, still wearing braces. I had no idea I had a current passport.

I unfolded a cream piece of paper. A pressed daisy floated onto my jeans from an invitation for my parents' wedding. It was held at the most famous church in Dublin—Christ Church. A postcard enclosed with the invitation featured a photo of the medieval-looking church. I put the flower and postcard back inside and refolded the paper.

A new thought pinged. Did Dad *take* me from my mother? I heard stories like that all the time. What if he was the one who did the abandoning? Were we in hiding? Why else would he have changed my name?

I tried to calm my racing heart and mind. Other legal-type papers declared my mother missing or deceased. *Deceased.* My head and heart ached. Their marriage was annulled. I set the papers on the bedspread next to me, tears blurring my vision.

At the very bottom of the box lay an envelope. Neat script across the front read *Benito*. I wiped my eyes and opened the letter.

Dearest Benito,

I know you don't want to hear these words. My dear heart, I don't blame you. But I can't let you stop me from saying them. It's too important. There may come a day when I don't come home. The more I learn, the more frightened I become. Someone doesn't want me to continue my research. I wouldn't be the first to disappear. You know that.

Strange things are happening. My research points to a truth even I have trouble comprehending. Perhaps I should listen and leave Ireland with you. But I'm too close to the truth about myself to stop. If I am right, it could change everything we think we know about what it is to be human. Perhaps I'm too close to the truth about all of us to stop. As a scientist you must understand. No wondrous thing was ever discovered were it not for someone brave enough to seek it.

My biggest concern, and what prompts this letter, is our daughter. Promise me, a vow as sacred as the day we pledged our lives together, that if anything strange should happen, if

I do not come home one day, you will take my little, dark Daisy and get out of Ireland immediately. Do not look for me. Trust me, I'll be as lost as my parents.

The ones who disappear do so forever.

Go to our special place. You must hide what I've enclosed. Bury it under the ghost so no one will ever discover it. As badly as I want to expose the truth I believe it holds, I want your safety more. I will find you there if ever I can.

I weep as I write this, but you must do what I ask to keep her safe. Know that I can't imagine a day when the two of you are not with me. But if that day ever comes, I will keep close the memory of your pure heart. How I could see your spirit the first time we met. You hid nothing from me (not that you could). And you gave me everything. Acceptance. A family. Boundless love that gives without fear of running dry. Ever.

And you gave me Daisy. I will long for the smell of her wild mane. The way her hands curl in her sleep like she's ready for a fight. The way she is lit up from the inside out. Protect our little treasure, for she truly is rare and special. I love you both.

Yours,

Grace

I read the letter five times. Afterward, I'm sure it was a full ten minutes that I sat staring at nothing. I didn't know whether to be grateful my father had apparently honored her wishes, or angry that something awful happened to my mother and he ran away.

But she didn't abandon me.

She loved me.

I couldn't pretend that the heart-sting I had lived with for so long had miraculously healed. It hurt differently. Cold fear pulsed through me. Regret at so many lost years. Anger that my mother chose some kind of research over her family. Even when she knew she was in danger. What truth could change our views of humanity itself? That's not something you say lightly. My questions looped endlessly around themselves with no clear answer.

A car passing outside my window reminded me of the time. I hurried to copy the letter on the printer in Dad's office so I could put all the items back in the treasure box. Then I rushed to get the ladder and replaced the box.

Mari answered her cell on the first ring. I could hear the noise of kids at school in the background.

"I need you."

"I'm there."

I peeked out my window when I heard Mari's car pull up. Dun's lanky figure unfolded from the passenger side of her little car.

"Hope you don't mind me coming, too," he said at the front door.

I fell into his chest for a much-needed hug. His sunny aura wrapped around me, enveloping me in its sweet warmth. "Shut up."

"Shutting up," Dun said with a big squeeze.

"I've never heard your voice so shaky," Mari said. "If Cora's rattled, the whole world must have tilted on its axis. You okay?"

"Not even." I pulled them into my room and explained everything I'd discovered about my mother.

"You're telling me," Dun said, stretched out on my bed with his feet dangling off the end, his long black hair fanned out over my pillow, "that your mom was mixed up in some kind of crazy research, *knew* she was in danger, and *told* your dad to get you out of Ireland? And then he freaking *did*?"

"I'm not telling you that, *she* is," I said, brandishing the copy of my mother's letter in the air like exhibit A. "My dad never told me anything. He's hidden this from me my whole life. I swear, I don't know which reality is worse: her abandoning us or us abandoning her."

"Reminder: we don't know what happened," Mari pointed out. "Only that she was worried when she wrote the letter and she's been gone for a long time."

"Maybe I've watched too much television," Dun said, "but the question ought to be, what is this truth that someone would want to keep secret so badly?" He folded his hands over his chest and stared at the ceiling. "Not to be cold, but I doubt she's alive. If she was, she would've come looking for you just like her letter said. Whatever she was scared would happen—dang girl, it musta happened."

"What truth could my mother possibly have known that would 'change everything we think we know of what it is to be human'?"

I stared at the letter again.

No wondrous thing was ever discovered were it not for someone brave enough to seek it.

"Guys, get me out of here. I can't face my dad anytime soon. I don't want to hear what he has to say. Everything's a lie."

"What will you do?" Mari asked.

"Dig up the truth."

FOURTEEN

ari drove us through the busy streets of Santa Cruz, past the boardwalk with its looming white roller coaster and candy-colored buildings, past the jagged knuckles of the cliffs on Highway 1. We had no destination. I needed to be out of my house and have a private place to make a plan.

I wanted to go to Ireland immediately, an idea Mari supported in the spirit that all quests were daring and noble, and if they weren't, at least I would have an adventure for once in my sad, sheltered life. She offered to use the rest of her airline miles to get me a ticket, and we tallied my savings with a couple hundred dollars she was willing to lend me. If I stayed in youth hostels, it might buy me a couple of weeks to search for information.

Dun remained doubtful. "What, you're going to roam the Irish countryside by yourself and go door-to-door asking if anyone knows anything about your mother?"

"Maybe she won't go alone. Maybe *Finnegan* will escort her," Mari teased.

Dun jumped in. "Oh, and rule number three of the Articles of

Friendship states that when you go on your first date with Gorgeous O'Guinness, we have a debriefing. How'd it go?"

I tore my eyes from my mother's letter once more, thinking of my afternoon with Finn in the forest. "You want to know what it was like? Surreal. We were a movie. We were my favorite book. Dreamlike. Sweet—and hot—and you guys will tease me for saying this, but I feel like I've known him forever."

"Aaaah. Love and lightning," Mari said with dramatic pause. She tucked her straight hair behind her ear and winked at me. "They both can strike sudden and hot."

"And they can burn you crispy!" Dun shouted from the backseat.

"I still can't believe it happened." I exhaled. Truth.

Dun pinched the back of my neck. "So, the kissing didn't suck?"

I shrugged him off. Now wasn't the time to think of Finn and replay our spectacular kisses. I had work to do. I wanted to go straight to Ireland, try to find information on my mother, and arrange all my extremely confused feelings into tidy little mind-files.

Anger: that belonged with Dad for taking my mother's love away by telling me she left us. He could at least have let me believe in her love for me. Anger had a subcategory for my mother, too, for forgetting that when you have children, you're supposed to put them first.

Concern: a woman named Grace Sandoval loved me for five years but risked her life and our future for a mystery. Also file under: driving need to unravel that mystery.

It seemed I inherited that need to know the truth. Would it cost me what it did her?

"Where'd he take you?" Mari asked.

"Who?"

"Finn!"

"He didn't do the taking. I took him," I said, irritated we were still on the topic of Finn when everything I thought I knew about my life turned out to be a treasure box full of crap. "I wanted to show him the redwood grove and the albino—" The faintest trail of an idea formed in my mind.

"Mari, will you take me to the redwoods?"

"Right now?"

"Now. Yes, now. I have to go there now."

Dun poked his head between us from the backseat. "Intriguing. Could not have anticipated that request. I almost thought you were going to say 'airport,' but the woods, much more logical."

The parking lot at the state park was empty, probably due to the rain that pattered steadily on the windshield. I threw my hood over my head and climbed out of the car. Mari leaned over. "I love you, girl, so I'm staying here to, you know, keep the car warm for you."

"Want me to come?" Dun asked. I wondered if he knew he was shaking his head as he asked.

"I just need a few minutes," I said and jogged toward the entrance.

Moments later, I was swallowed up by the forest. My forest. A gift from my father. The circular trail through the groves was the only place when I was little that Dad let me run free, out of his immediate vision. And it was the only place he ever opened himself up. I think he felt as I did, that no matter what we said, the trees would keep our secrets.

The rain was less intrusive under the large fingers of the redwoods, their foliage covering me in all directions. Steam rose from the split-rail fencing along the trail, and large spiral spiderwebs, so much like Finn's tattoo, stood empty. I pondered what a perfect design the spiral must be if nature herself utilized it in so many ways. Water droplets fell from strand to strand, and the spiral web vibrated with the music of the rain.

My breath blew out in a vapor. I shivered, cursing myself for the fool's errand I'd undertaken in the chilly drizzle. I stood in front of the albino redwood and stared.

Bury this under the ghost so no one will find it.

I'd written it off as an obscure Irish turn of phrase or perhaps something buried in a grave somewhere. But when Mari asked about my date with Finn, I immediately thought of the only ghost I'd seen with my own eyes.

Slowly, I circled the phantom tree. Hidden from the trail was a small hollow—like a fairy door—at the base of the tree. I squatted down, ran my finger lightly over the tiny hole, and immediately sensed the impression of panic. Not my own. It was like the tree had a memory and mine weren't the first hands to do this. I dropped to my knees and started to dig.

First, I scraped away a layer of albino pine needles, white and spent, like tiny bones left out to dry. Then, the moist earth, dark and pungent with life. Water trickled down my nose as I clawed at the rain-soaked ground until the tips of my fingers were raw. Was I crazy to think there might be something here? In this sea of dirt, did I really think I could feel an emotional memory at the base of the tree? Despite my doubts, I couldn't stop. Through the pain of tender skin, I kept my hands searching. The moment they fell upon something unnatural, I dug faster and seized a small velvet sack, ripping it up from the soaked ground like a dirty purple flower.

I yanked the top open and dumped the contents into my palm: a delicate silver key, no longer than my pinky and weighty with a sense of age. The top was ornately scrolled in the almond shape of an eye with two shimmering red crystal pyramids—connected at each apex like an hourglass—suspended in the middle where the iris would be. When I touched it, the gem spun, as did the forest around me.

I fell backward, hitting the ground with a thud. I tried to anchor myself by focusing on the trees above me, but my vision faded to black. I gasped for air as images flooded my mind, a kaleidoscope of whirling pictures and sensations.

Symbols and images from around the world fired at me, one after another. Triangles and pyramids, the triple spiral, the Star of David, Borromean Rings, the pagan triple moon, golden Hindu statues of some three-headed god, triquetras, and an ancient stone with a carving of the maiden, mother, and crone. Trefoil symbols in church windows in Moscow and on bridges in Central Park. The father, the son, and the holy ghost of the Christian trinity. Every manner of horrific death. Every method of inhumane persecution. The last of the images was an emblem I'd never seen before until I found this key: the two pyramids connected at the tips. All of these spun past my vision, demanding I capture their meaning.

My mother had clutched this key in her palm. I heard her voice in my head saying, "*The Light Key.*" I could feel her fear and see her trembling hands as she walked through a beautiful, cavernous library. She had needed to hide her journal, the written record of what she'd uncovered so far, knowing that someone very powerful wanted to keep its truths silent. Words on a sign spun past my scope: TURNING DARKNESS INTO LIGHT. A wisp of memory, like smoke, carried her thoughts through time and space, and they somehow landed with me. Whatever truth about humanity she was uncovering was a huge one and an old one.

People killed to keep this truth buried.

And I was digging it up.

When the vision stopped, I lay gasping for breath in the mud, surrounded by ferns and clover. Mist fell upon my face as I looked up into the canopy of redwoods. They reminded me of a circle of elders looking down on me, witnesses to my absurd new life. My right shoulder burned fiercely as I clung to the key and stood on wobbly legs.

I stumbled from behind the albino tree and froze, thinking I heard the crackling of footsteps in the brush. I waited, listened, but heard nothing else over the calm patter of drops around me. I wanted to run but was shaking too badly. What the hell was happening to me?

How was it possible to touch objects and be battered with images like that? When I felt my shoulder sting again like I'd been burned with a hot branding iron, I yanked the edge of my jacket down my arm and gasped at the unmistakable marking of the silver key above my biceps. With cold, trembling hands, I stuffed its physical twin in my pocket.

Somehow, one step after another, I reached the car. Exhaust trailed out of the tailpipe into the fog. Muffled music blared from inside the car where Mari and Dun sat in the front.

"Holy crap," Mari said when I opened the back door and slid in.

"It looks like the mud won," Dun deadpanned. My shoes were caked with deep-brown earth. My pants were soaked and muddy at the knees. Every nail was a crescent moon of dirt. I stuffed my hands between my legs to stop their violent shaking.

Mari asked in a quiet voice, "You wanna tell us what the hell happened?"

All I'd have to do was show them the key or expose my newly tattooed shoulder, and they'd believe me. They couldn't think I was lying or crazy. But I saw death in that vision alongside the symbols. I knew that the people who wanted to protect the secrets the key held would kill anyone to do so. *Had* killed to do so. Death echoed in nearly every one of those strange images. That made it okay to sit quietly trembling and tell them I was fine.

"Dead end," I finally answered.

FIFTEEN

I had never felt so alone. So freakishly, echoingly alone.

My cell phone rang. I stared at the phone as it trilled. It was my father. The call went to voice mail. Mari and Dun didn't say anything, and we silently waited for the voice mail chime.

He wanted to know where I was, said he knew that I hadn't gone to school and that Mari and Dun weren't there, either, and demanded I go home immediately and wait for him there.

I wouldn't be doing that.

"Is a mounted posse going to come after us now?" Mari asked.

"I love it when you say things like *mounted*," Dun joked.

"You're twelve."

I rolled my eyes, and my phone rang again. Irritated, I answered without looking. "What!"

"Pardon? Cora?" Finn's gorgeous voice.

"God. I'm sorry. I thought you were my father."

"You and your friends aren't in school. And besides the bothersome fact that I didn't get to inscribe something cleverly stupid into your yearbook, I got worried." There was an adorable pause.

"Truth is, I was afraid you were sick again."

"No. I'm not sick. I've… There's something I had to do."

"Are you okay?"

Finn's asking made the sadness pressing just under my heart's surface swell and rise to my throat. "No."

"Can I help?"

I was about to say no, but who else could wrap me in his warm aura and comfort me? I wanted Finn's arms around me. I wanted to sink into him. But I had an ulterior motive, too. I didn't know when, I didn't know how, but finding my way to Ireland was suddenly very crucial. "Yes. Meet me at the rec center in fifteen minutes?"

Dun squeezed my shoulder as I slid from the car. I tried not to wince when he touched the tender spot where I'd been inexplicably tattooed. I hurried to the rec center with a new alertness. The flood of images from the key rotated over and over in my head. Besides the dirt, fear stuck to my skin, making me feel the need to be more on guard. I looked over my shoulder more than once as I walked through the tree-lined parking lot. Finn hadn't arrived yet.

The copy of my mother's letter and the key rested against my heart in my inside coat pocket. Emotionally wrung out, I leaned against the wall. Without warning, I burst into tears, crying into my hands. I cried for my mother, who was either massively brave or massively stupid. I cried about my father, who had let me down while trying not to let *her* down. I cried for myself. I couldn't stop. Tear after tear dropped into my dirty palms.

There's a difference between old tears and new. The old ones you've held back scrape from the inside when they come up. My throat ached with the effort to battle them. I'd been battling them for so long. Too long. The new ones flowed freely, a faucet of emotion that felt like it would never run dry.

There was more to my mother than the few memories Dad thought he could hide in a box. We had something dangerous in common, and I had a right to know what it was. I was at the core of a secret storm swirling around me, and my father wanted to cover my eyes.

I would not let his secrets blind me anymore.

Two warm hands covered my own and a tender kiss graced my forehead.

I knew who it was; I'd felt him approach.

Finn pulled my hands from my face and wiped my tears with the hardened pads of his fingers. "What's the matter, Cora?"

"Everything. My father lied to me about my mother. He let me believe she left us." My sobs grew louder, a torrent of emotions unplugged. "But she didn't abandon me. She didn't. She's somewhere...I mean...I don't know what happened to her."

"Oh, sweetness—"

"I have to find a way to go to Ireland."

"I'm not surprised at all that you want to go there. Ireland's in your blood, Cora. It's familiar to you in some part of your soul." He leaned in close, his eyes alight, sparking gold and soft brown and so understanding. "Of course you want to look for your mother. Is there any way I can help you?"

Our faces moved closer, the kisses and warmth I needed just a fraction away, but then I stopped him. "Wait." I ignored his raised eyebrow. His pretty lips. "You have a way of saying the exact thing I'm thinking."

He kissed me softly, nibbling my bottom lip. "You must know your eyes broadcast every thought you have." He cocked his head. "But sometimes you surprise me with what you say or do. I figured you're extraordinarily direct."

I didn't like the idea that my thoughts and actions weren't always my own around Finn. I'd have to be vigilant not to reveal too much.

"No. Extraordinarily direct is not normal for me. That's Mari's job. Also not normal is grabbing your shirt like a thug in the hospital because I was curious about your tattoo." My mind puzzled over it. The fever could have permanently scratched my record. But if that was true, why wasn't I out of control with everyone the way I was with Finn?

"You're curious about my tattoo?" he asked with a brash grin. He started to pull his shirt up, exposing the taut ridges of his stomach.

I shoved his shirt down and looked around us frantically. "Stop that!" I liked the laugh that pushed up out of me through my tears.

He shrugged. "Fine. Maybe I'll show it to you some other time."

I reached up and tugged the neck of his T-shirt away, trying to see more of it. "It reminds me of the triple spiral." The flash of iconic and violent imagery from the key played in my mind again. "But it looks sort of like stars, too. Like a spiral galaxy."

Finn nodded. "Fair play to ya, Cora. You do know your Ireland. It is what you say."

"The triple spiral? But why?"

"It's a family thing. If you're familiar with Irish mythology, you'll know they haven't a clue what the triple spiral means. Loads of theories. My mum used to tell me the triple spiral was a puzzle that was important to our family's history. It's something of a family crest to her. Personally, the fact that no one knows what it means is what makes it cool. I see it as a tale with no beginning and no end."

I traced my finger over the top of the labyrinthine constellation. "Maybe that's the best kind of tale." He covered my hand with his and pressed it to his skin.

It was our tale.

Finn hugged me. Strong arms around my back, almost lifting me from the ground. His heated embrace cocooned me, and I buried my face in his neck. My hysteria receded like a tide. He'd warmed me, soothed me. Pulsing, sweet energy swirled around my heart and expanded, pushing out through my chest. It was a door, opening for only him.

His mouth moved softly against my neck. "Since I met you, nothing else exists. No one has ever touched me the way you do. You're like a *fookin'* hypnotist. I don't know what you do to me, Cora Sandoval, but I can't stay away from you." He released me and stood back. "I can't. I'm here, standing in front of you because I can't."

"You're here because I said I needed you."

He shook his head. When he ran the back of his fingers across my cheek, a slab of resistance fell away like a chunk from a glacier, melting under his heat. When he bent to look deep into my eyes, I was sure I cracked open and bared my soul.

"I'm here with you and I'm here *for* you. I have dramas and confusion in my life, too. But it feels better when we're together. Don't you feel that, luv?"

I did.

When he kissed me, I was irretrievably his.

I waited in his car, holding my hands up to the heater vent, and watched him walk around to the driver's side, his long legs flexing under his jeans, his shoulders flaring beneath his shirt. He smiled as he got in, and happiness surged through me. My dad would call it "smitten." He'd used that word while walking among the redwoods one day, describing how he'd felt when he first met my mother when she was visiting Chile. I recalled the exact word because of the wistful longing in his eyes and because he so rarely spoke of her.

Finn kissed my dirty knuckles, feather soft. He touched the back of my mud-caked hair and laughed. "There's got to be a story about why you look like you were dragged through a bog."

Telling him about my dad and my mom was one thing. Parent issues were universal, right? But I couldn't bring myself to tell him I was an aura-seeing, New Age nut job who unburied a key in the woods that seared its twin on my arm. Besides, I never forgot Faye's warning not to tell anyone about myself.

I wouldn't put Finn in danger.

"I went to the redwoods." He squinted curiously but didn't push for more.

I bit my lip as he stroked my hair. Every once in a while, an unruly strand caught on his beaded bracelet and he'd gently slip it free. His eyes were so sincere, his aura clear of the sludge I'd come to associate with people's ambivalence. Warmth and caring rolled off him and surrounded me. Like luxuriating in a patch of sun on a brisk day.

His fingers slipped from the top of my hair to weave through the curls at the nape of my neck. A conflicted look passed over his face. He was fighting the urge to pull my head to his. I got that. Even appreciated his restraint because it showed he cared about the state I was in. But I wanted him to kiss me. Desperately.

"It's okay to kiss me, Finn." I hooked my fingers on the pocket of his gray shirt and pulled. "You *have* to kiss me."

"Good," he said in a tight voice. "Because I *need* to."

His fingers clutched tighter at my neck. He brought my lips to his, but he stopped short of a kiss. Our lips barely lit upon each other's, so light it tickled. We stared hard into each other's eyes. Our breathing swirled around our mouths, merging, our auras doing the same. We were trapped together in a bubble of pulsing energy.

Finn smiled against my mouth and teased his face away from mine, then gently tugged my head back and grazed my neck with his lips. He planted soft kisses down the slope of it. His spiked hair tickled my cheek, and I gasped when he sucked gently on my earlobe.

I tasted his neck, tasted the upper curve of the tattoo that had beckoned me since we first met, bit the firm pad of flesh where his neck and shoulder joined. Something about him made me feel primal and strong.

"Damn," he groaned and pulled us face-to-face again. We still clutched the back of each other's heads. "You are a force to be reckoned with." As he leaned away from me, his bracelet caught in my hair and split apart. Crystalline orange drops rained down on us, slipping down my shoulders, into my shirt, onto the seat. Finn laughed.

I started to scoop them up, scavenge for them between the seats, but he waved me off. "It's no big deal," he said. "It's just a bracelet." I curled my fingers around a few beads. Their tiny facets dug into my palms as he started out of the parking lot.

"I don't know how to pull off getting to Ireland to look for my mom. Saying it out loud makes it sound even more absurd. My father will be one hundred percent against it." I clenched my hands together in my lap and sighed. "I want something impossible."

Finn glanced at me with a wry smile. "So do I."

I knew instinctively what he meant. Deep inside me, a girl twirled with happiness while tears flew from her cheeks. He lived in Ireland, yet he wanted…us. We drove a minute in silence while I tried to pull myself together. This day was too big. Too much of too much. I leaned my head back on the leather seat and closed my eyes.

"I hate to see you so low," Finn said. He flicked the turn signal. "I know what you need." The car pulled to a stop in a darkened parking lot.

I looked around, confused. "I need a fifteen-minute oil change?"

Finn flashed me a megawatt smile. He rummaged in the backseat for something, producing a bandanna from his guitar case. "I need to blindfold you."

"Kinky much?"

A chuckle. "Do you trust me?"

The pause was, perhaps, extraordinarily long. "Okay. Not entirely. Um. Okay." How strange that I'd come to rely on seeing auras so much that I was nervous about the ability being gone.

He folded the bandanna in a triangle and placed it gently over my eyes. "Hold this." I pressed my fingers to my eyes while he tied the back. It smelled like him, like sun and leather and cloves.

We drove a bit more, turning this way and that, finally coming to a stop. I couldn't see anything except that it seemed lighter than before. He got out and opened my door, then took my hand.

"I feel stupid."

"Hush, vixen, and follow me."

Finn led me through a chiming door. The luxurious scent of sugar assailed me. "Is that buttercream?"

"Sit here a moment. I'll be right back."

I swear my mouth actually watered. I tapped my fingers and smiled. It felt good to smile. I detected Finn's approach before I heard him. His aura was unmistakable. There was always the familiar pull, the energy infused with warmth, sex appeal, and a sprinkling of trouble. He slid into the seat next to me. "Smell this." Something delectable waved under my nose.

"Vanilla and…is it oranges?"

"You could work for search and rescue. Here, taste."

His finger touched my lips. Rich vanilla frosting and tiny bits of candied orange peel swirled over my tongue. Heaven. He untied my blindfold. I blinked and looked around. We were in the biggest cupcake shop I had ever seen. I'd heard about the new place and really wanted to go but hadn't made the time. My cupcake-loving soul was thrilled. In front of me sat six cute little miniature cupcakes lined up in a row. Each one different.

"I figured we should do a taste test to choose our favorite."

I threw my arms around his neck and squeezed him. He couldn't have picked a sweeter way to cheer me up, and obviously one can better formulate radical plans of running off to foreign countries when fueled by cupcakes.

I caught him looking at me strangely. "What?" I asked through a mouthful of chili-spiced chocolate.

"I don't know," he answered in a very non-answery way, studying me as if seeing me with new eyes.

"Okay. Let me have it."

He cocked his head, blinked, and grinned. "You're radiant, Cora. It's the only word I can think of. You have a special light about you. People try so hard to shine. You do nothing, and you eclipse them all."

I gasped. "You mean you see light—?"

"No. No. I can't literally *see* it." His brows pinched together. "I feel it. It's something brilliant about you that draws me in. You gaze at me with those incredible eyes of yours, and it's like a drug. I want another hit. And another."

I kissed his sweet lips. I swear he gasped a little.

"Funny," I said, peeling back the accordion paper of the pink-lemonade cupcake. "I'd say I'm the moth attracted to your light. I know at some point, I'll get burned."

"Burned?"

"I'll fall for you. You'll go home to Ireland, and even if I see you again when I go to look for my mother—because I will find a way to do that—I still have to come back to America. Fiery hole in my heart. Crash. Burn. That kind of thing." I gulped. Geesh, I needed to put a restraining order on my mouth, or put another cupcake in it.

Finn blinked. "You could fall for me?" he asked in a reverent whisper.

The next words tumbled out in a cupcake-soaked garble that didn't sound like the English language. "So hard."

"I think I just swooned."

"And look, you're still manly."

He took my hands in his. We sat that way for a few moments, marinating in affection and buttercream frosting. I watched our auras bleed into each other. Mine shooting off sparks of silver. His gold, brightening into a starlike glow. Together we became a comet, racing into the sun.

SIXTEEN

Finn waved good-bye to me from the driveway. As I was poised to slide my key into the lock, the door opened and Janelle greeted me with an overly dramatic face. "He's been waiting for you, honey. Better get in there and face the music."

"Well, he'd better brace himself. I've got some music of my own to make."

I walked into the living room and looked for Dad in his leather club chair but found it empty. The sound of ice clinked in a glass from the couch. Dad never sat on the couch, let alone reclined on it with a highball of amber liquid. Not on a weekday. His tie coiled on the floor like a waiting snake.

We stared at each other a moment, waiting to see who would strike the first drum.

"I can't believe you—"

"I am very disappointed that—"

Our opening statements overlapped. The room reverberated with quiet again.

"What's with the drink?"

"I'm an adult, Cora. I don't need to justify my actions. You, however—"

"I'm seventeen, Dad. I'd be on my way to adulthood if you'd let me."

"Where. Were. You? I had no idea where you were! You didn't answer your phone. Something could have happened to you. You just— just disappeared." He sounded more like a scared boy than my father.

Looking for the truth. Reading hidden letters. Crying over my mother. Digging in the forest for a possessed key. Freaking out. Falling in love. "What difference does it make where I went?"

"You *cannot* disappear like that!"

"Why? Because *she* did?"

Just tell me the truth. Tell me or I'll never have faith in you again.

"Yes! Dammit!"

I flinched. He actually admitted it. I was too stunned to reply. I wanted to yell at him, to accuse and force-feed him the poison of his secrets, but he looked so devastated. I could see it etched in the lines of his face. He'd carried it for so long. He'd lied to me, but he'd lost her, too.

Dad swirled the cubes in his glass. The melting ice left trails of crystalline liquid in the heavy alcohol. Despite my sympathy, I was about to light into him with all my questions. Tell him everything I knew, show him the key he'd buried under the ghost, when he said softly, a lone tear streaming down his unshaven cheek, "You remind me so much of her, Cora."

"How?" I whispered. I felt like I did as a little girl when a butterfly landed on my arm, and I held my breath so it wouldn't fly away.

"There's something different about you that draws people to you. Grace was like that." He glanced up at me, then quickly back down at his glass. "It's always been this way. When you were little, it was animals. Any stray thing would follow you home. No sooner would I take you to a park than a bunch of kids would be trailing after you.

Even adults, they'd *stare*. It always made me—"

"Proud?" There was too much hope in my chest. It hurt.

"Uncomfortable."

I swallowed hard. He couldn't be proud of who or what I was or trust me because I was too different, too much like her. "What you said before was wrong," I told him. "I think you *do* need to justify your actions."

He shook his head but didn't reply, except to take a large gulp of his drink. Finally he spoke in a choked voice. "I loved her very much. That doesn't go away even though…even though she did. I love you, too, sweetheart. I don't want to lose you."

"Then *talk* to me, Dad. This is your chance." I ventured out a little on the ledge, unsure of what to reveal. How much tighter would the chains get if he knew what I knew? I had to find a way to get to Ireland. "I—I know you're keeping things from me. If we can't trust each other—"

"There is no one you can trust more. If there are things I've kept from you, it's only been for your own good." The hairs stood up on my arms. He let me believe my own mother didn't want me. *That* was for my own good? He kept the truth of her from me. There was something strange and different about me, and he'd known it my whole life.

He kept *me* from me!

My anger flared anew. I clenched my jaw and spoke through gritted teeth. "I'll go to Ireland, and I will find her. Maybe she'll tell me what you won't."

Dad's eyes flared, wild and bullish. "You will not step foot on that island as long as I live."

"Someday what I do won't be up to you!"

"Someday is bullshit! It's a wish your heart makes when you want things to be different than they are!" Dad's red anger muted, and his voice softened. "I believed in someday for a long time, too. Hate me if you want, Cora, but Ireland is forever out of the question."

SEVENTEEN

Someday is a wish your heart makes when you want things to be different than they are.

That was the truest thing my dad had ever told me. And the saddest.

I showered the forest mud from my skin and hair, but the key and the clover ring would never wash off. These two marks were permanent, and so upsetting. I didn't even wear makeup, and suddenly I'm tattoo girl? If this was going to keep happening to me, how was I supposed to hide it?

I swallowed my misery and dialed Finn's number, hoping he didn't mind me calling so late.

"I was hoping we could talk," I said through the lump in my throat. "I just had the worst fight I've ever had with my dad."

"I was about to call you," he told me. "Can I see you again, Cora? I miss you already. I'll come by for just a few minutes, and we can talk in person."

I hesitated. My father would freak out if he caught Finn at the house.

"Please don't say no. I've got to see you again. It's like an ache," he said. "I'll give you a quick kiss, you can tell me your troubles, and I'll be gone. I promise."

"You can't keep that promise."

"What? Beg your pardon?" I could hear his smile under his insulted voice.

"'Cause I don't think *I* can. Okay, come on by, but be stealth about it. Dad and I are at war. My window is the first one on the left side of the house."

Fifteen minutes later, I heard a light tap on my window. I kneeled on my bed and slid the window open, poking my head out into the cool night air. Finn reached up and ran his hand down the length of one of my long curls.

"This is very Romeo of you," I said.

He clasped his hand to my cheek and whispered, "*O' she doth teach the torches to burn bright.*"

I stared at his smiling honey-brown eyes. A corona of light flared around his body and extended toward me, sweeping through me. After he returned to Ireland, would I ever feel his warmth again? I wanted to stay with the boy who convinced me that what made me different was what made me beautiful.

I threw down my kisses, one after the other, onto Finn's waiting lips. Somehow, as we kissed, he slowly climbed halfway through my window, crawled over me, fell into my room, and onto my bed, knocking my pillow into the lamp, which thudded onto the carpet. He wound me in the embrace of his arms and legs. He woke every sleeping want in me.

I loved him. I could waste time wondering how or why this improbable, beautiful emotion had gripped me so quickly, but why? I knew I loved him. And I'd have probably said it if his sweet mouth wasn't covering mine with deep kisses that made my body achy and hungry. Instead, I did something I had read about in Faye's books.

I *sent* Finn love. Pure, loving energy. Right from my heart to his. I imagined my light pouring into him, around him. Without words, I declared my devotion. I was powerful and weak all at the same time.

Finn gasped. "Cora, there's something I have to tell you—"

A burst of white light blinded me.

The light in my room blinked on. My father stood in the doorway.

EIGHTEEN

Spanish is a lovely language, but not so much when it comes in the form of profanities. Finn scrambled off me and onto his feet, but strangely he didn't look at my father. He stared at me through heavy-lidded eyes that gleamed as if he were drugged. His aura pulsed with every color in the rainbow, the green being especially vibrant and, surrounding it all, a halo of gorgeous white light. He stepped toward me but stopped when my dad's voice seemed to penetrate his fog.

"This is the trust you asked for, Cora? See it? It's on the floor. Smashed! And you!" Dad pointed at Finn. Finn's head snapped to my dad. He looked confused, like he'd just remembered that my dad was in the room. His hands shook slightly. What was wrong with him?

My dad continued his tirade. "You have to know that climbing into my daughter's bedroom window is the epitome of disrespect to this household. To *her*! Did you think about that?"

"It wasn't my intention—"

"I know all about your intentions, kid. I was your age once, too. Get out!"

"Dad!"

My father pointed his finger. Brownish-red flowed from his hand toward me, like he was trying to cast a spell, and I could do nothing to deflect it. He threw his fury at me like filthy garbage. I recoiled.

Finn held up his quivering hands. "I'm sorry. It's my fault. All of this is my fault. Please don't yell at her."

My dad strode over to him. Right up in his face. "You keep your Irish ass away from my little girl, you hear me? I don't want you anywhere near her! Ever!"

"Stop it, Dad! Finn, just go. I'll talk to you tomorrow. Go."

Finn held a shaky hand up to touch my arm. But it fell to his side. His eyes were tortured as he left. I wanted to run after him. To comfort him. Screw my father and his heavy anger, his smashed trust. His controlling. It hurt me to see Finn's defeated colors, to feel his pain. He looked positively tormented.

My feet moved me toward the door, but Dad stopped me. "You are not to leave this house. I will lock you in, Cora. I swear I will."

Meanness like I'd never known burst out of my body. "No wonder she left you!"

Dad shuddered and I knew, true or not, my strike had hit its target. We stared at each other. His body went as rigid as steel. He left my room and, a few seconds later, I heard the car screech out of the garage, leaving me with more rage than I knew what to do with. I wanted to get it out of me and had nowhere to direct it. So I did what I always did when I was upset. I ate. And every bite was like swallowing my own venom.

NINETEEN

I didn't sleep at all and sneaked out of the house at six in the morning, taking my gloom to a coffee shop I'd never been to before and where no one would find me. Bits of the day before still clung to me. Remnants of mud under my nails and humiliation in my gut. I had left a note for Dad, telling him that he was unreasonable and unfair. I was going to school, and he'd either have to send the police or come himself to get me.

Finn waited for me at my locker. He wore a condemned look, miserable and slouchy. I walked straight up to him and wrapped my arms around his body, latching my fingers at the small of his back. Heavy arms draped around my shoulders as he buried his face in my hair. His heart slammed against my chest. Something was very wrong. I could feel it radiating off him in the waves of colors that mixed together in a confusing blend, like milky paint spilling from his body.

"Last night was awful. I'm sorry, Finn."

"No. You're not to be sorry. It's all on me."

The bell to first period rang shrill and insistent. I wasn't ready to leave him.

"Come on." He took my hand and led me to the greenhouse. We slipped inside. The world outside ceased to exist behind the doors. This was our chrysalis, warm and muffled. Finn had a reckless, wild look about him. He stared at me a long moment as I hopped up to sit on the potting bench. He stepped in between my legs, then grazed his lips over mine, a brushstroke of desire and anguish. What was wrong with him? Every color he had was unclear. Emotional grime tinted his aura.

He leaned in close, making my heart ram against my chest. "Innocent Irish lad jaunts over to America and look what happens to him." His eyes flickered with mischief, but there was a hint of something so sad, too, that it made my stomach cave in on itself. "Why'd I have to fall in love with you?" he asked.

My heart went off in my chest like a confetti bomb. Little mini-hearts floated into my bloodstream. "Love?"

He practically glared at me. "You know I am. Mad in love! It's *fookin'* insane. I talked to my mother last night after what happened at your house. She's angry at me for becoming so involved and for sneaking into your room and jeopardizing you. I know—I'm not good for you. I have to go home, Cora. My flight for Ireland leaves tonight."

Tonight. I couldn't breathe. He may as well have kicked me in the heart.

Finn closed his eyes. His head tipped back.

"Why did you tell your mom about sneaking into my room?" I asked.

"Something happened to me last night. I felt things—physically, emotionally—that I've never felt before. I wasn't myself. It was so strange. It was like I lost control. I shouldn't have done what I did." He shook his head, casting off the memory. "My mum's made the arrangements. You have no idea how controlling she can be. I have to go home."

Worry radiated from my center, up to my chest, closing off my throat. I swallowed hard. Had I done something to him? I was simply trying to give him love last night, from my soul to his, but maybe because I was this silver aberration I had inadvertently affected him badly. My love felt like a weapon.

I stared, disbelieving. Our parting sounded like a choice right now. His choice. I knew good-bye would eventually come, but it was too soon. He was breaking my heart. My voice was small and shaky. "Do you want to leave?"

"Cora." His hand cupped my cheek, and he shook his head sadly. Gone was the boy who was open to me. Globes of self-protection floated in his aura. "What difference does it make what I want? You always knew I'd be going back."

"When I go there—"

"*If* you go. And if you do, it won't be for me. It's time to say good-bye, Cora." One tear snaked down his cheek.

An aching freeze started in the middle of my chest, spreading outward like cold fingers. My breaths were a puff that barely came out. I was slowly icing over, numbing my heart to the pain. "Go then."

Finn looked down at the floor for too long. When he looked up, his eyes were full of things he'd never say to me. He reached for me, desperate. "Maybe someday—"

"Don't say 'someday' to me!" There was no way we would see each other again. I tried to push him away. "Go," I whispered again, but then found myself grabbing his neck, my fingers tugging at his dark hair. I pulled him against me. Even when his good-bye was the truth, I couldn't deny my need to feel him close before he was gone.

"Just leave," I cried in his ear, clutching his T-shirt. His hands found their way to my skin, ran possessively up my back. He slid my hips forward, stealing a gasp from me.

"Go away," I moaned, with my legs wrapped tightly around his waist. Tears mingled with warm kisses that tasted like love, staining our lips.

"I don't care if you go," I said against his mouth. Then, the truth I couldn't hold back any longer. "I love you."

"I'm not the same person since I met you. You've affected me forever."

"You're so mean. It was cruel to tell me you love me and then tell me you're leaving."

"I'm so sorry." His words were spoken in a choked voice against my collarbone, but my heart recognized the truth. The empty promise of us. "I have to do this now, but someday things may be different—"

I shook my head solemnly and whispered into his hair, "There is no someday. People leave me, Finn. They don't come back."

TWENTY

I had a phone number and an e-mail I knew we would rarely, if ever, use. I had one text that said Finn would miss me, that he felt weaker with every mile away from me. His last text had simply said, "Good-bye."

Two long weeks without him.

In that time, I delved into my research about silver auras and ended the school year with plans to go search for my mother as soon as I could. My head was busy, but my traitorous heart replayed memories of clove-scented kisses and the limitless depth of Finn's gaze. How he ensnared everything in me when he was near. I had my own light, but Finn returned it to me, magnified. His eyes were a mirror for everything beautiful in me, things I didn't see in myself until he reflected them back. With Finn, I was my truest self, a girl who knew what she wanted and went after it. I liked her. I vowed not to let her go, even if he had.

My father barely let me out of his or Janelle's sight. The final week of the school year was miserable, amplified by the fact that I could barely concentrate on final exams. As soon as the last test was over,

I walked numbly through the throng of kids with excited, summer-is-finally-here balloon colors around their bodies. I just wanted to be alone.

If I walked long enough and hard enough, I might be able to expel the ache in my chest. Maybe I'd get distracted by a vine exploding with purple flowers, clambering up a stone wall. I'd notice how the stray cat darting across the street had markings identical to a leopard. Marvel at the surprising beauty of a child's pair of red patent-leather shoes clipped to a clothesline, collecting sprinkler-water in the toes. Maybe, if I kept my mind busy with these things, I could stop myself from thinking of the boy who took my heart to a moss-covered island five thousand miles away.

Ireland was a thief.

Eventually, I sat down on a bench in the park. Water immediately seeped into my jeans, pressing cold against my skin. Perfect. I leaned forward on my thighs and watched an ant heft a comparatively huge crumb, struggling to get where it needed to go. I had a sudden, mean impulse to put my foot down in front of it, to halt its progress the way my father always did with me.

A camera flash burst in my peripheral vision. Maybe it was a birthday party in the park pavilion, or a student taking close-ups of the miniature roses around the fountain. But when I looked up, I saw the pulsing, flashing white aura of the man who had stalked me. My breath stilled.

He was in close conversation with a woman wearing sneakers and a tracksuit. I shivered but stared, almost defiantly. The alarm ringing through my body was a welcome cloak over my heartache. I watched him, bent on understanding what he was, why he affected me so badly. His eyes met mine and a half smirk played on his mouth. He tore his gaze from mine, reluctantly it seemed, to refocus on the runner. Her small dog yanked frantically against its leash.

I couldn't take my eyes off the man's aura. It was so unusual, so startlingly void of the color that radiated from everyone else. It was beautiful and strange, like the albino redwood. It captivated me yet my blood ran cold with fear. What *was* he? Was I witnessing the heavenly aura of an angel on earth? Is that why I saw him in the hospital when I was on death's door? When Mrs. Oberman died? If so, why did he keep appearing to *me*? If he was the messenger of my death, would running make any difference? Wouldn't Death be able to find me anywhere?

The woman's hands waved animatedly, gesticulating as if pointing directions to a lost tourist. The man listened and nodded. The cloud of his aura reached out to her like an embrace. In response, her aura narrowed to a point in front of her chest and beamed toward him.

So slowly, like the taffy-pullers at the boardwalk, the man dragged her aura into his own. His eyes closed briefly. He sighed with a rapturous look of content as his own light brightened and enlarged.

One of the woman's hands reached up instinctively to cover her heart, right over the leak she couldn't see but could surely feel. It did nothing to stop the flow of energy leaving her body. She swayed a bit. He didn't reach out to steady her, though she was obviously struggling. She reached toward him.

He took a step back. His hands stayed tucked stubbornly in his armpits.

I jumped to my feet. I wanted to run to her, help her. I wanted to run away and save myself. But my legs wouldn't react to either thought. I was inexplicably frozen in place. I could only watch the terrible beckoning of her energy into his.

His gaze moved to mine and held. The sounds around me faded, the warble of pigeons, the squeals of kids jumping in puddles, everything receded so all I could hear was my heart beating hard in my ears. I felt a tug at my own chest, and an infusion of energy when our auras collided that I knew instinctively was coming from the woman.

It was as though he had shared a bite from his fork.

I shuddered with revulsion. Her terror coated my skin like oil.

He smiled.

The dog growled.

The woman stumbled.

I watched in horror as he siphoned her energy, her very soul, into his own. Her aura dimmed, then finally snapped from her like a rubber band. The white shroud around him burst like a solar flare as she fell to the ground.

The air around her went still.

A breath, held forever.

He stepped toward me, a shadow of a man obscured by his own white light. I held out my hands as if to stop him, but he kept coming closer, closing the distance between us in a few steps. The sensation I had while lying in the hospital helpless, of being pulled from myself, came rushing back to me.

"Stay away from me," I shouted, panic making my voice shaky. I'd just watched a woman die. I didn't want to die. "I'm not ready!" My own silver aura popped and sparked wildly. It burned coming out of me.

His eyes longingly devoured my aura. "I've waited too long for this," he said, so low I barely heard him. "It's folly to deny myself. We can search for another like you. Ready or not…"

My chest jerked violently again as he greedily tugged my light from me. I couldn't breathe or move. My entire body grew weak and numb so that I couldn't feel my hands or feet. This couldn't be happening. My vision faded in and out. A fiery hole burned in my chest, burned my heartache to ashes, and spread throughout my body. Would the world forget I existed when the wind scattered me to the stars?

His ravaging halted seconds later when someone ran up to us, asking if we knew the woman on the ground, if we knew what had happened to her. The man's eyes turned angry, but he covered it with a quick look of alarm. "Oh, good Lord. We should call an ambulance!"

Dizzy, swirling, I faltered. She didn't need a freaking ambulance! She was already dead. He towered over me, radiating stolen light. This man with the white aura, he was no angel. *You killed her,* I wanted to say, tried to say, but my voice was gone.

He was evil. I knew it with everything inside of me. I'd witnessed a murder. One I could never prove. He never touched her, just like he never touched me. His menacing gaze was the last thing I saw of him before a crowd gathered and swallowed him up.

Only then did my legs obey. I backed away and ran. Faster, harder, farther than I had ever run before, with only one thought: *I'm not safe. If someone can do that to people, kill with an invisible, evil hook of their aura into another's, then none of us are safe.*

Twenty-One

Erratic silver sparks flared from my body as I ran. I was a girl on fire and had to remind myself that no one could see the flames. Except perhaps *him*, the man whose aura flared pure white, who had the ability to drain people of their life's essence, who affirmed that mine was different, and who would have killed me, too, if he could have. He had tried. I was lucky to get away.

As soon as I reached my bedroom, my energy plummeted to my ankles like wrinkled socks. He *took* from me! His body had lapped up my silver aura like a greedy cat. Why? I knew without a doubt that people gave and took energy from each other every day. I could see it. I could feel it, and anyone paying attention to how their body responded around certain people probably felt it, too. But this was different. My breath came out in ragged, shivery bursts.

This was *death.*

He knew what I was, confirmed it with his venomous whispers before he tried to rip me from my body. I looked in the mirror. I had to know if my aura was affected, diminished somehow. Would I be able to see if I had less of it? But I saw a petrified girl with dark curls stuck to her sweaty face, freaked green eyes, and the same vibrating band of silver around her body. Too wobbly to stand any longer, I sat on my bed.

My arms prickled with fear. Had he been trying to kill me that night in the hospital? And if so, why hadn't he succeeded? I had been weak, defenseless. I remembered only the sensation of coming out of myself, of crossing my arms over my body, before he backed away and disappeared. Faye had talked about people taking energy from others, but nothing I'd read online or in her books mentioned people who killed doing it. Her ominous warning sailed like a banner across my brain: *There are those who want nothing more than to find someone like you.*

He'd said something like that: *We can search for another like you.*

Apparently, I had fallen asleep at some point, still dressed, shoes squeezing my feet too tightly. The pillow draped over my head, and I tossed it aside only to have it hit my dad sitting next to my bed in the moonlight. I peered at him from between the streamers of my curls and started to sit up, but he stopped me. "No, baby. Don't get up." Tenderly and slowly, like he might never get to do it again, he brushed my wild hair out of my face. Even in the dark, his parental love was a rope of light, reaching for me.

"I have a surprise for you." The crack in his voice was thunder to my heart. "I'm sending you to Chile with Mari and Dun."

I was wide-awake at that point. "Really?"

"Your grandmother, she'll—she'll take care of you while you're there." Dad bent over and hugged me. "I love you. I hope you know that, always."

My mind was racing. "It's a great surprise, Dad. Thank you. But you're not coming, too?"

I really wanted to meet Mami Tulke. I wanted to look into her eyes and watch her aura when I asked her about the phone conversation with my dad. I wanted to find out what she knew about my mother. But this sudden trip was too uncharacteristic of my father. "I need you to be straight with me. Why are you suddenly agreeing to this, and why aren't you coming?"

"I can't. Not yet, anyway. Remember I told you in the hospital that I'm on a team studying some mysterious deaths? Well, they're on the increase. And it's not confined to one place. These deaths are happening all over the world, including here in Santa Cruz."

Yes. I've seen people drop dead like that. It's beyond terrifying.

"Unfortunately, I'm needed here," he said, "for the time being. We hope to rule out a virus, but the clock is ticking. It's only a matter of time before someone in the media connects the deaths, and that would cause widespread panic, especially when we don't know what's causing it." He leveled a serious look at me. "I'm trusting you not to say anything. I'm telling you because you asked, but I don't want you to think my work is more important than you. *Nothing* is. I'll come to Chile as soon as I can."

Despite the deep chill in my bones that wouldn't leave me, I found myself getting excited when, two days later, my uncle Eduardo showed up with Mari and Dun to take us all to the airport. Janelle insisted on going to see us off.

The opportunity to get out of town was too good. It didn't mean I wouldn't be on guard in Chile, though. There were two fears I harbored: the killer with the white aura, and the fact that I had dug up a dangerous mystery in the forest. From the harrowing visions I saw in the key, death was the method most used to smother the truth.

The key nestled against my chest under my shirt. I didn't know what the Light Key meant, but I wasn't letting it out of my sight. My mother had held it and, somehow, it was like having her hand over my heart once again, like in the picture.

Grace was a constant presence in my thoughts. What happened to her? How would I ever find out? *People who disappear do so forever,* she had written. Who else was disappearing and who was responsible for the disappearances? Was it people like that man? It seemed to me, if I had the answer to that, I'd be one step closer to knowing her fate.

Uncle Eduardo parked at the drop-off curb at the airport. He gave Mari and me big, squeezy man-hugs and a hearty handshake to Dun.

"I'll just go in with you," Janelle said, absently twisting a button on her cardigan. "To see you safely to security."

"Afraid I'll sneak off to Ireland?" I asked without needing an answer. Janelle squeaked in surprise when I pulled her into a hug. "You don't need to escort me to security. Just tell him you did."

When I drew back, Janelle cupped my cheek and looked into my eyes, probably the most intimate gesture we'd ever shared. "*I* trust you, Cora." Then her voice lowered. "But I've been in love, too. I can see you've been hurting pretty badly since Finn returned to Ireland. You've been so withdrawn, not yourself. Just don't—" She stopped herself and smiled ruefully. "Well, like I said, I trust you." To prove it, she hugged me again and slipped back into the car.

Mari breathed deeply as they drove away. "Smell that?" she asked. "That's the unique and overpowering scent of *freedom.*" Looking pointedly at me, she raised her eyebrows. "Onward, travelers." She tilted her rolling suitcase and strolled toward the doors of the airport like a movie star, leaving Dun and I to pad after her like adoring fans.

Inside the airport, I shifted from one foot to the other and scanned the crowd with a watchful eye. I was being paranoid, perhaps. But I shivered anew at the memory of my soul being yanked out of my own body. It was too easy for him.

I thought our souls were connected to us with stronger threads.

Through my T-shirt, I fingered the outline of the silver key. A tremor of violent energy rolled through me with the memory of the images I'd seen in the forest. Each image had seemed so random. Some were religious, but some weren't. The only commonality was that many of the images were triplicates. *Threes.* What could that mean?

I was most intrigued by the vision of my mother, the memory of her hiding her journal in a vast library. The library looked familiar, but I couldn't see a name. Just a flash of the immense room, and then a spiral carved in wood with a daisy at its center. She knew she might disappear but didn't want the truth to disappear forever.

My eyes trailed over the throngs of people in the airport as we waited in line. My search for silver auras had become habitual, and I was always disappointed. But something caught my eye as I scanned the airport: a three-leaf clover on an overhead sign. *Three.* It was the symbol for the Irish airline. A quickening fluttered in my gut.

Ireland.

Where I was born. Where my mother disappeared. Finn's Eden. The truth was in Ireland.

All my ghosts were in Ireland.

"Guys," I said, my nerves twanging like guitar strings. I grabbed Mari and Dun's arms. "I need an enormous favor."

Twenty-Two

The pilot announced our descent to the Emerald Isle, but when I looked out the window, there was nothing but a sea of white clouds below. It didn't seem fair. I should be able to see Ireland coming at me. I should be able to get a good look at my adversary, the one that swallowed up the people I love.

As soon as my father got wind of what I'd done, he'd probably call out the Irish version of the FBI. I swore Mari and Dun to secrecy, or at least enough quiet to give me a head start, but was sure Mami Tulke would also give them hell for being my accomplices. Besides going online on her phone and buying my ticket, Mari had slipped me some additional cash. Because I was seventeen and had my passport, I was good to go.

I don't know why, but when I hugged them, tears spilled over. I found myself staring at them, memorizing their unique and beautiful lights.

Hopefully I would find my mother's hidden papers in a mystery library before my father found me. I wanted to hate him, but I had an abnormally sized fairness gland. I couldn't blame him for what he did.

Her letter *was* ominous, and she had vanished as she had feared. She had been very clear he should protect me above all, and he'd kept his promise. But if he'd just been honest with me, maybe I'd be better at protecting myself.

I couldn't help thinking of Dad as a coward. If someone I loved disappeared, I'd turn over every mossy rock in Ireland to find them. That's what I intended to do. She might not be in Ireland. She might not even be alive. I knew that. But I was determined to be brave, braver than my dad, braver than he ever let me be. I thrilled at the step I'd already taken, claiming the freedom to do what I had to do.

As we dropped into the misty clouds above Ireland, I thought of Finn. How could I *not* think of him? I tried to ignore the crushing heaviness in my chest. I fought stinging tears. I missed him like I'd been split in half. But I wouldn't contact him. Even if I saw him again, we were another good-bye waiting to happen. I didn't want that. Our one good-bye was hard enough.

The plane dipped below the clouds and suddenly the lushness of Ireland came into view. It was flatter than I'd imagined, but undeniably beautiful, a patchwork of green and gold floating in a universe of blue.

I was born here.

There had to be an inner bell that rang when you stepped on the soil of the country of your birth. I wondered if it would ring for me.

Right after we landed, I ducked into the bathroom to splash my face, brush my teeth, and tidy my nest of hair. I was so tense, my ears felt like they were riding on my shoulders. My stomach was queasy. *Suck it up, girl.* Quests sure weren't for sissies. I was in a foreign country without a soul in the world to guide me. *One step at a time. I'm a big girl. I can get a cab, get to a hostel. I'll be all right. I'm going to be all right. Be brave.*

The customs counter experience made me woozy. I was sure there must be an APB out on me already, but the clerk stamped me back into my birth country, and I was on my way. The baggage carousel snaked lazily past me. I realized too late that my bag had already gone by. I didn't have the energy to chase after it. It would come back around eventually. The crowd became a sea of legs and movement and color, and I, I was a still stone in the river.

Until a flash of silver darted past.

My head snapped up. My whole being startled. Silver! An aura like mine!

On the other side of the baggage carousel stood a guy maybe two or three years older than me. It was hard to tell. Some people have faces that carry the shadow of their young selves forever. Finn was like that—half rock-star man, half boy poet. Others, like this guy, had a man face, mature, all traces of the boy gone. He had probably looked twenty when he was thirteen. His silver aura shone like a beacon in the current of colors.

My hand came away from my mouth. I hadn't realized I'd covered it in astonishment. I couldn't help staring unabashedly at the pewter flares leaping from his skin. It was beautiful. Breathtaking. *Is that what I look like?* My heart pounded as I watched him gather his suitcase and head for the exit.

I had to talk to him.

I pushed through the migrating crowd to get my bag and dragged it to the exit, then burst through the doors into the drizzle. I looked left and right but couldn't find the silver guy anywhere amid the travelers and cars. I kicked my bag. How could I lose the only other person I'd ever seen with a silver aura? With a throbbing toe, I hauled my luggage along like a reluctant mule, looking for the correct shuttle bus to take me to the youth hostel Mari had e-mailed for a reservation.

I'd brought no umbrella, having packed for the summer sun in Chile, so I pulled my hoodie over my head, tucking my misbehaving curls into the sides. "No wonder this place is so green," I remarked irritably to an elderly couple who stood with me, waiting for the buses.

The old man grinned, showing a flash of a gold tooth as he

tipped his hat to me. As quick as his smile came, it disappeared. His expression switched to alarm, his gaze froze. He collapsed at my feet.

I gasped and knelt down to him. "Mister? Are you okay?"

Just as suddenly as he had fallen, his companion's body dropped on top of him, her arm smacking my shoulder hard as she fell. Her eyes were fixed open, their blue irises exposed to the rain. I felt for their pulses, but my ability told me everything. Their auras were gone. Doused.

They lay in a tangled heap at my feet, bodies contorted haphazardly, rain falling softy on their colorless forms. They'd just dropped dead. A choking fear gripped me and adrenaline surged through my body. My muscles pumped with fire and every sense heightened. "Help!" I screamed into the rain.

Suddenly, a hand grasped my forearm and hauled me to my feet. Shocked and confused, I blinked at his silver aura. I'd lost him and now he was here, tugging urgently on me. "We've got to get out of here." His English was swaddled in a thick accent. I followed his anxious gaze across the busy street. A man in a trench coat and a flat tweed cap walked with his back to us in the other direction, but his white aura blasted more terror through me.

"Come! *Andiamo!*" I grabbed my bag. The guy gripped my arm as we ran down the sidewalk puddled with rain, leaving those two poor people, fatally stilled, behind.

Twenty-Three

We were soaked by the time a bus screeched to a stop in front of us. He pushed me in front of him onto the stairs. I fought for breath and scanned the aisles for an empty seat. Auras rose in waves above the passengers' heads like steam off their soaked bodies. With my silver shadow behind me, I made my way through the mist of colors to the rear of the bus.

The mysterious guy openly watched me as, vibrating with shock, I took off my backpack and sat down. His silver aura wreathed his head and cascaded over his wide shoulders. Drops of water darkened the tips of his sandy hair before slipping to slanted cheekbones. He slid into the seat next to me. I removed the hood from my head, wiping rain from my cheeks with my sleeve.

"You are cold." It was a comment more than a question. "And afraid."

"Yes," I answered. Those deaths and the sight of a white aura chilled me to the bone. "Those poor people," I whispered.

I could feel his eyes on me, his intense *energy* on me. It was all I could do not to stare. Not because he was attractive. I mean, he was, in a classic statue sort of way. But what attracted me was his metallic aura. I appeased myself by looking at his hand resting on his thigh. I placed my own hand on my leg as well, trying to appear as normal as possible. I wanted to see our hands next to each other. To compare the glows radiating from our skin.

Our auras were identical. Silver beams leaped from our hands in spikes and flares. The longer I stared, the more pronounced the flickering became. All the hairs stood up on my arm.

It reminded me of the time my dad and I had watched a lightning storm a few miles away from our home in Santa Cruz and felt an electrical charge surge through the wire fence we were leaning on. I remember him grabbing me by the waist and running frantically into the house.

The stranger's aura and my own shot toward each other. My arm buzzed like electrically charged ants marched all over it. Sitting next to him was like being plugged in. His fingers tensed and dug into his jeans. I jerked my hand away but found myself staring at his face, and he at mine. Searching blue eyes. Hair like the beach. Waves of wet sand. He was all rolled rocks, sea glass, and wind.

I tore my gaze away and faced the window, pretending to be absorbed in the city I'd always wanted to see, when really I had never wanted to stare at anyone more in my life. I was so excited to see an aura like mine. It made me feel…less alone. I looked at him again, trying hard to keep my eyes on his and not above his head, or over his broad shoulders, where I could see his silver flashing in time with my own pulse.

He looked at me, knowing and sad. "I believe we are here together because like attracts like."

I raised my eyebrows. It was either the most arrogant come-on ever or completely, cosmically right. But my breath caught at his next words.

"You see it, of course?"

My response rushed out in an awed whisper. "Yes."

He nodded. A lock of curly hair fell across one of his eyes. "I've been searching for someone like you." He blinked slowly and smiled with a secret thought. "For someone like me," he said, holding his hand out to shake mine. "I'm Giovanni Teso."

I couldn't deny an instant tie to him. I knew what it was like to be searching, too. "Giovanni." I rolled his name around on my tongue.

"You can call me G if you like."

I wasn't sure I wanted to call him G. Giovanni sounded much more exotic. His name was like gelato, cool and flavorful. We shook hands and a palpable shock wave ran up my arm and into my body. Not painful, but startling. He must've felt it, too, because we both snatched our hands back.

"*Christo*," he whispered.

I sat on my hands. "I'm—I'm Cora."

"Well, Miss Cora. I think we have much to talk about."

I leaned back in my seat and tried to calm down. I was having major trouble getting the dead couple off my mind. I told myself they were gone even before we ran. There was nothing I could have done to help them.

Now here I sat with the silver guy. My head was a little dizzy and I fought for equilibrium. "Okay, but can we start with the basics so I can catch my breath? Where are you from?"

"Italy."

It did explain his accent and his straight, prominent nose. The high cheekbones. He had a proud face. Imperious. I could practically envision a Roman toga and a laurel crown over his curls. "But you're a blond with blue eyes," I blurted stupidly.

Giovanni smiled and gave a slight nod. "My mother, she was Danish. I take after her a bit on the outside. But on the inside, I'm pure Italian."

He sure was. Mix a young Nordic Viking with a Roman emperor

and you'd have Giovanni Teso. "How old are you?"

"Nineteen. You?"

I gave him my basics. Born in Ireland but grew up in California with my dad. Came here to work on a special, er, project. But all too soon the topic turned to the obvious.

"How long have you been able to see auras?" he asked me matter-of-factly, as though he could be asking how I took my coffee.

"Um. Only a couple of months. I'm still trying to figure it all out. You?"

"Always. Ever since I can remember."

"Wow." I tried to imagine what it would be like to be a child who saw auras all the time. How long before he realized it wasn't normal? I had a million questions. Suddenly, a rogue memory filtered out the way memories sometimes do, lying dormant until triggered by a smell or kicked up by an offhand comment. I had forgotten all about it, until now. "When I was little, I used to have dreams that there were rainbows around people."

"How do you know it was dreaming?"

I pondered that. "I guess I don't. But it stopped when I was four or five." *Right about the time my mother disappeared.* "Recently, I got incredibly sick, and then the colors started up. I thought something was wrong with me. Like maybe the fever gave me brain damage or something."

He nudged my shoulder softly with his own. "There's nothing wrong with you. Except I think, perhaps, you have no idea how rare you are."

I stared into his eyes, then let my gaze roam, exploring his aura. "How rare *we* are." I shifted slightly away so that his shoulder would stop kindling against mine. "You are the only other person I've met whose aura is—"

"Beautiful?"

I bit my bottom lip. He was a wily one. "Silver."

Giovanni leaned his face close. I could see silvery-gray specks in his blue eyes. I tried to ignore the obvious merging of our auras when he was that near. Happy agitation skipped through me, but I couldn't tell if the thrill I felt was his or my own at finding another silver person.

"*Scintilla.*"

"What? What does that mean?" The word was wine-red and silky. It sounded like *schinteeela* in his accent.

"It's what we call people like us." His sky-blue gaze traveled over my face, to my aura above my head, and then slowly raked over my body. His nostrils flared a touch before he added, "*Spark.*"

TWENTY-FOUR

A mighty flame follows a tiny spark.

My fingernails dug into the seat cushion. After a few stuttering attempts at speech, I found my voice again. "There's a name for people with silver auras? Are there more of us somewhere? Why do we have no color?" Questions tumbled from me. This was better than any book from Say Chi's.

Giovanni held up his finger, hovering just over my lips as if to quiet me. I wanted to be offended, to swat his hand away, but I couldn't seem to conjure up enough insult to override the other sensations I felt. "Do you know why we have this little indentation above our lips?" he asked in a hushed voice.

My lips snapped with electricity. I could hardly breathe. "No," I murmured against the shadow of his finger, which slid slowly away from my mouth.

"My mother told me that when we are new babies, needy and helpless, an angel comes to quiet us. Presses its finger to our lips and forever marks us with the touch of an angel. You are like that baby now."

I bristled. "Does that make *you* the angel?" I asked with a bit of shaky sarcasm.

"Hardly. But I can see you feel very alone. I do as well. I've been alone most of my life."

I leaned away from him. It was one thing for me to see into people's energy, read their emotions. But I'd never had anyone do it to me. It was creepier than the naked-in-school dreams.

Giovanni looked away, as though he knew I needed a break from his gaze. "I've spent my life studying this," he said. "And searching for people like myself. I couldn't believe it when I saw you. I'm afraid we are extremely rare. I think, Miss Cora, we are an endangered breed."

Fear and incredulity slithered into my body, raising every blade of hair on the way. He meant it literally. It brought to mind my mother's letter about changing our very beliefs about humanity.

"But we're humans, not breeds. We may have differences, but there isn't more than one kind of human."

Giovanni's head rolled against his seat. His eyes were serious and unwavering. "You are wrong about that."

I could have argued, but my notions about humanity had already been rocked. I looked down at the clover tattoo around my finger. I had to be willing to concede there was a lot I didn't know.

"Why endangered?" I didn't like that word. It made me feel like I was surrounded by hunters, with red dots of lasers trained on my skin. It made me feel one shot away from death.

"That's what I'm trying to figure out. There are so few of us. I've heard of Scintilla hiding in pockets around the world, but I can't seem to find them."

"I think I'm looking for one myself."

His gaze shot back to me, blond eyebrows raised. "Yes?"

I rubbed the smooth bed of my thumbnail over and over. "My mother."

"How long has she been missing?"

"More than twelve years."

He studied me with a haughty expression. I narrowed my eyes. I didn't know this guy. I only knew we were the same. And he had more information than me. Information I might need. The muscles in his jaw tightened. "Well, good luck to you." His tone was a bitter young apple, hard and sour. "She is likely gone forever."

The bus rolled to a stop. He rose, but I pulled him back down.

"Where do you get off quashing my hope like that, you—?"

"This is my hotel," Giovanni said calmly, pointing to an old but classically lovely building on a busy street corner. "Where are you staying?"

I looked around with no idea where I was or where I was supposed to be. I'd been so absorbed in talking to Giovanni that I hadn't paid attention to our route. He smiled sympathetically and stood again. "You are not alone, Miss Cora. Come with me, and I will buy you something to eat. We can talk more. Then I'll help you find your lodging, yes?"

Somewhat reluctantly, I followed him through the elegant lobby of his hotel, which gleamed under tiered chandeliers. Polished marble floors reflected everything, like I could dip down into it, into an alternate reality. I took off my wet hoodie, squished my damp self into a leather chair, and watched Giovanni as he checked in and arranged for our bags to be taken to his room. I leaped up and rushed to him.

"Don't assume you can send my bag to your room," I fumed, staring up into his eyes.

"You misunderstand—" His hand swept to my shoulder. A charge ran down my arm. "I merely wanted to give you the opportunity to have a hot shower, maybe warm your chill." His fingers traced the goose bumps on my skin. I shrugged his hand from me, unsure whether the shiver came from the rain or from his energy. "Perhaps you'd like to change into dry clothes before we eat. I'm going to stay down here and have a drink until you return."

"Really? I—well, I—" There was the uncomfortable chill of my wet clothes pressing against my skin. I glanced at the clerk behind the desk, who tried to look as though she wasn't listening. "Thank you," I said with as much grace as I could muster. Giovanni handed me his room key.

Once in the room, I bolted the door shut. There was something too knowing and canny about him for his age. Giovanni Teso was worldly, as if he had walked this earth for hundreds of years.

The hot water did warm me, though, and I was grateful for his thoughtfulness. I slipped into jeans, a soft emerald-green cardigan, and my favorite polka dot scarf. From the looks of this hotel, I'd need something better than a wet T-shirt for dinner.

Downstairs, I could see through the floor-to-ceiling windows of the lobby that the rain had washed the day away and night had fallen in its place. I found Giovanni in the bar as he'd said. He was on his cell phone but uttered a hasty good-bye and clicked it shut as I approached.

"My God, that was no time at all," he said, taking in my new appearance. "You get ready faster than any woman I've ever known."

"Yeah, I pitch my tent in the low-maintenance camp."

He appraised me with his silver-blue eyes. "Not all women are so blessed. Please, sit. I've ordered a cheese and fruit plate for us to start."

I'd never had the experience of being with someone other than my father who was so in command. I wasn't sure I liked it. I'd spent the last six months, and certainly the last day, breaking free of my father's imposing will.

Then again, I'd never had much experience with guys, other than Finn. It stung to think of him, mostly because I'd never understand his abrupt departure. I sighed and sat, deciding it wasn't such a bad thing that Giovanni ordered fruit and cheese for me after the long and dramatic day.

"I want to say," Giovanni began, "that I am sorry about earlier, about your mother. I only said it because both of my parents disappeared when I was a boy and were never seen again. They were both Scintilla, and now they're gone. I had to face it long ago."

His parents disappeared? My mother's parents had disappeared, as did she. "Oh." Shocked breath rushed out of me. "Wow. Both of them? Who raised you?" I asked, fighting the urge to comfort him but knowing I couldn't. Not really.

He smiled sadly, shaking his head. His stormy eyes said I couldn't possibly understand. "I did," he answered with a proud lift of his chin.

It was the first hint of the boy in him.

Raised himself? What kind of lonely life had he led? No wonder he seemed so worldly. Sympathy surged in me for Giovanni Teso, and admiration as well.

Domineering as my dad could be, at least I'd had him. We'd had each other. "I'm sorry, too." I touched his hand softly, and we both jolted at the current of energy spilling into our skin.

"Very intriguing. I haven't touched another Scintilla since my parents. I don't remember it feeling quite that way. I like it very much."

I blushed. It was impossible to speak on just a surface level with him. Everything seemed deeper. "You definitely speak your mind."

We gazed hard at each other before he spoke again. "I see no point in trying to hide from someone so like myself. I assume you can see the truth." Then he looked at me with scrutiny. "But this is new to you. Perhaps you've not yet learned all you can do."

"I bought some books—"

He waved his hand dismissively. "The best teacher is experience. I will help you."

My toes tapped excitedly on the marble floor even as my stomach crackled with jittery energy. With it came a smattering of guilt. I felt strange about this sudden alliance. But that was probably because I liked the exhilaration of putting my hand on the wire.

"Any idea where you'll begin your search for your mother?"

"I have some ideas, yes. I need to go to a library. A big one."

"There is, of course, the library at Trinity College."

My mouth hung open. "Of course. Trinity!" I'd seen pictures of it. That's why it looked familiar. And my God, the name…

"Pardon my asking, but why would you think any information about your mother would be hidden at Trinity College?"

I nibbled a square of sharp Irish cheddar and a tangy green grape. "Because she put it there."

"How do you know?"

"I saw it." I expected Giovanni to question me further, and I didn't know how, or even if, I could answer, but he simply nodded his head in acceptance. "I'm going to go there tomorrow."

He took the last bite of the cheese and fruit. "Would you like more to eat?"

I rocked my head from side to side, stretching my tight neck. "Honestly, no. I think I'm ready for massive sleep."

Having settled the bill, we stood to go. I thanked him, but Giovanni's eyes latched onto something over my shoulder. Behind me, a television hung in the corner of the bar. Many of the patrons stopped talking to watch the big news headline of the day about the mysterious deaths at Dublin Airport. The newscaster spoke of the couple who had collapsed outside the airport, and then footage from an airport security camera showed the scene: their bodies buckled on the ground, and a side view of me, kneeling among them with my hood over my head. All that could be seen of Giovanni was his hand grabbing my arm. Our silver auras were invisible, of course. We looked normal. Well, except for the fact that dead bodies lay at our feet. It was surreal to watch the scene from an outside perspective, like it wasn't us. I could almost pretend it wasn't. Until now.

Above the reel read a caption: "Authorities seeking witness for questioning about mysterious deaths."

And then the newscaster's voice: *"Authorities are searching for the person seen on this airport security footage, who inexplicably ran from the scene where an unfortunate elderly couple mysteriously collapsed and died outside Dublin international airport today."*

I couldn't breathe, couldn't speak. My legs went numb. "They're looking for—"

Giovanni wrapped his arm around my waist and led me from the lobby bar out into the cold night. It wasn't until we were a good block away that one of us finally spoke. "It's not just me, Giovanni. You were on there, too. They showed you grabbing my hand and running."

His jaw was rigid. "I realize."

"What do we do? I can't let them find me. Oh God. If my father sees the footage, he might recognize me."

Giovanni stopped and turned me to face him. "You mean he doesn't know you're in Ireland?" When I shook my head, he nodded decisively. "Well then, luck would have it you had your hood partially covering your face."

I gave Giovanni the address to my hostel, and I followed him toward it. "Do you not wonder how those two people died at the same time like that?" he asked me. "And why *you* didn't?"

"Of course I wonder. There was a man there with a white aura. You saw him, too. We're obviously rare, being nothing but silver, but the pure white ones are also different from everyone else. They scare me. I think he had something to do with the deaths. I don't know. This is," I said with a sigh, "it's all new to me. I wish I knew more."

"I saw him, yes, and I have reason to share your fear about the people with all-white auras. I have a contact, a doctor, who is very keen to help us know more about ourselves. Perhaps you would consider coming with me to see him? He's one of the reasons I've come to Ireland."

I nodded. I wanted to meet anyone who knew about the Scintilla.

"But first, I will help you find information about your mother."

I stared hard at the silver halo of light around him, suddenly frustrated that I couldn't see more of his true temperament like I could with other people. If he thought my mother's case was hopeless, what was his motivation to help?

"Why do you want to help me?"

"I have an interest in doing so."

I'm sure my eyebrows shot up about a mile.

"Survival," he added.

I began to ask him what he meant, but he stopped walking and pointed to a modest brick building on a side street. "This is your place here," Giovanni said. "I will come by in the morning, yes?" He looked at me intently and added, "Meeting you, Miss Cora, has been a delightful surprise. To have met another like myself is… Well, I was beginning to feel quite solitary in the world."

I would have said the same, though maybe in a less aristocratic way.

Giovanni went into himself for a moment, thinking. "I believe it's important we help each other. It's our best chance against them."

"Them?"

He smiled, ruefully. "There's always a *them*, isn't there?"

TWENTY-FIVE

The afternoon sun played peekaboo behind threatening clouds. Trinity College library hadn't opened until after lunchtime, and so I'd had to impatiently postpone my investigation with a lunch of bangers and mash at a small local pub.

THE BOOK OF KELLS: TURNING DARKNESS INTO LIGHT

The sign outside of the library actually said those words. The same words I'd seen in the vision when I'd unearthed the key in the redwoods. My body hummed with excited energy, and I wished for a fleeting, sad moment that Finn were here with me to share my excitement.

I fingered the key, rotated the small red crystal, and slipped it back inside my shirt. Would I need this key today? Did it unlock something that housed my mother's research? Would it lead me to her?

Giovanni waited in the long line with me, the strap of his messenger bag slung diagonally over his broad chest. He towered over the heads of everyone like a general surveying his troops. I had to smile. His attention was focused on something up ahead. With us, people-watching was a different sport entirely.

His gaze, which could be called cold but wasn't if you looked deep enough, flickered to me. He'd caught me staring. I blushed, and a knowing half smile turned up his lips. It was maddening because blushing was totally redundant. Apparently, he could read into the silver in my aura. I wanted to learn to read the subtleties of silver, too. I wanted to know what he was thinking, feeling.

"Any idea where we might find this journal of your mother's in a security-tight library with over 200,000 volumes that we are not permitted to touch?"

I rolled my eyes. "I don't answer questions that aren't questions." I knew the odds were against me, but I'd gambled on this trip for a reason. My mother had hidden something here. I knew it. The sign outside proved it.

The line of tourists shuffled into the Long Room of the library. I gasped as soon as I entered. My hand flew to my heart, pressing the key against my skin. The long, narrow room stretched out before us with two stories of books housed in dark wooden shelves soaring up to the barrel-vaulted ceiling like a huge, elegant ship turned upside down. Dozens of alcoves, sections upon sections of books, lined the length of the room. Ornate spiral staircases wound upward in some of the alcoves, while others employed tall, narrow ladders. The alphabet was etched in gold letters up the sides of each row of thick shelves. The brochure said there were over 200,000 volumes in this room alone. It made my book-loving heart race.

In between each recess stood a marble bust upon a wooden pedestal, over forty of them, giving the impression of a fleet of ghostly sentries guarding the ancient volumes—guarding my mother's treasure. But how on earth was I supposed to find anything here? I didn't voice this thought, not wanting to see any trace of smugness on Giovanni's face.

I walked slowly, looking for a box or something in which the key might fit, despairing more with each step. It wasn't likely that anything was going to jump out at me. I was surrounded by a vast sea of leather tomes with no idea how to find the one precious volume I needed.

Waist-high shelves stood in the middle of each alcove. I stopped abruptly. The warm air of Giovanni's breath and the flare of his energy rippled over my neck and shoulder. "What is it?" he asked.

"That carving there, the spiral." It was the one I'd seen in the memory bound to the key. I walked to the next alcove and then the next, past the busts of Jonathan Swift, Sir Isaac Newton, Socrates, Shakespeare. Beneath the stern faces of the world's great writers and thinkers, every single pew of books had this same scrollwork carved into the end pieces of the shelves: a winding spiral with a flower in the middle. I rubbed my temples as I racked my brain for ideas. Where would my mother hide her journal in a place like this? If she and my father and I had anything in common, she'd have hidden it in plain sight.

I walked down the length of the enormous room a second time, hoping against hope that if her journal *was* here, she hadn't tucked it away on the second floor with no public access. As it was, double ropes cordoned off parts of the floor, keeping the public from handling the valuable books. Even if I found something, I wasn't sure how I'd get my hands on it. My eyes scanned for anything with a lock in which the key might fit. The faces of each marble bust mocked me with blank, staring eyes. One bust in particular ridiculed me more than any other: Cicero. My father kept a handwritten quote of Cicero's under the glass on top of his desk at home. It said:

Are you not ashamed as a scientist, as an observer, and investigator of nature, to seek your criterion of truth from minds steeped in conventional beliefs? -Cicero

I'd had to stare at that quote a million times as I sat at his desk during the years I was homeschooled. I retrieved my mom's letter from my pocket and examined her neat, slanted script. Yes. It was the same as the script in my memory. I looked again into the colorless eyes of my messenger. When you have nothing to go on, you'll go on anything. I tilted my head to look at the books on the shelves in the alcove next to Cicero.

"What would it be titled?" Giovanni asked.

I gave him a tired look. "I'm guessing it will be titled *X Marks the Spot: The Musings of a Missing Scintilla.*" Giovanni's eyebrows shot up and he walked past me. I scanned the rows and rows of books all in shades of mud brown, faded blue, and maroon. I was about to move on when a red book caught my eye. One word was written in silver script where all the other books had gold: *Grace.*

"Giovanni," I hissed. With long strides, he stood back at my side. I pointed at the book. "That one. That's it, I know it." I was so desperate to touch it that my fingers tingled. I hopped up and down on my toes. I leaned against the teal ropes keeping me from the book I was sure was my mother's. Her name, Cicero's bust, even the color of the shiny foil lettering. "I have to have that book." My voice was a desperate plea, and my stomach knotted like cable.

Giovanni pointed at the security personnel in the room. "Go ask him what is required to gain access to the upstairs section."

His command stymied me, but I trusted he had a reason, and I believed he wanted to help. I walked along the glossy planked floor toward the man he'd pointed at, willing myself not to look back at the book.

Before I'd even gotten my whole question out, Giovanni was next to me. "We're running late," he said with a curt nod to the security guard. "Maybe next time?" He took my elbow and led me out of the library.

"Listen, I—you can't just—"

"Don't worry about it, Cora."

"How can you tell me not to worry? We need to go back in there!" I tugged on his arm, but he held it firm against his waist.

Giovanni stopped outside the gate to the college and opened his jacket a fraction. The silver lettering inside gleamed at me. I stared openmouthed. He winked.

I held out my hand. "Let me see."

He began walking again. "Not here. Let's find a coffee shop where we can sit in the privacy of a crowd."

We walked without speaking for a couple of blocks. I didn't ask how he got the book. Honestly, I didn't care. I'd have snatched the book if I could have, and I supposed he probably didn't survive his entire childhood on his own without using some sleight of hand once in a while.

The coffee shop was warm, and I was grateful for the respite from the chilly breeze. Giovanni and I scooted into a café table in the back corner. He slipped the book from his jacket and held it out to me. I thought about my apparent new affliction: psychometry—the ability to pick up information from an object. As best I could tell from the Internet, that's what had happened to me with the phone and the key. As if seeing auras wasn't crazy enough, I got to add another extrasensory ability to my repertoire. Not surprisingly, my search didn't yield anything on "spontaneous tattoos."

I took the journal and inwardly winced, expecting a rush of object-memory to overtake me, but nothing happened.

Nothing.

"Why do you wait?" Giovanni asked. Then his large palm covered mine. "Your hands are shaking."

Despite just meeting him, I was thankful to have him with me. "This might not be it," I said. I had been so sure my mother's journal would be infused with memories accessible with a touch, its silence crushed me.

He ran his fingers soothingly over the tops of my hands, then removed them, leaving a cloud of energy over my skin. "Open it."

I did.

The first thing I saw was the quote by Cicero in the same familiar script as my father's note. My head bowed and a sob-laced breath fell from my lips. I let the book fall open, deciding it would tell me what it wanted to tell me.

The pages were covered in scribbles, the first one a sketch of the pyramids tip to tip, like in the key. She seemed particularly interested in *Brú na Bóinne*, the Irish name for Newgrange, as there were pages of notes and drawings of that one place alone. It was majorly important to the Irish, who could boast in a superior "Our megalithic temple is one thousand years older than your Stonehenge" kind of way. It was important enough that even Finn had the triple spiral tattooed on his chest. Talk about pride of place. But why was Newgrange so important to my mother?

There were also newspaper clippings, quotes, pictures of religious icons and saints, many of which I'd seen when I held the key for the first time. This was my mother's journal, a piece of her in my hands. I couldn't wait to devour every word. "If—if we could walk back now, I'd like to go to my room and read a while."

Giovanni nodded. "If you don't mind, I'd very much like to know anything that might pertain to us."

"You got this for me, and no one has told me more about myself than you have, Giovanni." I took a deep breath. "I'll tell you. I promise."

TWENTY-SIX

The book weighed down my purse, but it wasn't a burdensome weight. It was heavy with my mother's history. I was going to catch hell for it, but coming to Ireland hadn't been a mistake.

We crossed a busy street in front of a large park called St. Stephen's Green. The sun fell behind the buildings, casting intermittent shadows on the edge of the park. Giovanni and I walked through the shadows, heading toward the Temple Bar district and my hostel. My mind was on one thing: to get back and immerse myself in my mother's world. It was like she was waiting for me to get to know her.

I barely registered Giovanni, and finally realized how much we had walked today. "This is totally the opposite direction from your hotel," I said. "You don't have to walk me."

"I'll not leave you until you are there safely, Cora. You must realize what constant danger you are in." He gave me a wry and bitter look. "Scintilla have a way of vanishing with no trace."

Giovanni scanned the crowds filing into the park. "God, but it's busy here tonight. I'm going to the toilet right there." He pointed at a row of portable toilets. I grinned, thinking how it must confuse the rest of the world when Americans ask for the "restroom."

"Looks like you're gonna have to leave me alone," I joked.

"Be right back," he said and jogged away.

Applause rolled out from the center of the park. The sound of a guitar vibrated across the air. Then singing. I stood on my tiptoes but couldn't see over the heads of the vast crowd filling St. Stephen's Green. The colored lights of the stage mimicked the auras in the audience, so all I saw was a lake of outlined bodies and a raging storm of color rising into the twilight above the trees like the aurora borealis.

The singing continued, dreamlike. The sensation of irresistible magnetism was strikingly familiar. The last time I felt so overwhelmingly compelled to move toward a song was…oh. I could barely breathe. I left my spot and pushed through the crowd toward the stage. If I didn't confirm who my heart believed was up there singing, I'd always wonder why it took my breath from me. I looked back, but I couldn't see if Giovanni had returned. The place I'd been standing was lost in the undertow of people swaying to the music, so I returned my attention to the soulful voice singing of a girl and how he wished he'd never left her.

"*Her love, her pain, were my own. Flowers of the seeds I'd sown. Watered by her cry, the day I said good-bye.*"

Just hearing it made my heart hurt.

The stage lights cast millions of colored gems on our heads, sparkling on our skin, swirling through the tinted auras of the crowd like we were the center of a vast galaxy in motion. I shoved through the rows of spectators and stumbled forward, stopping at the base of the stage. But my heart continued to stumble.

It fell at Finn's feet.

I looked up and watched him sing, perfectly curved lips barely opening as though the lyrics hurt coming out of him. The blue stage light shone down on his jet-black hair and bathed his golden aura so that he looked like a candle burning on stage. His eyes were closed as he sang.

See me, I thought, willing him to open his eyes. *Look at me.* Just once again so I could see if he would feel as stunned and shaken as I did. If he felt anything, anything at all. Perhaps he'd left it all behind in America when he decided to leave.

His long fingers plucked the guitar strings, and I instantly remembered how they felt behind my ears and on my jaw as he kissed me. I closed my eyes and listened to his tender voice. It was almost enough, having had this last glance at the boy I loved. A moment with him I thought I'd never have. I understood then why they called them stolen moments.

Once Finn's image on the stage was forever burned in my heart, I forced my chin up and turned away. I needed to be as strong as he was the day he let me go. The singing stopped. I faltered but kept pushing sideways, swimming across a riptide of auric energy.

At first I had wanted Finn to see me but now...now I wanted not to endure this fierce, pulsing ache in the center of my chest. I had enough pride to walk away without him seeing me.

"Cora!" My name echoed across the crowd like a slow-moving wind.

I kept moving to the right of the crowd, but it parted in a wide circle around me. Except for one person who stood in my way. He must've run the length of the stage to intercept me.

Wordlessly, Finn cupped the back of my neck with his hand and clutched me against his chest. A tiny gasp escaped me, but I could form no words. He spoke for both of us, his words coming out in a reverential murmur, his warm lips against the hollow of my cheek. "You're here. Jaysus, you're here."

I was a million miles away from everything familiar—but in his arms, I was home. Why did Finn have to feel like home?

"How is it that in all the faces in this crowd, I opened my eyes and saw the one that was in my mind?" His lips moved softly against my skin. We both turned our heads so slightly, our lips only meeting at the sacred corner of our mouths where smiles and secrets hide.

I became aware of applause all around us. Finn must have, too, because he broke contact and peeked at me with a wide smile that soon faded. "You're crying, luv?" He swiped my cheek with the back of his fingers, then brought them to his lips. "Why are you crying?"

I sniffled. I hadn't realized I was. "Because you're here."

Finn led me to an open spot of grass. "Are ya letting on, Cora? I live here. You might be a wee bit far from home," he pointed out, enunciating his T's in his charming Irish way. "You said you'd find a way and you found a way. I never doubted you would." With a laugh, he swept me into his chest once more. "Christ, it's good to hold you again." My breath came in short puffs against his collarbone. "It's the sun on my back after days in the rain."

I reveled in the nearness of him, the delicious pleasure of his hands on me. He smelled so good, so familiar. The cloves and soap, the…

"So," said a woman's cold voice from behind me. "This is Cora."

Finn held on to my hand. "Mother, Cora Sandoval. Cora, this is my mother, Ina Doyle."

"I see it's too late." Mrs. Doyle regarded me with icy blue eyes, bordering on resentful.

"Too late for what?" I asked, unable to ignore the bait. Finn squeezed my fingers.

She smoothed her tightly drawn hair against her scalp. "I had hoped Finn was simply being melodramatic about his affections toward you. I had hoped it was merely a crush, as he is too young for any serious involvement. But I see it's too late." I'd never before heard someone use the word "hope" like a spear.

"Can we not go into this now? You're being rude," Finn told her, his voice sharp. His aura jabbed at her in angry spikes. Her aura responded like a Death Star force field, deflecting his blows. Amazing.

Ina's eyes flicked to mine. I tried not to look away but failed, my gaze landing somewhere near her impeccable shoes. "Am I?" she asked. "I do apologize for being rude. I'm a mother. We tend to want to protect our children."

That's when I lifted my gaze to meet hers. "From me?" I asked, barely able to mask my astonished laughter. I didn't want Finn's mother to hate me, but clearly she had already made that decision before we'd met. And if she really wanted to split hairs, he was the one who broke *my* heart when he left so abruptly.

Someone in a suit tapped Finn's shoulder. "One moment," Finn said to us. "My set was over, but I don't think they expected me to go darting off the stage."

Although their color was different, Mrs. Doyle's eyes and Finn's were identically almond-shaped. Hers would be beautiful if they held any of the warmth her son's eyes did. She leaned in close and whispered, "You've changed him. He wasn't ready."

"Ready? Pardon me for saying so, but I certainly didn't expect to feel like this. It just happened."

Ina clucked her tongue. "Oh," she said, "you thought I meant *love*." Her gaze raked my body. "Love is like smoke, dear. Sneaks in under locked doors. There's something about you, I'll give him that. What you bring is another matter. He can't handle it."

Finn sprinted back to us and grabbed my hand. "Enough." His steely words matched the hard, razing stare he gave his mother. "I'll decide what I can handle." Ina turned on her high heel and strode away.

"Sorry about her," he whispered. "It's not you she's cross with."

I was too stunned to react. I'd received an auric bitch-slap. Apparently, I didn't have the ability to deflect bad vibes as well as she did because my body was like an empty balloon after the encounter. "I'm so sorry to cause you trouble. I had no idea I'd see you."

"You mean you didn't come here for me?" he asked, sticking his bottom lip out in a very appealing, ripe fruit kind of way.

I bit my own lip. "No." When Finn gave me the truth serum look, I said, "Honestly. I came because of my mother. I never got to fill you in on everything—I never had time. I didn't expect to run into you. That's why I tried to leave. I wanted to respect your wishes not to see me." I couldn't look at him then. He'd see my pain.

"You know nothing of wishes," Finn said.

"But—"

"No, Cora. I'm awed that you're here," he said, his voice sure and strong. "I thought it would take a miracle to ever see you again. Now that you're here, I feel whole again. I may never let you leave." He kissed the top of my hand. "Will you stay with me awhile?"

"I can't. I—" Again, I looked around for Giovanni or the blaze of his distinctive aura. I didn't want to worry him.

"Please, luv. I'll take you to Mulcarr's Pub for some traditional Irish music. My uncle Clancy owns it. I just want to look at you. Christ, Cora, the reality of you is so much better than I've been dreaming."

Finn jogged over to the stage and had a quick exchange with someone before returning to my side. I had Giovanni's number and asked Finn if I could use his cell phone to make a quick call. He answered, reasonably frantic. I muttered a hushed apology, told him I'd run into someone I knew, and that I'd call him later. I could tell Finn was curious but he didn't inquire.

Finn.

This was surreal. He wanted to spend time with me, time I thought we'd never have again. I wanted that also, but I was torn in two. I had my mother's journal—and I really wanted to be alone to read it. But this unexpected time with Finn was something I couldn't make myself throw away. It would only be for a little while, I reasoned. The truth was, I believed in fate. And obviously our story wasn't over.

TWENTY-SEVEN

I was overcome by the force of Finn's energy. Something was different about him. Maybe being on his own turf infused him with more confidence. His aura was so big, and so strong, that it washed against the shores of my own with each step he took in my direction.

"The pub's not far from here," he told me. When he held my hand, it felt completely natural, like there'd never been a good-bye. "Let's walk."

Inwardly, I lashed myself for not being stronger, for not kissing his cheek and parting ways again with resilient grace, like a woman from an old movie, whose heart bleeds as she smiles politely through her farewell. I wanted to fully understand why he'd left as abruptly as he had. He seemed so happy to see me, though, that I couldn't make myself confront him. I was happy, too.

Finn and I strolled hand in hand through the streets of Dublin lit blue by the early evening light. I was charmed by the cobbled streets and the juxtaposition of the old and new in the buildings we passed. While we walked, I told him about my mother's letter and how I hoped to find out what had happened to her. Astonished, he promised he'd do what he could to help me, though he didn't know what. "A dozen years is a long time to be missing."

Across the street from Mulcarr's Pub, there stood a beautiful church and a rather imposing shrine of the Virgin Mary. I wondered if it made the people who had too much to drink feel guilty leaving the pub under the watchful eye of Mary.

The pub was quiet inside. A family occupied one table in the corner. A lone gentleman at the bar hovered over a brown pint of Guinness. Pictures and posters depicting the recent history of Ireland covered the green walls. The ceiling was a quilt of yellow tin stamped with intricate patterns. At the juncture of ancient beams above us was a carved wooden square—a *boss*, Finn called it when he saw me looking—engraved with three rabbits chasing each other in a circle. Three had become an eerie number. My eyes found it everywhere.

Within thirty minutes or so, a crowd filled the pub. From grandmothers to babies in strollers, families took seats around the perimeter of the room. "It's funny how many kids are in here," I said.

"You've got to know, Cora, in Ireland a pub is much more than a bar. It's a place of gathering. It's our tribal fire pit, in a manner of speaking. I grew up in this place. When I was a wee bit, my uncle said I'd toddle from table to table trying to get a dram off people's cider."

I tugged his short stubble. "Trouble, even then."

To my left, I noticed what appeared to be a small room adjacent to the bar. There was a red door with wrought iron looping over the top like cursive writing. A window opened to the back side of the bar. "What's with that little room?"

Finn smiled and grabbed my hand. "Come with me."

Inside, it was exactly as it looked from the outside—a tiny room no bigger than a walk-in closet. The window was painted with a family crest and the worn floor looked as though centuries of feet had smoothed its grain. We sat on one of the two benches that ringed the peculiar little space.

With one arm around my waist, Finn slid me closer. He brushed the curls from my cheek. We stared into each other's eyes, an epic, wordless conversation. He kissed the tip of my nose. I reveled in his tenderness but was scared to open to him again. I'd missed him. I'd hurt over him. But before I could fully marinate in my fear, he squeezed my chin gently, easing my mouth open. He held me and kissed me in such a way that I remembered my heart was still his.

It might always be.

"You don't mind, do you? I had to kiss you," he whispered against the sensitive corner of my mouth. "I've missed you so much, Cora." Longing amplified in his energy field. His aura enveloped me, leaving me breathless and light-headed. "This room is called a snug."

"Good name for it."

"Aye!" boomed a voice from the bar. "There's a bit of canoodling going on in this snug, isn't there now?"

Finn winked at me and whispered, "That'd be my uncle Clancy." He introduced us and slapped his uncle's arm. "What's the *craic*?"

Clancy Mulcarr had robin's-egg-blue eyes under dark brows, snowy hair flecked with gray, and a snowy beard. He looked like a seaman, rosy-cheeked and weathered. Unlike Finn's mother, he smiled warmly and kissed both of my cheeks through the snug's little window. "If this is how they grown 'em in the States, perhaps I'd better seek my romantic fortunes there," Clancy said with a wink.

"Actually, Uncle, Cora was born here."

"Is that so? Welcome home, daughter of Ireland."

I smiled and sat back down. Uncle Clancy passed two small glasses half-full of amber liquid through the opening. Finn took one and passed the other to me. I sniffed it.

"Bulmers. It's the cider I was after as a child," he said, leaning on the ledge of the snug's window. "Taste it."

Finn and his uncle chatted back and forth, and it took my kiss-addled brain a few seconds to realize I had absolutely no idea what they were saying. When Finn caught me watching him, listening intently, he smiled and bent to kiss me again.

"Were you speaking Gaelic?" I asked excitedly.

This earned me a stern look from Finn. "We do *not* call it Gaelic," he said in a serious, proud tone. "We speak *Irish*."

I nodded, contrite. "Noted. I want to hear more."

He leaned in. The hairs on my arm stood when his warm breath caressed my ear. He whispered the strange words slowly, seductively in my ear. It was beautiful. A language of old, salty winds and softly ringing, weathered bells. My brain didn't know what he said to me, but my heart did.

We left the intimate cocoon of the snug and joined the growing crowd in the pub's main room. Finn led me to a table made of a glossy square of wood affixed to the top of an old barrel. We sat on little stools topped with woven leather. The fire warmed my cheeks, or maybe it was the cider. Next to us sat a group of men. Each held a different instrument—a banjo, a fiddle, a small accordion-type box, and a guitar. Finn grabbed a guitar from atop an ancient leather-covered piano and sat on the stool next to me.

A young woman with braided hair sat alongside the men with a deep bass drum in front of her. She tapped her bare feet while she played. As the music got going, other people, women mostly, joined with flat drums, which Finn told me were called *bodhráns*. They brushed the drums with wooden sticks that resembled thick paintbrushes. Each beat thrummed deep in my chest like a pulse. I'd never view musicians the same way after seeing how their auras pulsed with the music as if their bodies were tuned to it. It was another moment of confirmation of something I'd always known subconsciously: music affected our energies. Music wove around us and asked our souls to dance.

Finn accompanied on guitar while his uncle Clancy sang a slow song. Clancy had a beautiful voice, river deep, that carried and fell like water over mossy stones. As when Finn had sung, I choked up. The song was so full of melancholic emotion, almost like a call to ancient kin, and I instantly understood what Finn had meant about their music.

The ghosts inside of me stirred.

When the tempo picked up again, the entire room exploded with energy and colors. We all clapped along, whistled, and cheered. Two elderly women stood up and, with their palms touching, did a kicking sort of dance together around the room.

"You so owe me a Riverdance!" I yelled to Finn over the music.

One of the women bounced over to me with her palm up. I shot a questioning look at Finn, who indicated with a tilt of his head that I was being invited to dance with her. His grin was wide and teasing, probably anticipating my goofy version of an Irish jig. "It is wrong on so many levels that I have to do this before you," I said. He just laughed.

Inside my body, there lived a quiet me, a previous version of me, who desperately didn't want to dance like this in front of a room full of people. But the newer version of me very much wanted to. Besides, how could I politely turn down an elderly lady, even if she was going to show me up on the dance floor?

The crowd hooted when I pressed my palm to hers. I took a big breath and kicked my feet around in my best approximation of Irish dance. She smiled approvingly, raised one hand over her head, and tossed her silver hair. For a moment, I could see the other version of her: the one who was my age, having her first taste of cider; the one who danced all night and kissed a boy in the snug. She was still in there, shimmering with light.

The music ended to raucous applause. I plopped down in an exhausted heap, having danced three songs in a row.

"Well played, Cora," Uncle Clancy said with a squeeze of my shoulder. "I'm so pleased you danced. Sibyl loves a new partner."

I was breathless. Happy. "Thank you. I actually had fun!"

"Of course you did!" Clancy looked at me with kind, sincere eyes. "It was a sight to behold. You were positively glowing out there."

Uncle Clancy left the bar in the care of his employees and walked us a few blocks away to introduce me to what he swore would be the best beef stew I'd ever had in my life. Once we were seated and eating, he poked me in the arm and raised a caterpillar brow at me. "Well?"

"You sure do know your stew."

He smiled so broadly it was as if he'd cooked it himself.

"Thank you so much for your welcome tonight," I said. "You've been really sweet."

"As opposed to my mother," Finn added with a bit of throat-clearing.

"I didn't mean—"

Finn waved a hand. "No worries, Cora. She was a wretch to you. That's just the truth of it."

Clancy took a swig of his Guinness. A spot of tawny froth remained on his mustache. "My sister give you a bit of a breezy welcome, did she?"

I shrugged, not wanting to criticize Finn's mother, even if she had made me feel like gum on her shoe. I kept my thoughts to myself. In my experience, the only people who are safely allowed to trash parents are their own offspring.

Clancy patted my hand. "Oh now, child, that's Ina, especially when it comes to her little prince here," he said, motioning to Finn with a tilt of his head. "Don't let her get to you. She puffs up and pecks like a goose, but she's all fluff and feathers."

That wasn't how I would've characterized Ina Doyle. She was regal, queenly, with sharp and efficient mannerisms that said she couldn't afford to make a wasted move or speak a wasted word. Or waste her breath on a girl like me.

"You'll not take it personally, eh." Clancy said it like a command. But she'd basically accused me of *doing* something to Finn. Of changing him.

Finn scooped the last of his stew from the bowl and pushed it aside. He ran his hand down my arm, leaving a trail of warmth. "She said no dating. How was I supposed to know I'd meet someone so rare?"

I choked on a bit of my water, and he patted my back.

"Surely Ina could tell how special this one is," Clancy said, pointing his fork in my direction. "I'm not surprised you were drawn to her." He winked at Finn. "And fair play to you for luring her here."

We finished our dinner and walked outside into a light drizzle. Clancy kissed both my cheeks and handed Finn an umbrella. "I'll be seeing you," he promised and strode down the street in the direction of the pub.

"Well, you've got Uncle Clancy charmed."

I sighed. "Why does it seem like we never parted?"

"Maybe because we were never supposed to." Finn leaned in to kiss me but stopped, leaving my willingness evident on my parted lips, which he touched lightly with one finger. "I've been beating the *shite* out of myself ever since I left you."

"Oh." My lips hungered to kiss him, but I held eye contact and whispered, "Well, I'm here now." Warmth heated in his eyes. "I'll take over the beating."

He burst out laughing and kissed me. A deliciously wicked kiss with my head cradled in both of his hands. My fingers dug into the back of his neck. Having him in my arms, his mouth on mine, left me breathless and my body hungry. He wrapped both arms around my shoulders. "God, you do things to me, Cora. When I'm with you, I feel ten feet tall and bulletproof." Our eyes met. "I'm greedy," he admitted, bending his head forward, speaking his words into his chest.

"I thought I could walk away, but in my heart I never did. I'm with you now, and everything in me wants to hold on. I want to keep you with me. Possess you. Am I wrong for feeling that way?"

I didn't think so. It was the same for me. I wanted Finn to adore me so completely, he'd never say good-bye again. He'd forever be ruined for any other girl. I wanted to claim him right back. Did that make me wrong, too?

We stood in the rain. Chest to chest. Heart to heart. I'd never regret coming to Ireland. No matter what disappointments the trip might hold regarding my mother, seeing him again was worth it. I'd fly across the world for one kiss from Finn Doyle.

Still, he wasn't the reason I came, and I'd be doing myself and my mother a disservice if I didn't honor that. "This has been so lovely," I said, aching already. "But I have to go back to my room now. I've got this journal of my mother's, and I was on my way to read it when I ran into you. The truth is I'm dying to read it. It's like she's waiting for me. She's been waiting for me for twelve years."

TWENTY-EIGHT

Finn wanted to walk me back to my hostel, and he wrapped his arm around my shoulder as we strolled. We came to a bridge over the river Liffey, and I got momentarily lost in the sight of it. I was in Ireland! Bronze seahorses reared under the bridge lampposts. The city lights glowed on the river's flat, wide surface like gold wax dripping into the water. I gawked and swiveled my head, relishing the sights of Dublin at night, disbelieving that I was actually there.

The journal in my bag waited like a bomb, ticking off the minutes. I was eager to get back to the small room, crawl into bed, and read it. Was it too much to hope that it might lead me to my mother?

Faye's words about people wanting to find someone like me played over and over in my mind. So did the strange man's yearning eyes and haunting threats. His white aura had already hooked mine, and I never wanted to experience that again. I hoped the journal would tell me more about myself, tell me about people with white auras, maybe how to protect myself so I didn't become one of the vanished.

As soon as we crossed the bridge, something familiar caught my eye. "That's the church where my parents were married."

"No *shite*?"

"I recognize it from the postcard in my mother's things. C'mon," I said, slipping my hand from his. I started for the intersection. A horn blared. Finn reeled me back by my elbow.

"Mind your step. You were looking the wrong way, luv. We drive on the opposite side of the road here." We crossed the street and descended the stone steps leading to the front of Christ Church. A bush with bright yellow flowers glowed in the moonlight in front of the large Gothic structure.

"This place is like something out of a storybook," I said, craning my head to see the peaked roofs, medieval turrets, and arched windows of the ancient gray stone building.

"It's a grand old place," Finn said. "One of the oldest buildings in Dublin, I reckon."

"I've got to see inside," I said, pulling on the handles of the huge wooden door, overcome with the need to see the place where my parents vowed to love each other until death claimed them.

The door didn't budge. "Past hours, I'm sure. Tell you what, we'll come back. I've got to work all day tomorrow. I tried to get out of it, but Clancy needs me to mind the pub while he looks into a new distillery."

"No problem. I'm a big girl. I can do a little sightseeing on my own. I briefly saw something in my mother's notes about Newgrange. I still can't believe I'll get to see it with my own eyes. I've dreamed forever about going there."

"It's impressive," Finn said. "And not far from my house. No one knows for sure who built it. There's much mystery and speculation about the place, makes me curious about your mum's interest with it."

"She seemed to have a lot of interesting ideas." I'd told him that she was researching something here in Ireland, that she was worried about me and my dad, that she disappeared, but I stopped short of the absolute truth.

"Ideas such as?" he asked. "And are you saying she disappeared because of whatever she was researching?"

I chewed on the tip of my thumb, trying to decide how to answer. "She thought she was on the verge of discovering something about humanity, something that would upset what we think we know about ourselves. Something that someone wanted to keep a secret."

His head jerked up. "That's a mighty notion, all right."

"I know. What could be so important that she'd keep looking into it even if she knew she was in danger?"

Finn blew out a big breath and wrapped his arm around my shoulder again. His apparent uneasiness fueled my own. "Makes me worried for you. She disappeared, luv. You said her parents did, too? That's not a coincidence. Maybe her work is something you ought not to be poking around in. Maybe," he said, gazing skyward and blowing out a big breath, "if it means your safety, then some secrets are better left buried."

"I have to poke around. I need to know what happened to her." I found myself thinking of Giovanni losing both his parents as a young boy and wondered how old my mom was when her parents disappeared. "Who'd want to hurt my mom to hide whatever truth she was uncovering?"

"Depends entirely on what that truth was. Conspiracies against knowledge…," muttered Finn. "It's ridiculous. I guess it's easy to speak of keeping secrets buried forever when it's *you* I'm worried about. Easier to think of someone anonymous, somewhere out there in the world, doing the uncovering." He paused, deep in thought. "There's something very brave about people like your mother and"— he touched my face—"like you, Cora. I mean, how can mankind evolve if we aren't searchers of truth?"

"My dad would actually like you right now if he heard you say that," I teased. My aura flashed with infinite love toward him. He thought my mother was brave. He thought *I* was brave.

Finn walked with a purposeful gait, his eyes focused on the sidewalk in front of him. I continued talking out my theories.

"The world is full of powerful organizations, religions, that all need us to swallow their existing beliefs about humanity in order to keep their machines running. I don't think they'd let go of that power lightly. Look at how the church threatened Galileo after he suggested that the sun, not the earth, was the center of our solar system."

Finn said nothing. I wondered if he'd even heard me. His aura, which was usually so generous, was reined in tight to his body. I slipped my hand over his on my shoulder. "You okay?"

"Aye. Just thinking maybe the world would be a more beautiful place if we didn't have so many secrets. If we could share the truth of who we are with each other." He smiled apologetically.

"You've got a beautiful soul, Finn Doyle." I wished I could tell him how beautiful. His aura expanded around him a bit, puffing up with the compliment. But I noticed he still held a ball of quivering yellow in front of his solar plexus, and I wished I could peel back the layers and know what he protected. I laid my hand on his arm. "Really, Finn, is something wrong?"

"Can't you wait to go to *Brú na Bóinne* until I can go with you?" he asked, concern pursing his full lips into a thin line.

"I don't know how many days I'll have before my dad comes looking for me. He could be on his way now. I don't want to waste a day."

"Right, but be careful. At least let me pick you up after. I'll be at the visitor center around five? We'll get a bite?"

"Deal. And don't worry. I'll be okay. It's a big tourist attraction with lots of people, and I befriended a fellow traveler who wants to go, too. I'm sure we'll be fine."

Twenty-Nine

I pored over my mother's journal into the late hours of the night. I had suspected, but now knew that she was Scintilla. She confirmed it with her writings about "silver" and about seeing auras. We were the same, and she had felt just as alone in her differentness.

Brú na Bóinne, or Newgrange, was mentioned numerous times. Excitement fluttered in my belly. No doubt the place was critical to my mother's investigations. The words "Origin story" were written in bold letters on the back of a postcard of the triple spiral. What could she have meant by that?

I thrilled at following a trail my own mother had blazed.

When Giovanni came to meet me at my hostel with a rental car, he was still miffed at how I had left him at the park the night before. I had called him right away when I ran into Finn, so I didn't get why he was still upset.

His eyes crackled with intense earnestness as he explained. "Finding another Scintilla was a miracle. Even a few moments of thinking I'd lost you was agony. I thought the worst. I'm not quite ready to face the world alone again."

I'd have told him that I understood more than he knew, but it wasn't necessary. That was the thing with Giovanni—he knew. Neither of us wanted to go back to being *the only one*. Our shared understanding rapidly connected us in a unique bond.

"I promise I won't worry you like that again," I said. To my surprise, he pulled me into a hug. The incredible whirling force of dynamic energy between us caused us both to step back. We exchanged awkward smiles. Hanging around another Scintilla was going to take some getting used to.

The *Brú na Bóinne* Visitors Center was a very busy place. We parked the car and got the last two tickets for the next time slot on the bus that ran between the visitors center and the historic site. I was relieved to get the tickets. I had to see as much as I could before my dad arranged for a military-style SWAT shakedown of Ireland to find me.

The photos of Newgrange I'd collected back home looked like big mounds of grass-covered dirt with some rocks around them, but in person they were enchanting. The very earth felt hallowed. Ancient energy rose up around me, grounding me in its history.

We tromped up the path toward the largest burial mound, a giant grass-covered dome with intricately carved rocks around the base like a stone diadem. There were over a hundred of the large stones, called kerbstones, all engraved with ancient megalithic art of spirals, zigzags, and drawings. I was intrigued to learn that exactly three kerbstones were never found. That number again.

Giovanni strolled ahead of me, taking pictures of the 5,000-year-old stones and touching them respectfully. I slipped around a corner to the steps that led up to the top of the largest mound, delighted to actually walk atop this ancient temple. I pulled out the red journal and turned to one of my mother's entries about Newgrange. The paper fluttered lightly in the breeze.

I am led again to this home of the Triple Spiral, like a compass pointing me to my true North. Could Gabriella have been right? Is this just one of many places in the world that was a base for people like me? It's not what we know about it that intrigues me. It's what we don't. Who built it? What are the true meanings of the markings in the stones? Why did the inhabitants mysteriously disappear, sometimes for hundreds of years, before another group would settle, only to also disappear? A theory is that the tomb was a solar temple for a prehistoric race of supernatural people. Doesn't seem so far-fetched right now. Our Irish mythology taunts me like King Nuada, the Silver Hand…Silver. Could the legends have only told part of the story? Too often in history that is the case. There are so many signs telling me this was once a place of people like me. And too many like me have vanished. I feel I'm on the edge of a discovery. One that could answer all of my questions.

The passage gave me chills. I shared her feeling—on the edge of discovery. I looked around at the green valley below. Satellite mounds dotted the fields in the distance. The river Boyne meandered past the great mounds. Ireland stretched out beneath me in all directions. The beauty of it created an alchemy inside me, transforming my curiosity into a deep affection. Ireland struck me as wild. A restrained wild, though. Not the messy abandon of a jungle. A tame fury simmered under every green blade.

Seeing auras was considered *supernatural*. When I pulled the word apart, examined it, I thought it meant natural but different, extraordinary. It didn't mean it wasn't real. From my inquiries online, I learned that auras were considered real by many people, doctors and scientists included. All over the world, people conducted research to prove and measure and study their existence. So that couldn't have been my mother's big discovery.

No. There was more to this. Being what Giovanni called Scintilla was just one part of the puzzle. If Scintilla was one race, were there others? If so, my hunch was they had white auras.

"What happened to you, Grace Sandoval?" I whispered into the wind.

Giovanni found me atop the tomb. His aura was so strikingly beautiful, it made me see mine in a new light. If only everyone could see the beauty radiating from our bodies, the truth of who we are, and how our energies merged, maybe the world would be a nicer place.

"Come, Miss Cora," Giovanni said, waving me over. "They say we can go inside the tomb now."

We went together to the doorway, first climbing stairs to get over an enormous oblong stone with spirals carved in its surface that was blocking the entrance, and then ducking under a flat lintel stone over the door. A slit above the doorway made it possible for the sunlight to penetrate deep inside the chamber for twenty minutes every winter solstice.

I'd finally found my way here.

Inside, a large pillar stone welcomed us, and I sucked in a breath. The actual triple spiral! This iconic stone saw sunlight only once per year on the solstice, and our guide said it was possible the original inhabitants believed it to be a connection from our realm to other realms of existence. It was pure mystery and magic. I wanted to sweep my fingers over the pattern that curled like tender new fronds, but a few people in front of us blocked our way. I remembered vividly how the picture of it spun in my mind's eye along with the other images when I unearthed the key. And I also vividly remembered the first time I saw its pattern tease me from under Finn's shirt.

"What does it mean?" Giovanni asked.

"It's called the triple spiral. It's known over the world as a Celtic symbol, though that's completely misleading because the people who built this place were here three thousand years before the Celts arrived. It's older than the Great Pyramids and older than Stonehenge. There are all kinds of theories about the triple spiral, but no one knows for sure. Some say it celebrates the sun since so many of the stones are astrology-based. Others call it the triple goddess: maiden, mother, and crone." My face heated. "And I might have slipped into know-it-all mode."

"Creator, destroyer, sustainer," offered an elderly woman from behind us. "I've read that interpretation as well."

"Life, death, and eternity," said someone else in a voice hushed with awe.

"A tale with no beginning and no end," I whispered to myself.

Giovanni's hand rested between my shoulder blades as we walked through the narrow passageway toward the small chamber room. I didn't know if it was the place or his hand causing the strange sensation, as though my heartbeat had shifted, settling closer against my back, beating hard against his hand.

"There is Viking graffiti in these tombs," Giovanni said, pointing excitedly. "Do you see?"

"I see," I said, smiling.

We entered the narrow cruciform passageway that led to a ceremonial chamber where cremated remains had once been found. The winter solstice event was simulated for us with lights. I shuddered in the cool cavern. The hair on my arms stood on end. "You can feel history blowing on you here."

The sun gifted us with its presence when we walked outside the tomb. I turned to Giovanni. "What did you mean the other day when you said I may not know what I'm capable of?"

Giovanni sucked his bottom lip when he concentrated. "How do I say it?" His blue eyes squinted as he searched for the words to explain. "People, they go around giving and taking of energy."

"That much I *do* know." Even before I knew about auras, I could sense it. It seemed to me it was the most widely used form of communication, whether the people were aware of it or not.

He frowned slightly. "Did you also know the Scintilla are a source? We," he said, holding his head up proudly, "are the spark that ignites the flame."

"I don't understand." But I'd heard similar words... *A mighty flame follows a tiny spark.*

Giovanni looked around. He zeroed in on a grandmother who was struggling with a very unhappy toddler currently in full meltdown mode, screaming, arms and legs flailing on the ground. "Watch," he said, leaving me leaning against a tree as he strode over to them.

I could not hear what he said to the woman or the child. But I could clearly see his silver aura flow out of his body and swaddle the little girl in its glow as he chatted with the elderly woman. The kid suddenly stopped crying and looked up at him like he was Santa Claus. Then his energy shifted a bit and wound around the elderly woman as well.

"Oh, gracious!" the old woman said. "I was at my wit's end. You have the magic touch with children, sure enough. How can I ever thank you?"

Giovanni patted the girl's head and walked back to me with a conceited smile. "You see?" he asked. "You can give them the spark. It's what they want. Their greedy bodies take it like candy."

I thought of the man in the park, who didn't give of himself. He took. Ruthlessly. "It seems like a violation to tamper with people's auras," I said.

Giovanni's brows pinched together. "It is not a crime to make people happy, Miss Cora. I've spent most of my life alone on the streets around the world, and I've learned you can get nearly everything you need—food, money, a place to sleep—in exchange for the one thing everyone in this world wants most: to feel good."

"But aren't you manipulating them?"

"Such an ugly word. I consider it currency, not manipulation. You should be asking how to do it. Not judging me for giving of myself. It's my choice who to give to."

Just as I was ready to tell him about the man with the white aura and argue about people's choice to receive or to be taken from, the bus pulled up in front of the waiting area, and we had to run to catch it. Giovanni and I sat next to each other, but he was brooding and silent for the drive. Twice now, I'd upset the one person who could tell me more about myself. But when we got off the bus he surprised me by asking me to walk with him.

"I'm sorry," I admitted as we stood outside the back of the visitors center on a small footbridge over a stream. "I shouldn't have judged. It's just that I've seen very violent attacks on people's auras. What you're doing is definitely not the same thing. You do what you have to do, and you make people happy. My best friend, Dun, does that, and I don't even think it's conscious."

Giovanni tilted his head in a charming, inquisitive way, and when he accepted my apology with a bright smile, I found myself thinking, *he hardly needs special energy to make people feel good.*

"Finn is picking me up, but if you don't mind, I'd like to talk to you again soon. I have so much more I want to ask. You showed me how you can give of your aura, but can you teach me how to block energy or"—my throat closed around the words—"stop someone from taking energy against my will?"

Concern and something like understanding registered in Giovanni's eyes, and he nodded gravely. "The people with the white auras…you wish to protect yourself in some way. I wish I could tell you how. I don't know the answer to that, but I will answer as many of your questions as I can." His hand ran from my elbow to my wrist. "Please call me. I'm desperate to see you again," he said, his tone pressing, his stormy eyes insistent. I couldn't look away. "You scared me to death when you disappeared yesterday. You have no idea how rare you are."

"That she is," Finn's voice said from behind Giovanni.

Finn strode toward us with an almost predatory gait. His tiger eyes never left Giovanni's face. The yellow-green aura was a color I'd never seen on him. Distress but with something else mixed in. Jealousy?

I walked over and took his hand. Finn curled me into his arms. His warmth was different. Infused with the fire of possessiveness. I mumbled an embarrassed introduction, then moved back to Giovanni to say good-bye. Finn's gaze raked my back.

"Thanks for everything, at the library and today." I held out my hand formally, which Giovanni took, giving it a jolt of energy. I gritted my teeth. "I'll call you."

Giovanni stepped forward and, much to my dismay, kissed each of my cheeks. Little circles of residual energy swirled on my skin. He whispered urgently in my ear, "Careful. You are not safe with him."

I stepped back. Blinked.

Giovanni nodded curtly to Finn as he passed us and tramped through the glass doors leading to the visitors center. His silver aura disappeared into the crowd.

"It's my own fault the lads are swarming, really," Finn said with a soft nibble to my bottom lip. "Leaving you alone like that. I don't know what those flippin' *eejits* in your town were thinking, but to the wider world you are enchanting."

"It's not like that," I said. "What you heard him say was soooo out of context." The memory of the physical charge between Giovanni and me rushed through my body. I flicked it away. "We just have a lot in common."

"I'll bet."

I stopped Finn in the parking lot and turned to face him. "You know, I don't give my heart to just anybody. Your accusing me of being fickle is an insult."

He nodded. I was warmed by the sight of his love, tinged with a little bit of insecurity. It was easy to forgive his jealousy when I could *see* his attachment to me, his fear of losing me. I wished he could see my attachment to him. I wished he could see how silver strands of energy from my body coiled and reached for his heart. I ran my fingers over the outline of his jaw and then behind his neck, pulling his mouth to mine. He kissed softly at first, almost reluctantly, until I bit his bottom lip and opened my mouth to a deeper kiss. His fingers dug into the small of my back.

The kiss was everything true, a claiming and a declaration.

Mine.

Yes. Yours.

Thirty

At the hostel, Finn parked the car and offered to walk me in. The lobby was relatively empty but for a twenty-something couple on a dingy couch, looking at something on their phone. I fished my key from my pocket and turned to say good-bye to Finn. There was everything but good-bye in his eyes.

"Food?"

I laughed. "We just ate!"

Finn drifted into my atmosphere, nibbled my bottom lip, and whispered, "Dessert?" in a voice as dark and tempting as chocolate.

"I could go for something sweet," I answered with a mock air of indifference, while my heart beat double time.

He kissed me again and sucked my bottom lip into his mouth just slightly. "So could I," he growled.

I snagged his hand and led him to my room.

Our impatient kisses delayed us at my door. Neither of us could suspend our need to close the gap, emotional and physical, between us. The bold girl I liked so much rose up in me again. I held Finn's narrow face between my hands and kissed him hard. His hands clutched the small of my back, gathering my jacket in his fists as he pulled me against him. Being pinned to the door by Finn's body was as heady as being pinned underneath him in my room that night back home. A small shred of me knew that unlocking the door and taking Finn into my room was reckless.

Freedom is its own kind of open door.

I fumbled the key into the hole, and we tumbled inside, wrapped in each other.

Cold hit me. A breeze that had nothing to do with air vents or open windows. The chill ran over my back like a bank of white clouds.

I slipped from Finn's grasp.

"What is it?"

Nothing seemed out of place. I couldn't put my finger on it, but perhaps I was looking with the wrong sense. I reached out with my subtle body, my aura. There was a ghost of energy in the room that hadn't been there that morning, the residual fingerprint of someone else's energy, lingering malice. I could feel them as if I'd walked through the vapor of their aura.

"Something's *off* in here," I said, unable to fully explain it to Finn. "I don't feel safe."

His eyes scanned the place for anything out of the ordinary. His chest expanded and fell with a testing breath. "I can't say why, exactly, but this place *does* have a bad vibe," Finn said.

I scrambled around the room, gathering my things, throwing one article after the other into my suitcase and shoving it closed while Finn watched me with a disconcerted expression.

"It reminds me of when my uncle Clancy took me to visit my grandmother in the hospital. We stood over her bed, and I swear I felt it when her spirit left her body. There was…a drift in the currents of the room."

I shuddered. "Spoken like a true sailor."

He crossed the floor, gathering me in the warmth of his arms, into the cocoon of his heartbeat. "If you don't feel safe here, luv, you shouldn't stay."

"Hence, the packing." I slung my duffel over my shoulder, plans formulating in my head. "Giovanni will let me stay with him until we figure out what to do."

Finn's eyes widened. A touch of anger and protectiveness flared from him and wrapped me in an unwelcome cloak of dull green and lifeless yellow. "That wasn't my first notion," he said. "You want to stay with some tosser you barely know rather than with me?"

"I—honestly, it hadn't occurred to me that I could stay with you."

I thought of Ina Doyle. I wasn't welcome in her son's life, so how would she like me being in their home? "What about your mother? Do you really think it will be okay? For just a night or two? Just until I can figure out what's next?"

"I'll call Uncle Clancy. I'm supposed to drive him home when the pub closes. We can pick him up, and he'll drive with us to my house. He's got a way with my mother." When he held the sides of my face, I gripped his forearms. Our eyes locked. "I don't know what's got you so spooked, but I don't ever want to see fear in your eyes like I see right now. Let me take care of you."

He didn't say what I'm sure we both thought. *Let me take care of you…until our time is up.*

THIRTY-ONE

About thirty minutes out of Dublin, the lights of the city gave way to dark country roads with occasional roundabouts and road signs written in both Irish and English. Finn, Clancy, and I rode in silence. I sat dazed, looking out the windows. Two things were definitely in abundance in Ireland: rock walls and pubs.

Finn had called ahead and told his mother I'd found myself in some very unsavory lodgings and that he'd invited me to stay with them. Uncle Clancy took the phone and spoke of how they had to help. After all, I was a young girl on my own.

We slowed, then pulled into a driveway with an enormous wrought-iron gate. A large iron sun adorned the top. "*Ag éirí grian mainéar,*" Finn said. "Rising Sun Manor." The gate opened to a long, winding, uphill drive lined with dense trees and brush. I had an irrational flash of fear when the imposing iron gates swung closed behind us.

My father must be sick with worry by now, I thought, then tried my best to unthink it. I had to focus on my mother for the short time I'd be in Ireland, for the short time I'd be free to find her. I didn't know how my dad did it all those years. I knew I wouldn't be able to live the rest of my days with the pendulum of unanswered questions swinging through my heart.

Finally, Finn's house came into view, stately and impressive. Like a summer cottage for royalty. Maybe that explained Finn's mother's disapproval. Perhaps I wasn't good enough for her son. I never imagined Finn living like this. The spiked hair, tattoos, and leather straps on his wrist. The guitar and the blues. The way one penetrating look from him could shoot fire through me. He had the same tame fury simmering inside him as his country: cool green on the outside, intensity underneath. Finn's fingers tapped a silent, restless tune on my thigh. His face was an impassive mask as we drove up to what Dun would gleefully call the O'LottaDough Mansion.

I realized there was so much I didn't know about Finn Doyle. But I could *see* that he had a good heart, and that allowed me to disregard Giovanni's paranoid warning. I knew what I knew. Finn was good inside and, right now, I was grateful for the refuge he could provide.

Clancy explained that the house had been built on a site where a castle once stood, but it had burned down centuries ago, leaving remnants of a cracked stone foundation and a tall circular building with a peaked roof. They had used the shell of stone, incorporating it and the tower into the home now known as Rising Sun Manor.

"Is that the ocean I hear?" I asked as we stepped out of the car onto a pea-gravel driveway. I hadn't realized we were so close to the coast.

"It is," Finn said. "I was born with sea air in my lungs and salt in my hair." He pointed to an old stone tower looming above us. "That was once a lighthouse."

We walked up the massive steps to the main house that splayed out like an open hand and through the wooden double doors. Finn set my bag at the foot of the staircase and pulled me forward. "C'mon. I want to show you around."

"Don't be long," Ina warned after she greeted us icily in the foyer. "We'll have dessert in the library," she added, casting a sideways look at me, "and get to know one another."

"I could get swallowed up in a house like this," I told Finn as he led me from room to room, through doorways and long corridors. "How many people live here?"

"Just my folks and me," Finn said. "Uncle Clancy lives in the old stable house on the far end of the property."

"Seems like a lot of house for three people."

"Aye, but you can be alone even when everyone's home," he said with a wink, pulling me into a hug behind a tall bureau.

"You never mentioned all this."

"Not something you go crowing about, is it? It's more than we need, aye. But my mother inherited it. The land has been in our family forever."

We took a dizzying route through the house, a blur of smooth polished wood, darkly spiritual paintings of angels and death. One particular black-and-white print arrested my attention. Two figures seemed to be standing upon the clouds, gazing heavenward at a swirling, spiraling mass of angels. "That's beautiful," I said, particularly entranced by the spiral design.

"It's a scene from *Paradiso*, from the *Divine Comedy*." Like the couple in the painting, we stared upward at the ethereal art. "C'mon. You ready for the meet and greet?" Finn asked, a hint of teasing in his voice.

Personally, I could have skipped the whole "getting to know each other" session with his mom. Ina Doyle didn't want to know me. Her mind was already made up.

"I love this room," I said when we walked into the library. It was moody in the best way. High walls covered in gray fabric wallpaper and polished black furniture with gray-and-black damask. Ebony bookshelves lined the walls from floor to ceiling. The dark colors could have made the room dreary, but it wasn't. It was heaven. A wide bank of windows overlooked the moonlit ocean. A fire blazed and crackled in the large fireplace.

Finn's mother's bookshelves could have competed with Faye's at Say Chi's. Apparently Ina was interested in all manner of metaphysical topics: auras, occults, chakras, psychic phenomena. I desperately wished to kneel down and riffle through the pages. Judging by the number of New Age bookstores in the world, and the number of websites online, many people were interested in this stuff. Still, I was shocked by the coincidence. Who'd have thought Ina and I would have something like this in common?

I picked up a book on auras and rested it in my hand while I paused to remember what Ina had said to me in the park. *There's something about you.* At the time, I had taken it as an insult, a judgment of my appearance or some other deficiency. Now, I wondered if she could see more, and it unsettled me.

Finn and I sat together on a gray velvet chaise. "So, what do your parents think about your coming alone to Ireland?" Ina asked, handing me a mug of tea and a tiny plate of shortbread.

"I was born here," I said. "This trip was, uh, long overdue."

She wasn't satisfied. "But to come alone, at your age?"

Finn shifted next to me. "I traveled to America alone."

"Regretfully, yes," she said, smoothing her hair, which she'd pulled into a tight chignon. "Though you were *somewhat* looked after, Griffin could have done a much better job of it. Who is looking after Cora?"

"I am." We both said at the same time. I giggled. It was a weary giggle that threatened to turn into a fit of inappropriate hysterics. I pinched the flesh next to my thumb.

"What do your parents do?" Ina asked.

"My father is a scientist."

She nodded, eyebrows up, perhaps impressed. "And your

mother?"

"She is…was…researching…" I took a deep breath and blew it out while she looked at me expectantly. "My mom's been out of my life for a long time."

"Oh. I'm sorry," Ina said. The smallest hint of a rose amid her thorns.

"Cora's exhausted, Mom. Can we interrogate her tomorrow?" Finn stood and helped me to my feet. "I'll show her to her room."

Ina nodded curtly when I thanked her for letting me stay. Her stare pressed against my back as I left the library.

My guest room was in the old lighthouse tower. "You're not going to lock me up in the tall, tall tower and throw away the key, are you?" I said, craning my neck to look up at the spiral staircase curling into the soaring ceiling like the inside of a seashell.

Finn kissed my fingertips. "If it'll keep you from leaving, luv."

We climbed the many steps circling the tower. Every so often, there'd be a rectangular pane of window above a stone sill, upon which burned a small votive candle. It was a nice touch, and surprising that Ina would do that for my arrival. My hand ran across the bumpy stone as we ascended, around and around, until we reached a door so aged and weathered it looked like it had been scrubbed with sand and bleached by the sun. It creaked when Finn pushed it open.

Broad, whitewashed beams arched across the ceiling. A stone-framed church window stood at one end with a circular pane above and three gothic points below. The walls were painted a calming shade of lavender, and a large white bed rested under the open window, where billowy grape-colored fabric rustled in the night breeze.

"Okay," I said with my hand over my mouth. "You can throw away the key."

"Want to know a secret?" he asked.

"Absolutely."

"This is where I learned to play the guitar. Instead of doing my homework, I'd sneak up here where no one could hear me and teach myself to play."

"I love that. Want to know a secret?"

"Give it to me."

"I'm scared I'll find out nothing about what happened to my mother."

He nodded sympathetically.

"And I'm scared I will."

"Sleep, *críona*. We'll plan and plot in the morning." I received a very gentlemanly but conflicted hug. Then he left me in the room alone.

I washed my face in the little white basin next to the bed, slipped on my tank top and a pair of girly boxers Janelle had given me for Christmas, and climbed into the soft bed. It was weird to think Finn was somewhere in this sprawling house, maybe lying on his bed staring at the ceiling, too. Would he dare a visit with me in the night?

Yeah. He would.

That thought alone made it hard to fall asleep. But finally, I did.

I dreamed. My mother called out to me from underwater, and I tried to shine the massive spotlight from the lighthouse down on the ocean to find her, but it wouldn't budge. That dream reel switched to me running through a busy airport. The man with the white aura followed me. I kept trying to convince security he wanted to hurt me, but they didn't believe me. I ran through the airport and lost him by walking among a crowd of Red Hat ladies.

On the plane, a man sat down next to me, his tall body filling the space. He put his hand on my wrist. Laid it there, almost soothing. Heat swarmed over my skin. Instantly, the tugging started. An invisible knife lashed at my chest, opening it for my aura to be ripped from my body.

The air was sucked out of the atmosphere. I gasped for breath, tried to lift my hand to cover myself like I had before, but he pressed my wrist down hard. I couldn't yell. I couldn't move through the heavy air surrounding my numb body. I could do nothing but stare into his eyes and silently beg him not to kill me.

My silver aura flashed in angry lightning strikes, objecting as it left my body to be swallowed up in his expanding white aura. My head fell back and somehow I screamed.

I opened my eyes as his aura exploded in a blast of white.

My depleted energy snapped back into my body. The shadow of Finn's mother leaned over me, but my eyes still burned with the white flash of my dream, bathing her in its ghost.

"You were screaming," she whispered, with her hand on my wrist. "Bad dream?"

I couldn't nod or answer. Weighted down, limbs heavy.

Ina's fingers slipped from my skin, and she backed away. "*Codladh sámh*. Sleep well. I'm sorry."

THIRTY-TWO

Something tickled my face, and I bolted upright. The plum curtain lifted in the breeze from the window above my headboard. I squinted against the bright room. Unusually bright. The clock said it was past ten. I had slept way too late.

My legs wobbled when I stood, like my muscles hadn't caught up to the fact that we weren't sleeping anymore. The awful dream revisited while I showered, the memory of it making me tremble. Had Ina actually been in my room, or was she part of the dream, too? I stood in the hot water an extra couple of minutes to erase the chill.

I wound my way down the spiral stairs, listening for signs of life. A world of green rolled away from every window I passed. I followed the clatter of dishes and the warm, sweet scent of sugary pastries to the kitchen. Ina stood at the sink with her back to me. When I entered, she turned slowly, almost reluctantly, and met my eyes. Her brows furrowed, and she turned back to rinsing her teacup.

I swallowed hard and slid a chair out at the table. "Good morning."

Ina glanced at the clock. "Travel sure does take it out of a person. I'll bet you're hungry."

"I kinda am. I can make something—"

"Nonsense. I've got some scones baking. You're obviously fond of sweets."

Sucker punch. Well played.

I gritted my teeth. "It sure smells good." I watched her bustle around the kitchen, seemingly doing twenty things at once. My mind was obviously still on slo-mo.

"Um, I was wondering if I might use your phone to make a quick call to my father."

"Of course," she said, nicer than usual. "He'd want to know where you are and that you're safe. Finn says you have some special inquiries you need to make while you're here," Ina said.

"Yes. Is he here?"

"I'm sorry, no. He waited but didn't want to wake you. He had to go with his uncle to unload a shipment at the pub. He wanted me to tell you he'd be back after lunch. The phone's right there," she said, pointing to the counter next to her.

I felt too shy to ask if I could use one in another room. I took a deep breath and dialed Mari's number. Dun answered it on the first ring. The bizarre conversation-in-code went like this:

Me: Hi, *Dad*!

Dun in a scoldy voice: It's about time you called us, young lady! You should have called sooner. So the eagle has landed?

Me: Um, yes? I'm good. How are you?

Dun: I've been better. Mari is giving me a makeover. We're starting with a Brazilian wax. I'm in a compromised position right now.

Background sound of Mari smacking him.

Dun: Ow! Dammit.

Me: How are things with you, *Dad*? Busy at work?

Dun: Totally busy.

Me: Okaaaay. So, I thought I'd better check in.

Dun: Are you with McSexy? Has he showed you his big *shillelagh*?

Me: I *do* love it here. It's beautiful.

Dun: Great. Don't go getting into any wild shenanigans, you hear? Shenanigan is an Irish word, yeah? Hey, Mari, is shenanigan an Irish word?

Me: How's the *weather* there?

Dun, in a serious hushed voice: We've been questioned. Your dad could totally work for the CIA. And your wee little grandmother is in a snit. I think Mami Tulke is making a voodoo doll of you. I'd give you a couple of days before he shows up.

Me: Okay, thanks. Love you.

Dun: We love you, too.

I hung up with a knot of worry threading around my veins like a weed. In a shameless and defiant display of anxiety, I scarfed down two scones and a huge glass of orange juice. I didn't want to, but I had to ask. "I had a bad dream I can't shake. By any chance, were you in my room last night?"

"I was," Ina said with a thoroughly apologetic expression. She looked pained to admit it. "Forgive me," she whispered, then sped away. I stood in the kitchen and wrapped my arms around myself, trying to understand why my hairs stood on end.

Thirty-Three

"That's the second bit of surprise I've had today," Finn said as he greeted me on the sprawling lawn of his property that afternoon.

I'd been reading my mother's notes on the cliff overlooking the ocean and trying to quell my impatience to leave. I detested that I was without transportation. Not that I knew where I'd go next, but Christ Church was definitely on my list. I tried to use the computer in Finn's library, but it was password protected, and no one was home to ask. I took the opportunity to look through Ina's books but found nothing on Scintilla or legends of people with silver auras.

Later, I figured I'd go to an Internet café and research the historical significance of threes. I had found my mother's journal but hadn't needed the key to unlock it. So what was the key about and what was it trying to tell me? The only reference to a key was this entry in her notes:

> *We have a name! Scintilla.*
>
> *It means "little spark." What it means to me is there are, have been, others like me. It means I have a history, even if I*

don't know what it is. It means…I'm not alone.

South America was a gold mine. The spirals led me there. Seems that spirals have marked the depth of human history and the breadth of the entire world. What began as a foray into pre-Columbian artifacts featuring spirals, led to learning about Earth's most energetically charged location, the Elqui Valley, in Chile. Earth's magnetic center. It's a magical place. I discovered so much there, so much about myself, and I discovered love sweet LOVE.

An offhand comment about the Scintilla holding the "keys to heaven" has me pursuing another avenue…

I snapped the book closed and laid it on my lap. "What surprise?" I asked Finn.

"You'll get to meet my *da*. He's home."

"Oh?" I said, trying to sound upbeat. "Great." *Another parent to loathe my presence.*

His brows rose. "He'll adore you."

I changed the subject. "Did you tell your mother about me running away? The way she talked this morning, it was like she knew my dad would be worried about me."

Finn looked at me, startled. "I told her nothing. But it wouldn't surprise me if my mother was two steps ahead. She always is. Could be that she assumes your dad worries abnormally about everything like she does."

I studied his profile. "You *sure* you said nothing?"

He gave me a sideways glance. "I tell my mother as little as possible. It's like giving *fookin'* bombs to terrorists." He winked and tossed a rock over the cliff's edge.

We walked in the house, hand in hand. I squeezed harder as we entered the large blue-and-white sitting room. It was like walking into the sky. Aged, painted clouds floated above us on the soaring ceiling.

His parents were already there, seated in two high-backed chairs with a little table between them. Two crystal glasses of wine rested on a doily.

Finn's father jumped to his feet. His hip bumped the table and the wine wobbled and splashed a bit, leaving dots of red on the white lace. Ina settled the table with one hand. She didn't get up but managed the barest hint of a smile at me.

"Cora, my father, Fergus Doyle."

"Nice to meet you, Mr. Doyle," I said, extending my hand.

"F-Fergus is fine," he muttered. His hands shook a bit when he took mine between them. He looked at me like I was an apparition. A ball of energy rolled together in our pressed palms. Then the creepy sensation like someone pulling a vein out of the middle of my hand. I pulled away. "Welcome, Cora."

I felt a little dizzy and concerned that someone so unsettled was a doctor. I hoped he wasn't a surgeon. "Thank you."

Fergus walked back to the chair next to Ina's. I couldn't see his face, but I could read hers. It said, *What did I tell you?* His aura flared erratically, shifting colors—red, seaweed, white, and yellow—like he didn't know how he should feel.

Finn clearly detected it, too. His skin creased hard above his nose as he watched his father slam his wine in one long gulp and refill his glass.

"Sit down, won't you?" Fergus said.

"No, Pop. I think I may take Cora out for a bite."

"Nonsense," Ina spat with a smile—a real skill. "Your *da* has just gotten home and wants to spend time with you. We have family coming for supper."

"Oh, thank you," I said. "But I'll be getting a cab to town. I-I have some things to do there."

"We'd love for you to stay and join us," Fergus said. His aura pulsated with more excitement than should be healthy. He was so different from his self-assured, easygoing son.

"Sounds great," I ventured. I hoped it didn't drip with sarcasm the way it did in my head.

Finn rubbed a small circle on my back, leaving a swirl of warmth. "You sure? I'd really enjoy it so much more with you here."

I looked at the clock and reasoned that it was already late afternoon anyway. By the time I got into Dublin, the church would be closed. Maybe I could use a computer here at the house after dinner. I sat down while Finn walked over to a cabinet and pulled out two more wineglasses. He poured the garnet liquid into both and handed me one.

"Finn," his mother called to him softly but laced with warning. "I don't think that's entirely—"

"Cheers, Mum." He raised his glass in her direction. "Here's to being together." Then he clinked his glass with mine.

"Already starting on the wine without me!" boomed a voice. Uncle Clancy burst in the room, and I actually exhaled in relief. I offered him my glass. "Thank you, child. It'll be whiskey for me. Sure you don't need that to warm up? Atmosphere is like cold, hard *shite*."

I stifled a laugh.

Clancy hugged Fergus warmly. "Good to have you home," he said. They gave each other big man-pats on their backs, the kind that sound like they're trying to knock the teeth out of each other's faces. I eased back in my chair.

By the time dinner rolled around, Clancy was so boisterous that he took up all the space in the room, leaving none for my unease. Still, Ina would scarcely make eye contact with me, and Finn's father treated me like a rare breakable. How did someone so normal come from such odd parents?

"I've never had a meal so fancy in my life," I whispered to Finn. "Not even at a restaurant."

"It's because of you," he whispered back.

I'd perhaps indulged in too much wine—no surprise, since I'd never drunk before—because next thing I knew, I found myself saying to Ina, "I saw your books in the library and noticed you have an interest in auras. I share your interest."

Fergus choked a bit and took a sip of wine.

Ina's aura shrank back a few inches. "It's merely something that fascinates me," she answered coolly.

"Yeah, the way a banker is merely fascinated with money," Finn retorted. Ina gave Finn a warning look, and suddenly both Fergus and Ina were passing dishes around the table.

Finn leaned in close to me. "You, too, huh? You never mentioned auras before."

"Yes, I—"

"How long are you home for this time?" Clancy asked Fergus, who shot a look at Ina and murmured something about it being indeterminate.

The dinner talk soon eased into a rhythm that was obviously familiar to them, chat of the pub, and work, and neighbors. Eventually, Clancy burped and scooted his chair back loudly. "Welp, I'm off. I'm *fluthered* and *flah'ed* out. Night!" He squeezed my shoulder, and Ina and Fergus began clearing dishes, leaving Finn and me alone in the dining room.

"They're insane. I'm going to be the one to say it. What is it about you that's got them all acting like gits?"

"My sparkling personality?" I asked. Giovanni's voice suddenly rose in my head. *Scintilla. The spark.*

Finn watched me closely. "Where did you go, just then?"

I smiled. "I'm here. With you."

His fingers traced the line of my neck. "I want to kiss you."

"Do."

"There," he said, tracing my collarbone. "And right here." His finger ran along my jaw. "Definitely here." He teased his fingertips over my cheek.

A warm blush flushed my face.

"How is it possible that every kiss is the most satisfying in the world, and still it's never enough?" He leaned in, his breath heavy with wine that smelled of chocolate and blackberries. I wanted to know if his tongue tasted like that, too.

Before I knew what happened, we were in each other's arms. Our mouths dancing, our hands clutching. I gasped when he tilted my head back and kissed the soft slope of my breast. Suddenly, he pulled away and stood. His voice strained to say, "I'm sorry, Cora. I have to get a bit of air."

"What did I do?" I asked to his back.

"No. No. It's me. Right now, I feel like I can't control myself with you. It's mad. I want you so completely. I've never been this way. It's more intense than anything I've ever known. It's not right. I'm…I'm sorry."

He left me sitting in the dining room with my lips on fire, my body wide-awake and aching. He was worried about taking what I wanted to give?

I tiptoed past the kitchen in search of the doorway that would lead to my princess tower. I didn't want another attack of the awkward, so I hoped no one would see or hear me creep by. I could hear Finn's parents in the kitchen in the middle of a heated, whispered argument.

"I disagree," Fergus whispered. "I think it's amazing he's found someone like her. A miracle."

How could I walk away after hearing *that?*

Ina responded, "You and I both know the implications."

"What's the drawback? He's found what the rest of us could only hope to find in our lifetimes."

I suddenly liked Fergus Doyle very much.

"Dammit! You *know* the drawbacks!" A hand slapped loudly on wood. "And what are the odds that someone like her would fall for someone like Finn?"

I chewed my lip. I couldn't even pretend to understand what she meant. Finn was amazing, and before this, Ina had acted like I was garbage.

Fergus's voice remained calm. "If the legends about Scintilla are true, it could benefit him. It could benefit us all. It was all I could do not to…"

Silence. Every pulse point in my body slammed in alarm against my skin. Faye had told me there were people who wanted nothing more than to find someone like me.

These two knew what I was.

"You can't tell me you haven't thought of it yourself," he said, defensively. "What's the matter?"

A great sea of silence. I slipped under its current. Waiting. My fingers dug into my palm.

"Look at me, Ina. Have you *taken* from her?"

Sniffle.

Footsteps moved. I lurched back into the shadows behind the door.

"Do you have *no* control? How could you? What happened? Tell me what happened!"

"I couldn't help it!" Her voice lashed the air and cracked against my body. "I wish I hadn't, Fergus. She gave me a power, my sortilege. It's true what we've heard, the Scintilla's energy gives us our sortilege. I always wondered what mine would be, fantasized about it, even. But now I know, and it's bloody dreadful. Now…now I can see the blackest hole in every heart."

THIRTY-FOUR

I backed away. Their whisperings faded under the pounding of my pulse in my ears. Shallow breaths escaped in loud puffs no matter how I tried to reel them in. I yearned to find Finn, but how could I explain my trembling body, my cold, shaking hands, my complete terror from what I'd overheard?

Finding the doorway that led to the lighthouse tower, I took the winding stairs two at a time. My foot slipped on one of the smooth stone steps, and I tumbled forward. My hand scraped against the stone wall, pricking my palm with the sharp sting of a cut.

Blood made my hand slip on the doorknob. I shoved my shoulder into the wood and barreled through, then quickly locked it.

Did you take from her?

I thought it had been a dream. That she had heard me scream and came to check on me. But of course she couldn't have heard me so far up in the lighthouse. Unless…unless she was already in my room.

Shakily, I rinsed my hand, wrapped it in a towel, and sat on my bed. I knew it was possible to take from someone's aura because I had seen it with my own eyes, and I had felt the terrifying pull of it from my own skin. Finn's parents were like that man? No, wait, their auras weren't white like his. How could Ina do that to me? Was it because I'd been asleep, defenseless? If so, it was spineless thievery.

I watched Giovanni give of himself to that little girl. It calmed her, seemed to make her happy. Was that what Ina was doing? Taking a little "hit" off me? Getting what Giovanni said everyone in the world wants most: to feel good? Her knowledge of auras and energy must have taught her that she could do it consciously. I placed my hand over my racing heart. I needed to stay calm.

I should leave this place tonight. Maybe I could go to Giovanni and then find a room at another hostel in the morning. But it was night. I had no real idea how or where I was going to go, dark roads, foreign country, whispering ghosts, and all that…and I was still really concerned that someone with an ugly soul had been in my room in Dublin. I had no idea if the person had been there for me, but if so, who was to say they wouldn't find me again? Staying put for the night behind a locked door seemed the lesser of all evils. I'd call Giovanni first thing in the morning and break away.

I remembered the stash of hard candies at the bottom of my purse and dug for the bag. I leaned back on my pillows and swirled the cherry flavor in my mouth. I kept my clothes on, even my shoes, and packed everything back into my duffel. That took all of five minutes.

I'd managed to calm myself enough to let sleep drag its heavy hand over my eyes, but one thought kept me from giving in to it. What did Ina mean when she said she could see the blackest hole in every heart?

A rattling sound startled me. I lay in the darkened room with the flavor of old candy on my tongue and listened. My hand was throbbing. The doorknob rattled again. A light flipped on outside my door.

"Jaysus!" It was Finn's voice. He banged on the door, causing me to startle. "Cora!"

"Yes?"

"There's blood on your door."

"What are you doing here?"

"I wanted to apologize. No. I wanted to see you. I couldn't lie there another minute knowing you were so close and not come to you."

I tiptoed across the plank floor to the door. I kneeled down and peeked underneath. I couldn't see Finn's aura, only his bare feet poking out from beneath his jeans. I stood and put my hand to the door, trying to absorb the warmth of him through the wood.

"What happened to you? Why is there blood?"

"I-I slipped. I'm okay."

"Want me to kiss it?"

I smiled. *Yes, so bad.* "I'm not dressed."

"Even better." I could hear the smile in his voice. "I'm sorry about earlier."

"That's okay," I answered. "I'm not mad at you for wanting me."

"I still want you."

Silence and longing.

"I'm so tired," I finally answered. It was true, but I was unsure why I made an excuse not to see him. I think I was afraid that if he came in, I'd find myself spilling every detail of my eavesdropping. How do you tell your boyfriend that you can see auras, that your own aura is rare and coveted, and that you think his mother is a nasty, aura-snatching thief?

"Can we talk tomorrow?" I asked through clenched teeth, knowing I was going to have to give him a good reason for leaving.

He sighed. I'm sure he had the same thought I did. *How many tomorrows did we have?*

THIRTY-FIVE

I couldn't get back to sleep. I spent the whispering hours between night and day reading *Grace*. Much of it didn't connect together at all. There were articles about the existence of auras, newspaper clippings of people who disappeared, and her handwritten notes.

> *Dr. M spoke about "categories" of humans, as though there are delineations beyond our known differences such as ethnicity and blood type.*
>
> *He thinks this difference in certain humans directly relates to a measurable output and exchange of energy. He theorizes that there has been crossbreeding of two groups of humans over thousands of years, resulting in an energy "soup" where some people drain energy from other people. Then there are transmitters—natural givers of energy.*
>
> *He is seeking "pure" examples of both for genetic testing.*

A mysterious doctor sought people like my mom for some kind of genetic testing? I wondered how I could find this doctor and whether she had. I wondered if Dad or Giovanni would know of him.

Through my window, a pink sliver of sunrise crested the horizon. I put the journal in my bag. I hoped Giovanni wouldn't mind my calling so early. I had to get out of this house, and I wanted to talk to him. My mother's note seemed to confirm what he'd told me about different breeds of humans, and I had promised to tell him what I learned. I wished there was more to go on than the cryptic "Dr. M" in her notes.

I tiptoed downstairs to the kitchen to use the phone. Giovanni answered on the first ring.

"I'm sorry to call you so early," I said softly.

"Miss Cora." His voice sounded groggy, his accent more pronounced. The word Miss came out like *meeees*. "I hoped you'd call."

"Though probably not at sunrise."

"Anytime. Come to have espresso with me. This man does not wake without espresso."

I could easily imagine him right now: blue eyes, half-lidded from sleep; blond, tousled hair; long body stretched out… I stopped, a fist of guilt punching my stomach. I should never think thoughts like that about Giovanni.

"Okay," I said, "coffee sounds insane right now. I'm going to go to Christ Church after." Guilt stabbed me again. Finn wanted to go with me. I supposed I could leave him a note to see if he wanted to meet me there.

"I will take you."

"I'm not sure. See, Finn and I—"

Giovanni sighed impatiently into the phone. "I know about Finn and you. You don't need to tell me. I could see it."

I switched the phone to my other ear. God, he was being irritating. "Good. So, I'll see you soon. I want to ask you some more questions."

"I will answer your questions. Of course."

"Okay. Thanks."

"If…"

"If?"

"You meet me at the church without him."

"What's your problem?" My voice sounded too loud to myself, bouncing around the empty kitchen. I whispered, "You don't even know him. I don't even know *you*, for that matter."

"Have you told him what you are?"

"No."

"No?"

"No, okay, I haven't told him about us."

"Then I'd say you and I know each other on a whole other level."

I faltered, irritated because it was true. It suddenly seemed wrong that I hadn't told Finn anything about my ability or my strange aura. What was my problem? Nervousness about Faye's warning, yes. But if I were being brutally honest with myself, it had also been fear that he might think I was really strange. Too different. Would he, this beautiful guy who had his pick of girls, have still fallen for me if he had known? My insecurity would look like distrust from Finn's perspective.

I should tell him.

"We'll be meeting at a church, Cora. I think you know you can trust me. I have nothing but your safety in mind, which is why I'd rather he not be there. If you want coffee, come to my hotel at eight. Otherwise, I'll be at the church at nine." He hung up. The bastard actually hung up! I stuffed the phone in its cradle.

"Making plans?"

I jumped. Finn stood in the doorway of the kitchen with his guitar hanging from his hand. Fatigue rimmed his eyes and tinted his aura a deep twilight blue. "You're up early," I said, trying to sound casual.

"I couldn't sleep."

"Me neither."

"Looks like we both had someone on our minds."

I started to come toward him, but his aura shrank back as I approached. "I'm sorry, Finn. I need to go see Giovanni."

"Obviously." He stared hard at me, like he was waiting for me to say something. When I didn't, he blew out a raging, garnet breath. "I heard you, Cora. You said, *I haven't told him about us.*" He held up his hands. The look on his face was pure pain. "So, tell me now."

God. He'd heard me, but he'd misunderstood. "That is *not* what that comment meant. I'm just going to talk to him. His parents disappeared, too. We're trying to help each other."

"With all your things?" he asked, gesturing to my duffel bag at my feet.

"I think it's smart to have everything with me. Just in case. I don't really have a choice."

Finn pulled a chair back from the table and plopped into it. His guitar sang out as he set it a bit roughly on the table. "Life is nothing *but* choice. Do I get up today or stay in bed? Do I turn left or right? Should I be a doctor and make my parents happy or please myself and study music? Do I stay in Ireland or do I find a way to go back to America to be with a girl who wants to spend time alone with some other bloke?"

"I don't want him! I want to find out what happened to my mother. I need answers. Don't you see, Finn? I don't just need answers about *her*. I need answers about *me*. It's like…life or death important to me. You don't understand."

"I understand how important this is to you. We all want to know about ourselves. Where we came from—"

"No, Finn. You *don't* understand. You can't possibly because there are things I've kept from you."

More hurt flashed in his eyes. "Clearly."

That whipped at the pain rising in me. I couldn't indulge in it. Finn, his parents, they were distracting me, and I didn't have much time left. "Seeing you again has been magic, but I didn't come here for this. For us. *You* left me, remember? This is all confusing me and getting me off track. I have to do what I came here to do, Finn. I have to go."

He stood abruptly and crossed the space between us. He took my face in his hands. "Are *you* trying to say good-bye now, Cora?"

I was right. Our first good-bye had been hard enough.

I swallowed hard, choking on my love for him, and answered. "You're wrong about Giovanni and me. *You* have my heart. But my father's likely on his way, and I have to go right now. I'm sorry."

THIRTY-SIX

I needed to get my hands on a phone book to call a cab—and perhaps I could look up doctors whose names started with M, which would probably be a major exercise in futility because she most likely wasn't referring to the medical kind of doctor. Finn was gone. He had walked out of the kitchen without another word. I'd never forget the colors of his heartache.

The phone book was on a shelf near the phone. I flipped it open.

"What'll you be needin'?" Uncle Clancy said as he swept into the room. God, these people were early risers. He grabbed a scone from a large jar on the counter and stuffed it in his mouth. Crumbs dotted his shirt over his round belly.

I smiled at him and his sunny aura. "I'm going to call for a ride into Dublin."

"Come with me, child. I'm going into town to open the pub anyhow," he said, tossing me a lemon scone.

We walked together to the car. Clancy opened the door for me, which was very sweet. I wondered if Finn was watching us as we drove away. I know Ina was. Clancy waved at her. Ina's cold stare from the front window was the last I saw of Rising Sun Manor.

"You come all this way to see that boy of ours?"

"I've always wanted to come to Ireland. It's held a certain fascination for me my whole life. You might even call it an obsession. But I have to admit," I said, picking at the seam on my jeans, "I'm glad I got to see your boy, too."

Possibly for the last time. Pain rolled in my chest.

Clancy grinned through his white beard. "You're sweet on each other, that much is clear. Do you have family here?"

"I-I'm not sure. I'm looking."

He gave me a sideways glance and patted my arm consolingly as he parked in front of Christ Church. Giovanni leaned against a stone wall. He smiled when he saw me.

"You know him?" Clancy asked, peering at Giovanni with his eyes narrowed.

"Yes. He's helping me, um, find my people. Well, thanks for the ride."

"Good luck on your search, lass. I'll be seeing you back at the house, I reckon."

Giovanni didn't move. After his ultimatum that had snowballed into my parting with Finn, I wasn't in the mood to smile back. "Tell me you've had your espresso. Because I have a lot of questions and you're gonna need to be alert."

He raised one eyebrow and cocked his head, silver-blue eyes twinkling in the morning sun.

Giovanni opened the large church door for me and swept his arm in an exaggerated bow when I walked past him. I was about to start in on my list of questions, but the inside of the church vibrated with such a reverent hush I stopped in my tracks, causing Giovanni to bump into me.

"*Scusi,*" he whispered. His hand lingered on my shoulder a moment, making it tingle all the way down to the cut on my palm.

I stepped away. We walked through the church in silence, awed by the ornate beauty and history. I came upon a beautiful rectangular table fashioned of scrolled iron, topped with a copper tub full of sand. Votive candles nestled in the sand, prayers for peace from pilgrims who came before us. To the right of this table was a painting with three figures—they looked to be women with ornately braided hair— seated around a pedestal table. All of them were painted with disks of light around their heads.

The longer I stared, the more sure I was. "Auras."

Giovanni's hushed voice answered from over my shoulder, so close his breath fell against my temple. "Of course. Go to the Bible. Even it says, 'There is a natural body and a spiritual body.'"

"I've seen this in paintings before. I always thought it was how the artists depicted divinity."

A quiet, sardonic laugh came from over my shoulder. "*Sí*. The divine in all of us."

I turned to look at him, close still, staring at me with crystalline eyes. So close, shock waves of pleasurable energy darted back and forth between our auras. We stood there a moment and gazed at each other, our silver auras flickering, competing with the luminosity of the votive candles next to us.

Giovanni's eyes settled on my mouth and his lips parted a little. His aura pulsed faster with his heart rate, and mine sped to match. He moved his head a fraction closer. I'm sure he could see my aura flare wildly as I realized what was happening. I put my hand on his chest to stop him. "Tell me everything you know about us."

He covered my hand with his for a moment, then held on to it and led me to a row of wooden chairs. We settled in, facing each other. Sparks ricocheted from where our knees touched. I shifted slightly. At some uncomfortable point, we were going to have to discuss the obvious energy between us. I thought it was the unique alchemy of two Scintilla, but a girl knows when she's about to be kissed.

"Since I was a boy, I've been researching this. References to auras are prevalent in many cultures: ancient Egypt, India, China, all over the world. The energy that dwells within us and around us has been called by many names. Chi, kundalini, Odic force, prana, electromagnetic fields. Hell, you could even look at pop culture: Obi-Wan Kenobi and the damn Force."

I looked around, hoping no one heard his increasingly excited rant. He softened his voice. "There is evidence everywhere of what you and I can see—in art, literature, and history. For a time, it was common to talk of someone's *light*. Now it's been suppressed, except in New Age circles, which sadly are not taken very seriously."

I thought of that New Age nut from TV, Edmund Nustber, and had to agree. "Why has it been suppressed?"

Giovanni shrugged. "Why is anything true hidden away? Fear? Greed? Control? The existence of auras and spiritual energy isn't easily provable, but there are people who are working on it, who've been working on it for a long time."

"Like my mom."

He patted my hand and pulled a Bible from the back of our chair, flipping the pages to a certain passage. "See here," he said, pointing to Ezekiel 1:22. "'Over the heads of the living creatures there was the likeness of an expanse, shining like awe-inspiring crystal, spread out above their heads.'"

"Wow. I feel like I'm the only person on earth who was in the dark about all of this." Of course I was. My dad had purposely kept me in a darkened room all my life. I sighed. "Can you please explain what you meant when you said there was more than one kind of human, because my mother's journal spoke of that, too. If Scintilla are one kind, what are the others?"

"Here's what I believe." He held up three fingers. "There are three breeds of human: those who give, *Scintilla*. There are the *Arrazi*, those who take." Giovanni shrugged. "And then there's everyone

else, regular people. Though I do think some of *them* have faint traits
of Scintilla or Arrazi because of family history. The people with the
auras of all white, I believe they are Arrazi."

"So, people who drain you, make you exhausted when you are
around them, you're saying they are descendants of these *takers,* the
Arrazi?" That would explain people like Janelle and certainly Serena
Tate. "And people like us? According to you, we are givers?"

"Yes. Though, pure Scintilla are extremely rare. We are givers of
light, Cora. It is a beautiful thought, no? Problem is, the Scintilla have
all but disappeared."

"My mother. Her parents."

"My parents."

"*Why* are we disappearing, Giovanni? What's happening to
the Scintilla?" It was odd saying the name like I was talking about
characters in a mythic tale.

He leaned close. I could smell the hint of espresso on his breath.
His aura collided with my own again, and I felt a sudden infusion of
scintillating energy. "You want to know what I think is happening to
the Scintilla?" He looked around. "I think we are being hunted by the
Arrazi."

On instinct, my hands pressed together in front of me. I didn't like
the sound of being someone's prey. I'd had a taste of that in California.

"We're being wiped out. I don't know the reason. If I did, maybe
I could stop it. I couldn't stop it—" His eyes misted over with a teary
film. His voice suddenly choked, and his raw emotion choked me up
as well. Of course he would be emotional. He'd lost his parents so
young. I'd been searching for answers for a few weeks. He had been
searching his whole life.

"It's too late for our parents. I'm sorry, but I believe that in my
heart," he said with such surety it threatened to shatter my hope. "We
will never see them again. But we are here." He reached out to me,
but his hand hovered inches from my skin. The contact was as real as

if his hand cradled my face. He dropped his hand and stared intently into my eyes. "I thought there was no hope. Until you showed up. There must be a reason we're both here together, Cora."

"What reason?"

"To find out the truth. To protect the givers of light in this world." My hand was taken up in his. "To protect each other."

The chill of vulnerability slid over me. Like a baby deer in a wide-open field. "How do you know who's doing the hunting?"

"Like any prey, we have natural enemies. I'd heard the word Arrazi more than once in my life. And I watched people *feed*, it's the only way I can say it. One man took another man's aura in a pub. At first I watched with interest because I'd seen the give and take of energy, but not one so blatant, so violent. I had no idea he was killing him until the man slumped over." Giovanni snapped his fingers, making me jump. "Lights out. And the taker, his aura turned pure white, like that man at the airport we saw when the old couple died."

I gasped. "Yes. I know." I could barely breathe with the memory of it. "And there was one in California, too."

Giovanni's eyes went wide. He touched my hand.

"I saw him kill two women. He tried to kill me. It was the most terrifying thing I've ever been through."

His mouth opened in surprise. "It's true then, what I've heard. There are a few Scintilla scattered everywhere. And where we are, there is the Arrazi."

"But the woman he killed, she wasn't like us. She had a normal aura. Colorful."

"As did the poor man in the pub." He pinched the bridge of his nose. "There must be a reason they are killing regular people, too. We need to find out. I think there is a man who has been following me. He could be Arrazi. If we could follow him—"

I jumped to my feet. "I'm not volunteering to be bait for some soul-suckers!" An elderly couple looked over at me with shocked expressions. The woman crossed herself.

Giovanni got up and took my elbow, leading me deeper into the heart of the church. "If we could find out *why* they are killing and *why* there are so few Scintilla left in the world—"

I shook my head. "I came here to find out any information I could about my mother. I want to know about *her*. About myself. This is all too much." I started to cry, overcome. "I want to go home."

Giovanni pulled me into a hug. He was so tall that my face landed squarely in the middle of his chest. I could hear his heart rumble against my wet cheek, feel our auras commune and wrap us in an electrical storm.

One of us should pull away.

"Miss Cora." When I didn't answer, he held me back at arm's length. I blinked my tears away and looked up at him. "I know you're scared," he murmured, brushing my tears with the pads of his fingers. "I bet our parents were scared. We can't let them down. Please don't run back home. You've already said there is a killer there. If he comes after you—"

"He already has."

He squeezed my upper arms with a gentle shake. "You must understand, until we find out what they are after, we can't hope to stop them. Please help me do that."

I had to look away from his pleading eyes.

My gaze landed on a statue nestled in a marble column. Out of one smooth green-gold stone was carved a statue of Madonna and child. She held her child in front of her heart. I walked over, touched my palm to the smooth curve of the mother's head, and ran one finger over the baby's head. It didn't look like a baby at all.

It looked like a mother and a little girl.

Turn right, turn left. Stay here or go home. Get up in the morning and attack life, or stay in bed and pretend you aren't a motherless child who has seen murder right in front of your eyes. It was as Finn had said, all choices.

If I left now, I was no better than my father. Even if my mother was dead, I couldn't abandon her again. I finally appreciated her quest to uncover the truth. It wasn't just herself she was concerned about. She worried about me. About everyone like us. She was trying to understand the truth about humanity. I had to carry on in her place.

Giovanni approached, but he stopped shy of reaching me.

"I'll help," I said. "For as long as I can."

THIRTY-SEVEN

We walked from the calm of the great cathedral into the noisy hum of Dublin's city streets. "How can I get hold of you if I need to?" Giovanni asked, pulling out a very high-tech phone.

"For a wandering orphan with no family, you do pretty well," I said, motioning to his phone.

He shrugged. "Yes, well, I did say some people would give almost anything in exchange for what I can offer."

"I'll give you my cell number, but please try not to use it. I'm afraid my dad will figure out how to find me by the cell phone records. I'll give you a digit for every question you answer."

"I've already answered a kilo of questions."

I conceded that he had and gave him all but the last digit.

"I appear to missing one," he said, frowning at his phone.

I crossed my arms. "Why did you say I wasn't safe with Finn?"

Giovanni cocked his head to the side. "That's what I have to answer to get the last digit?" He looked down the street, apparently deciding. I didn't like the look in his eyes, but after the overheard conversation with Finn's parents, I needed to know.

"I felt from him a—" He squinted at something. "There is a man coming. I've seen him before." Giovanni grabbed my elbow.

"Are you trying to get out of answering my question?" I asked as he tugged me away from the church. I didn't know what he felt around Finn, but I knew what I felt. Still, I wanted an answer.

He looked over his shoulder. "Either this world is decidedly smaller than people think, or this man really is following me. This might be our chance. I wonder if we can turn the tables," he said. "His aura, it is white."

My heart thumped at that word. "White? I'm—I'm not ready for white. We have no plan!" Panic hammered at my heart.

Before I could think what to do, Giovanni abruptly turned a corner, hauled us into a recessed doorway, pressed me against the glass, and said, "Look over my shoulder. Is he still there? He's in a suit. Red tie. Do you see him?"

I tried to ignore the startling intimacy of our bodies pressed together, the charge of our energies colliding, the spice of him so close, and looked around his arm. The man who stared back at me from across the street let his mouth spread into a slow, sick smirk.

The hospital.

The grocery store.

It was the same smirk he gave me in the park after he drained the life from that woman. Terror hit me full force.

Something else hit me, too. Pure rage.

I was tired of this game. He'd had plenty of times to kill me and never had. Though I wanted nothing more than to be as far away from him as possible, I tried a different tactic. I grabbed Giovanni's hand. "Come with me."

We stepped off the curb and started into the street. Confrontation was a stronger, more potent brew in my blood than cowardice.

"What were those World War Two pilots called?" Giovanni asked, squeezing my hand. "The Japanese ones who—" He still had his phone in his hand and suddenly held it up, pushing record on the camera.

"Kamikazes," I answered, staring straight ahead at the man who had not moved. "And not a helpful image right now." I didn't know what kind of mix fear, desperation, a thirst for answers, and a dash of stupidity made, but it kept my feet moving toward him.

The man looked surprised at our approach, yes, but amused, too. I didn't like amused. *Screw this guy*. I wanted answers. If this man was what Giovanni had called an Arrazi, he was another piece in the puzzle. If we could get him to talk, maybe we'd be closer to having a full picture.

We crossed the street and stepped up onto the sidewalk where he waited. His arms were folded over his red tie, his dark eyes no longer amused. They were ravenous. Predatory.

"Two of you," he sneered. "And you," he said, cocking his head at me. "Hello again."

"Yes, two of us, *one* of you," Giovanni said.

The man with the white aura laughed. "Oh, you think there's but one of me?" He stepped even closer and bent forward, almost conspiratorially, to say, "There's an *army* of us."

Giovanni glanced around us nervously. I clasped his forearm. This was not someone to take your eyes off. The man sarcastically waved to the camera, mocking us.

An explosion of aggression fired from me, propelling me forward. I shoved him in the chest. "Why are you following us? What the hell do you want?"

He stumbled back, caught his balance, and fixed me with a deadly gaze that stopped my heart. "It's not what I want that matters." He smoothed the lapels of his suit jacket down calmly and spoke with mock civility. "But since you asked so very politely, I will tell you. I want nothing more than to devour every…last…drop of your precious life and leave you dead on this sidewalk."

I shook with fear and adrenaline but pressed on. If I could just get more information from him… "I've seen you do that. I've seen you murder," I seethed. "But you won't kill me. If that's what you really wanted, I'd be dead already."

His fingers gripped my chin, lifting it up. "Are you actually *eager* to die, young lady?"

I slapped his hand away.

"Don't touch her! We know what you are, Arrazi," spat Giovanni, literally, on the man's shiny black shoes.

Whips of white energy stretched toward Giovanni like tentacles. His body lurched forward violently as the man pulled his glorious sparks from his chest. I leaped onto the man's back, throwing punches as fast as they would come, though my arms felt leaden and ineffectual. The man reached back and tossed me to the ground. My teeth clattered with the impact.

The distraction I offered was enough to stop the ravaging of Giovanni's aura. He punched the man in the mouth but was apparently too weak to do any real damage. Pulling on Giovanni's arm, I spun him away. "Run!"

We tore down the sidewalk, skidding around corners, swerving around pedestrians, weaving in and out of traffic. I was in a panic. Running for my life from a *taker*. A murderer. How stupid to think we could confront him. I'd almost gotten us killed.

Scintilla *were* being hunted.

I was being hunted.

Nausea crawled up my stomach, into my throat. My legs burned as I sprinted across a bridge. My lungs threatened to implode from lack of oxygen. I had to stop. I had to catch my breath. I dared a glance behind me. Giovanni was gone! Throngs of businessmen strolled the sidewalks. I scanned the crowds manically, first for silver, then for the blaze of a red tie, for the flash of a white aura. I had to get off these streets.

Around another corner I saw the most welcome sight in my life: a sign that said MULCARR'S PUB. I slammed through the doors, and as soon as I saw the sweet face of Uncle Clancy I burst into tears. I fell into his open arms, sobbing incoherently about how some man was after me.

Clancy rubbed my back and clucked, "There, there," while I sniffled and snorted about being followed. He looked at me with kind, sympathetic eyes and gave my chin a little chuck. "You're all right now, girl. No one is comin' after you. Where's your friend?"

"I-I don't know. We… I ran, got separated. I don't know if he's okay."

He sat me down in the snug, which was perfect, hidden and insulated from the outside world. "Just you sit there a wee bit. I'll get Finn from the storeroom to come and gather you up, take you back to the manor."

I scooted into the corner of the snug, hugged my knees, and tried to calm myself. What was that man doing in Ireland? Did he follow me here? And if he wanted to kill me so badly, what was stopping him? And, would I always be so lucky?

My phone screamed at me from my pocket. I didn't recognize the number or the name on the screen: M.G.R.I.

I answered in a shaky voice. "Hello?"

For a moment, I heard only breathing on the other end. Then, finally, "Cora. It's G."

"Oh my God. Giovanni, are you okay? I thought you were behind me. I lost you. How did you know my full number? I never gave you the last digit."

"Well, there were only ten options," he panted. "I'm okay. The man was too close behind us. I deliberately split in another direction from you so he'd follow me, instead. Then I lost him. I've been looking all over for you."

"It was *him*. The killer I saw back home."

Silence. Then, "I wondered why you seemed to recognize each other."

"I'd know his face anywhere."

"Do you know what this means?"

My heart beat out the seconds before he answered his own question. My gut already knew the answer.

"It means he's after you. He's following you, too, Cora."

"Yes. He's after both of us. He and his…*army*."

"Do you think he wants to kill us?"

"Yes," I answered. "I do. He could easily kill us. I've witnessed how easily. And I think he wants to very badly. But he said it's not what *he* wants that matters. There's something stopping him."

Giovanni and I sat with that, silently sharing the fear. His sigh was full of weight. Then he said, "I don't like the way he feels."

"What do you mean?"

"I'm paying for the last digit, Cora."

The door of the snug burst open. Finn dropped to his knees in front of me. "Sorry, I've got to go. I'll call you back," I said and hung up.

Finn held my face in his hands. He placed tiny kisses all over my cheeks, chin, lips, forehead. "You're okay," he whispered, though I didn't know if he was reassuring me or himself. "I should never have let you go with that guy. I'll find him. I'll kill him." His aura flashed with large orbs of deep, bloody red and a darkness bordering on black.

"No, no," I said. "It wasn't Giovanni."

He pulled back and looked at me. "Who then?"

I wanted to tell him everything, to curl myself under the protective umbrella of his love. But this knowledge put people in danger. What if he disappeared like my mother? What if that man killed him? I'd never forgive myself. "It was a strange man, following me. I—I thought I had seen him before."

Finn searched my face. He held my hands and wrapped my arms

around his shoulders. "I won't let any harm come to you, Cora. I promise." I nestled my face into the crook of his neck. He had no idea how little power he had to protect me from this kind of harm, the kind that comes at you out of nowhere, reaches inside, and pulls your soul from its bindings.

"I have a surprise for you," he said into my hair.

"If it's all the same to you, I'd rather not go for cupcakes right now."

He chuckled and fished a paper from his wallet. "I reckoned if I could help, maybe you wouldn't need that tall Italian tosser." He grinned at me. "I wanted to show you that I understand how important finding information on your mum is to you, so I went to the General Register Office. This," he said, handing me the paper, "is your parents' marriage license."

I peered at the paper. There hadn't been a copy of this in the treasure box. There was my father's full name, Benito Raul Sandoval. And my mother's name in Irish, which I couldn't pronounce, but it did say "Grace" in parentheses. "Oh, Finn, thank you! I can't believe you did this."

"Look right here." He tapped the paper with his tapered finger. "It shows their address at the time of filing."

I gasped. "Can we—?"

"Way ahead of you. It's not far from here."

I pressed the paper to my chest. "Our house. I get to see our house." I bit my lip but couldn't hold back my tears. "Thank you, Finn. This means the world to me."

"Aye, *críona*. I know it does."

"What does that word mean?"

He smiled before answering. I thought I saw a blush warm his aura. "My heart."

THIRTY-EIGHT

The drive took on more significance because of where we were headed. Every thatched-roof farmhouse, every rock wall dripping with history, every corner pub and crumbling stone remnant of a building was something my parents and I would have traveled past years ago. These were the roads my parents would have taken to go to work or to the store for bread. These were roads my mother took to come home to us.

Before she didn't.

Despite the sun, I blew warm air into my cold hands and rubbed them together. The fear hadn't left me since my encounter on the street, but thinking of what might have happened to my mother only made it worse. Had she also been stalked, taunted, and threatened by a killer? Had someone like him found her but not held back?

The car slowed. Finn turned off the main road onto a narrow lane lined with trees and hedges. He parked in front of a tiny house ringed by a thicket. I grazed my hand over a leaf as we walked. "There are the best blackberry bushes in front of the house down there." I slapped my hand over my mouth. Finn peered at me curiously. I knew these bushes would soon be dripping with dark, plump berries. But there was no fruit now, only delicate white flowers with a secret inside.

"How did you know?"

"I have no idea. A memory, I guess." I saw a picture in my mind of a pudgy little hand stained with summer.

We reached a small stone cottage with an eave over a bright red door. "There's your house," Finn said, though I knew it already. Whenever I dreamed about a house, even the one I lived in now, it always had a red door. I'd never understood why, until now.

Do houses have memories, too? Can they recall the squeal of a little girl chasing after a grasshopper in the grass? Or the way young lovers gaze at each other over their sleeping newborn? Would this house be able to bring forth the smell of sugar caramelizing on fresh cinnamon rolls? Or the wail of a child sobbing, "I want mommy"?

We approached the stone half-wall surrounding the yard. I stood in front of the red wooden gate, ran my fingers over the weathered iron handle in the shape of a…daisy.

"You want to go to the door and ask if we can look around?"

"Do you think they'd let us?" I asked, taking Finn's warm hand in mine.

He gave the door a couple of hearty knocks, and then we waited. We heard only the quiet hum of a late spring day—the rustling of leaves, a dog barking in the distance, an occasional car passing, the zip of an insect on the fly.

"S'pose nobody's home."

"Maybe I'll have a quick peek in the windows." I walked around the side of the house, trailing my hand along the stone. It wasn't enough to see the house, I needed to touch it. Around the corner, I found a gleaming window trimmed in white. I cupped my hands around my eyes and, with my forehead pressed to the glass, peeked inside. A bedroom, perhaps a guest room because there were a few boxes, a vacuum, and odds and ends next to the bed that one would throw into a rarely used room. A layer of dust blanketed the items. Did no one live here now? I began to turn away when another image came into view like a holograph overlaid on the scene before me. A crib. A toddler with bright green eyes and black ringlets cascading around her face. Refracted light shimmered in my eye. An orange crystal hanging above the bed, casting rainbows on the walls.

The image vanished. Finn's hand was at my back. "You okay, luv? You look like you're seeing ghosts."

"I am," I said. "My own."

"That's a right eerie thing to say."

"Wasn't it you, telling me about the ghosts in Ireland?" I teased, trying to lighten the mood despite the disquiet on my skin.

"Aye. I did say that. Thank you for making it oh-so-real for me. Look at my arms!" Goose bumps sprinkled over his skin, and I smoothed my hand down his arm.

We walked around the back of the house into a lovely cottage garden. Along the entire length of the back wall spread row upon row of daisies, thousands of them. Another flash of a picture in my mind. My mother on her knees, planting, a long black braid down her back.

Pieces of my family lingered here. I had no idea why I could see the memories, but I was glad not to feel the awful sting and burn of a mark forming on my body. I had no idea why it happened at some times and not others.

Maybe, I thought, what marks us are our peak emotional moments—either scarring us or setting us free. Either way, none of us get out unmarked. My marks were just more literal.

"Was it good to have brought you?" he asked, concerned. "You look *affected*."

Unnerved, I looked around with a strong impression of being exposed, like there were eyes on us. "I am affected. I feel tender here. Ireland is a—a *thin* place."

Finn nodded, seeming to know what I meant. "Aye. The veil

between worlds *is* thinner here."

"Exactly." I turned to him. "I will love you my whole life for doing this for me."

⚜━━━

We held hands and listened to John Lee Hooker as we drove. "Did you ever get in trouble for breaking your mom's bracelet?" I asked, running my fingers over his wrist and recalling the intensity of that afternoon together and the powerful desire between us when we kissed in my room. I'd never felt emotions so all-consuming. It had felt like both the beginning and the end. Finn had said good-bye the very next day.

He smiled with a nonchalant shrug. "It's not like I broke the bracelet on purpose. Mom's odd. She was superstitious about them. Thought the crystals would keep me from being vulnerable to the negative energy of other people."

"I've heard of crystals doing that. I'd like to know more about it. She's tight-lipped about her interest, though. I'm guessing she's more into New Age stuff than she lets on."

His quick look made me wonder if I'd crossed the line. This time I didn't care. She'd taken my aura. If that wasn't crossing a line, I didn't know what was.

"Hey, I need to check in with Mari and Dun. I promised I'd call. Maybe they'll know if my father is on his way here yet."

"You think he can find you?" Finn asked.

"He won't stop until he does. And he'll obviously think I'm with you." Uncertainty crept in. "Truth is, I know I have to face him sometime. I'd just rather it be after I find out the secrets he'll never tell me himself."

"I dunno. Maybe it's better for the heavy secrets to ride on the shoulders of those who are strong enough to carry them." Finn grew quiet after that. We both did.

A short time later, he bypassed the turn into Dublin.

"I don't want to go to your house."

My body slammed into the seat as Finn stepped hard on the gas. "You had a strange man following you today." He peered hard into the rearview mirror and cursed to himself. "Maybe that and the stories of your mum have made me paranoid, but I think the black van behind us has been following since we left the cottage."

My hands squeezed the armrests. In the side mirror, I saw a van trailing close behind, even as Finn sped up. "Are you sure it's been there the whole time?"

"No," he said, making a sharp left turn. "But I'm not about to let them follow us to the manor, and I'm not going to let you out of my sight."

The tires screeched as we made a few abrupt turns and pulled onto a quiet, tree-lined road. The van was no longer behind us. He eased up on the gas, and we both sighed with relief, though I realized I was still biting my lip.

"Now tell me why you don't want to come to my house."

I fidgeted with my scarf. "Your parents make me uncomfortable." There. I said it. Well, part of it anyway. I kept my eyes fixed on the mirror.

"My *da* said they'll be going out tonight. It will be just us. I promise to steer them away from you as much as possible. One more night? I can't bear to end things the way we did."

I nodded my agreement and dared a look at him. "I know. I was afraid I wouldn't see you again and that would be your last memory of me. Of us."

"I was jealous. I'm not going to say I like your peculiar attachment to that chap, but it was wrong of me to doubt you."

At the manor, he showed me to a small sitting room on the first floor where I could use the phone in private. He backed toward the door and shut it behind him.

Mari: Dun wants to know, "How's my girl?"

Me: Tell him I said peachy.

Dun from afar: Excellent.

Mari: How's the sleuthing going?

Me: I saw my childhood home today, and the church where my parents were married. And I've got my mother's journal.

Mari: Anything on your mom?

Me: Some. Kinda. I'm going to try to find a doctor she mentioned in her notes, and I met someone who's been helping me. I wish I had more to tell you.

Mari: I don't know what you expected. It's not like there'd be signs pointing the way to her grave.

Me: Can you maybe *try* to filter yourself once in a while?

Mari: Sorry. So here's the scoop. Mami Tulke said your father is on his way to Ireland. I don't know exactly when his plane arrives, so prepare yourself. You probably only have a few hours before he gets there.

Me, with a pounding heart: Okay. Thanks. Love you guys.

Hearing their voices made me miss them even more. I wanted to call Giovanni as well since I had cut him off when Finn came into the snug. I started to dial, but Fergus knocked quietly on the door and peeked in.

My fingers poised above the keypad. I thought they were gone for the evening. "Hi," I said cheerfully. Maybe too cheerfully. My neck heated. Finn's dad had talked about me like I was a bottle of rare wine he wanted to sample. I stood behind a chair and grasped the edges. I swear, I'd bash it over his head before I let him take from me.

He tripped on thin air as he walked in the room. He still seemed so sketchy around me, and his nervousness was infectious. Why would *he* be scared of *me*?

"Touching base back home?" he asked.

"Yes. The required check-in."

He smiled. "Wish we'd had more of those when Finn was in America. But I'm glad he met you."

"Why?" Fergus looked surprised at my question. I was as surprised I had asked it. "I mean—I know you didn't want him to date yet."

"Perhaps we were waiting for him to meet someone like you," he said.

"Your wife doesn't seem to agree."

"Like all mothers, she's protective."

"Am I really a threat?"

'Cause I seriously couldn't be the dangerous one. I wasn't hovering over *their* bodies while they slept, siphoning off them for a hit of bliss. My fists clenched and I found myself throwing out the question I most wanted answered. "Mr. Doyle, how can I be the dangerous one when Ina took energy from *me*? Please, tell me what you know about me. It's why I came to Ireland: to find out everything I can about…about Scintilla." There, I'd said it, and it became even more real.

He cocked his head, his surprise evident. "Your parents never told you?"

"No. Nothing. I knew I was…different. I didn't know why until I came here."

"Does Finn know?"

Guilt again. "No."

One finger pointed at the ceiling, and he opened his mouth to speak, but Finn came in the room. "I'm afraid I'll have to steal the pleasure of Cora's company from you, Da." He gave his father a funny little bow. "If you'll excuse us," he said, winking and kissing my hand in a formal, gentlemanly way. "Don't you have a date to go on?"

Fergus nodded, mumbled something incoherent, and watched me in this confounded way as Finn steered me from the room, honoring his promise to keep us apart when I most wanted to hear what his dad was about to say.

THIRTY-NINE

A hundred candles.

There had to be at least a hundred candles in the library, shimmering against the windows, reflecting in the mirrors, scattered among the shelves and tables.

I gasped. "It's beautiful, Finn."

The full moon shone through the large picture window in the library like a polished alabaster plate. Finn and I gazed at it while leaning arm against arm at the open window. The back of his fingers brushed mine.

"I once read that the author Karen Blixen would curtsy to every full moon," I told him.

"Why?"

"I don't know. Out of respect, maybe? I always loved that idea. Of giving props to the moon just for being there. Just for shining."

He looked at me with a heavy-lidded gaze. "I could bow to it for the way it shines on your hair," he said. "Like silver stars spilling over your dark curls. You're beautiful, Cora. *You* shine."

I leaned into his shoulder. "And every night," I continued, a bit breathy, "she would stand for a moment at her south-facing door in Denmark, gazing out toward her beloved Africa." I curled my fingers around his arm. "I know I'll do that when I go back home. Face east. Face Ireland. And think of you." It hurt my heart to think of it.

Tell him the truth.

He coaxed me to sit cross-legged on the thick gray velvet couch, with our knees touching. His hands rested on his thighs, palms up, like an offering. I placed my hands over his, reveled in the familiar swirl of energy around our skin and the light music of his pulse under my fingertips. We stared into each other's eyes. His eyes were so familiar and yet so uncharted, like a well-studied map to a place I'd never been.

Knee to knee, palm to palm, soul to soul. When we first met, I was too shy to stare into his eyes for longer than a few dreamy seconds. I felt so bare, so…seen. Now I had no fear of Finn's eyes. They were toasty warm and filled with humor and life-lust. They spoke love when he looked at me.

After a few moments, an incredible thing happened: the conversation of our heart rates slowed, then synced. Our pulses fired at exactly the same time, thrumming softly in unison through our hands. "Do you feel that?" I asked, almost afraid it would stop if I moved or spoke or even breathed.

He smiled. "Every time I'm near you."

"It's amazing."

Tell him. "Finn, I—"

He broke the connection and grazed his fingers over my collarbone, sending rolling heat down my arms. I found myself tilting my neck to the side as his hand brushed whisper-light over my skin, so feathery, it was excruciatingly pleasurable. I sighed when he wound his fingers into the curls at the nape of my neck.

"Pleased with yourself?" I whispered, noticing the satisfied smile on his face.

"I'm pleased I make you feel good. I'm pleased with how you react to me." He touched my lips with two fingers, tracing the contours. They parted involuntarily. "I could watch you all day, luv," he murmured against my mouth.

His full lips melted into mine, his tongue teasing. My breath hitched when his kisses traveled from my lips to my neck, behind my ear. "I'll never tire of the sounds you make," he whispered.

My back arched against the pillows of the couch. He hovered over me, his aura pulsating with the warm orange-red fire of desire, tinted with the yellow of his affection. He was a sunset shining on me, warming me. Igniting my cravings.

As we kissed, my leg wrapped around his thigh, and I pulled him closer. Any restraint he had been showing fell away with the full contact of our bodies. I was pinned between the plush softness of the couch and his firm, muscled body. It was like sinking together into the top of a storm cloud. He pressed against me and kissed with more hunger. I moaned softly.

"That…sound," Finn gasped. "I want more."

My lips roamed down his neck to the soft crook where his tattoo flared out. I still hadn't seen it entirely. And I wanted to. Badly. I wanted to rip his shirt open and follow the spirals, trace them with my mouth.

Buttons skittered across my body. I realized I had yanked his shirt open to his waist. Shocked, I looked up to see him staring down at me more intensely than he ever had, full of love tinged with a fury that had nothing to do with anger. He was beautiful. Smooth lines and waves. The tattoo swirled over the right side of his chest, arching up onto his neck.

I tasted the stars.

We writhed together, arms and legs a tangle of need. It was as if we couldn't get close enough. My soul opened to him. My desire to give him everything I had was overwhelming. *This is what love is. Two storm-drenched, raging streams merging together, blending into one.* I lost myself in the tide, surrendering to the overpowering current.

He whispered my name over and over, like an incantation. "Cora. Cora. God, I love you."

I fell into him. Into an abyss of need. So excruciatingly good it hurt. I couldn't breathe. I felt faint, as if I were dissolving—dissolving into him, a comet hurtling into the sun, losing its own fire.

My ecstasy morphed into panic. A sharp spike of adrenaline consumed the rush of passion. I was coming out of myself.

Being drained of all that I was.

Dying.

I was a flame plunged into ice water. Biting cold tore at my insides. The numbness was so severe, I could barely feel my hands and feet. I gulped for air, my lungs and chest aching as if I were kicking for a surface that would never come.

"You're killing me," I choked out, my voice a whisper.

Finn's beautiful mouth was still locked on mine, his kisses strong, pulling me even deeper into him. I lost myself. There was agony in coming apart like that, at being reeled away from myself.

My leaden arms pushed against his smooth chest, but he was unmovable. Any strength I had, I used to bring my knee up into him. I clawed and struggled, but it was like moving a mountain. Somehow, I rolled out from under him, falling to the floor onto my hands and knees, my dark curls bleeding onto the red carpet beneath me. When I looked up, I couldn't see Finn. He was nothing but shadow. I could see only his aura. The brilliant, blinding, pure white light of it.

FORTY

Finn's face appeared closer to me now, dazed and rapturous. His eyes were as clouded as that night in my bedroom. My eyes registered the full view of the triple spiral on his chest. Did he realize he had his arms outstretched? That the light burst from his fingertips like some kind of sorcerer?

I tried to move my heavy body, terror and survival instinct telling me to get away from him. I couldn't feel my hands at all, though they supported me on the carpet. The room swung in and out of focus as I struggled to stay upright. Fearful thoughts struck like lightning. Searing. Burning away everything I thought I knew about Finn.

He had taken from me. Robbed me of my energy, the very essence of my life. His aura glowed with nothing but white light. Like that man in the park. He and my…my Finn, they were the same!

I tried to crawl backward, away from him, and fell onto my butt, burning my elbows on the thick carpet. Each breath was like sucking air through the eye of a sharp needle. His euphoric expression changed slowly, too slowly, to one of concern. He rushed to my side and dropped to his knees in front of me.

"Why do you look like that?" he whispered. "Don't you feel what I feel, Cora?" He ran his hands over his head and looked to the ceiling. "Amazing!" Then he looked down at me again and took my face in his burning hands.

I had no energy left to fight him. No strength left to fend him off. I couldn't even lift my arms. "Please, please don't," I choked out.

"No one ever told me love was so beautifully grand, so exquisite." He bent to kiss me, and even then, even as I came undone, even as I faded from myself, I loved his sweet words, his lips on mine. I could not fight. He was killing me. And something inside me still loved.

Suddenly, someone yanked us apart.

Ina shoved Finn away and stood over me, shielding me from his white glare. I closed my eyes and collapsed, rolling to my side, curling in on myself. I was so cold. *This must be what people feel like when they bleed to death.*

"Clancy!" she screamed, while putting two fingers to the pulse point on my neck.

I opened my eyes briefly when Uncle Clancy burst into the room, noted his shocked face as he looked from me to Finn. "What's happened?" he asked.

"Oh, shut up! We all knew this would happen. Get her out of here!"

Clancy scooped me up off the floor and carried me to the door. I began to slip out of consciousness but fought my eyes open to look at Finn. I couldn't believe he would hurt me like he had. He attempted to push past his mother. His long fingers reached out, clawed the air for me.

His mother's voice was angry. She pointed at Clancy. "Out! Now! Get her on the next plane back to America. Get her back to her father. We can't keep her safe here. She was never safe here." Her voice softened then. "That girl's not safe anywhere."

Ina touched Finn's cheek. Her words followed me down the long hallway. "Oh, son, look what she's done to you."

FORTY-ONE

I awoke in the back of a horse-drawn buggy, swaddled in a scratchy wool blanket smelling of wet animal. I had no idea how much time had passed. Warmth slowly flowed back into my body but only at my core. It was a small bit of coal smoldering inside my belly. I could barely move or stay awake. I stared up at the incredible scattering of stars and thought that if I wanted to, I could fall into them. Into forever.

The rhythmic sway of the buggy rocked me like a baby. Each *clop* of the horse's hooves took me farther from Rising Sun Manor and from Finn. One thought of him and my heart exploded, countless bursts of light competing with the stars.

His mother had said I wasn't safe. She must've known what he was capable of. But then why did she say I had done something to *him*? What kind of human steals the aura of another like a greedy child grabbing candy and then blames the candy?

The Arrazi. The ones wiping out the Scintilla.

I was so naive.

Thieving Ireland. My happiness was stolen. My beliefs about how the world worked—those had been taken, too. I had come no closer to finding my mother than I was back at home with a box of treasures scattered across my floor. I wanted to be home, safe, with my dad. I never should have left.

Warm tears seeped into my temples as I closed my eyes and drifted away.

I came to as I was being carried across a crunchy gravel walkway. Outlines of trees rose above me like black clouds. At my side, Clancy's deep voice whispered, "Praise be, he didn't sleep with her. It was a holy show back there, though." He snorted. "That's what happens when you send a boy to do a man's job. It's a good thing, aye, works in our favor. Can't have the maiden spoiled. This is good."

An icy fear clutched my belly. I pushed as hard as I could away from the arms that carried me and fell to the gravel. It bit hard into my cheek and lip. I tasted the iron tang of blood. For a moment, I could only see black shoes in front of me, and even that image faded in and out. It had taken everything I had to push away.

I willed my chin upward and tried to focus on the blurry faces. But all of my strength evaporated when I saw the man who had been carrying me. He'd finally caught me. He yanked me to my feet like a rag doll, holding my shoulders so hard I was sure I'd wear the bruise of his fingertips forever. He looked hungrily into my eyes, his smile curling up fast and sinister. "Just a taste? She's taunted me for months. You're the only reason I held back."

"You and I both know you're lying, Griffin. You didn't hold back. You're glowing like a *fookin'* candle. You took lives like you were taking seconds at dinner. You took from her in America, and had you gone too far and killed her, I'd have killed you."

Griffin looked down, contrite, but his hands still clutched me like a vise. "May I?"

Clancy waved him on. Answered with a nonchalant air, as if the man had simply asked for seconds of beef stew.

I was overcome by confusion and the bitter stab of Clancy's betrayal. I tried to kick my feet but wasn't even sure they left the ground. My aura yanked violently into Griffin's. I could not swallow. Could not catch my breath. It was like having an enormous hole ripped into my chest and bleeding into thin air. I was evaporating. Slipping away to the spiraled heavens.

FORTY-TWO

I woke swallowed up in a plush, comfortable bed. When I opened my eyes, it appeared as though someone had turned the calendar back about five hundred years. An ornate canopy of thick toile swirled overhead, gathering into a gold-sculpted cap in the center. The posts of the bed were wider around than my legs and carved with figures I couldn't see clearly in the flickering candlelight. I stared groggily at the candle. A dark wick, skirted in blue, rose to a dancing orange flame, fading to white like an aura.

I bolted upright. My head spun, and a wave of nausea rolled in my belly.

The memory of what happened to me, the sick certainty that I wasn't safe, hit me full force. I jumped out of the bed, fell to my knees, and crawled to the door. Gripping the doorknob, I hauled myself to standing and jiggled the knob. Locked. There were no windows in the room, except for an opening in the wooden door—roughly the size of a torso—which was barred. Another piece of wood on the other side of the bars stopped me from being able to see through.

I fought my rising panic. It made me sick to think of my father's misery. His fears had come true. Guilt coursed through me. No wonder he'd clipped my wings. Look what I had done at the first hint of freedom.

Clancy…he was supposed to get me out of harm's way. That's what Ina told him to do. Put me on a plane to America, back to my dad. But he hadn't. Instead, he brought me here. He let that man Griffin *feed* off me.

A sheen of sweat broke out on my upper lip as everything became clear. I'd heard the name Griffin before. He was the family friend Finn had been staying with in America, the one who worked at the hospital. My insides roiled. Was I destined to die like the woman in the park? Griffin stole her flame. Snuffed her out like a candle.

The way Finn almost did to me.

Did he know? Had he known all along and kept it from me? I remembered the constant ball of a secret in his aura, and how I'd wished to know what it was. But I'd been intent on keeping my own secret. I never thought his might be as big. Or so devastating.

My knees wobbled. I grasped the edge of the bed and bent forward, taking deep breaths, willing my dizziness to go away. Using a footstool to hoist myself up, I climbed back between the sheets. The air smelled faintly of warm lemons and herbs. A tray with a pot of tea sat on the nightstand with a delicate china cup and a full silver tea service. I lifted one small, gleaming lid to find sparkling cubes of sugar. My tongue ran over my parched lips. A carafe held ice water, and though I was suspicious of anything offered, I couldn't resist. If they wanted me dead, it was not going to be by poison. I gulped down two glasses.

I had no way of knowing what time it was, whether it was day or night or even how much time had passed since I arrived. I was depleted to my core, far weaker than I'd been when I was ravaged by fever in the hospital. I pushed myself into the crisp sheets and curled up on my side against the pillows, thinking a body as terrified as mine, a mind as chaotic as mine, and a heart as broken as mine would never sleep.

A woman's voice woke me. "Drink the tea."

I rubbed my eyes and focused on the lady standing next to the bed. Real, actual daylight cast shafts of gold across her high cheekbones and on the floor at her feet. I glanced around for the source, then followed her eyes to the ceiling.

"Skylights," she explained. "Too too high to fly." Oh yeah, this woman definitely had ghosts. They crowded her eyes.

She reached for the silver teapot. "Here," she said, handing me the tiny cup filled with warm tea. "To help."

I eyed it dubiously but took a few sips while she watched with eyes like cracked green leaves. "Little bird, little pet…how did they trap it?" She wasn't asking me. It was more like a conversation with her invisible friend. I set the cup down and spoke slowly, as one should do with a crazy person.

"How—do—I—get—out—of—here?"

Her eyes snapped from the cup I held back up to my face. "You don't."

I swung my legs over the side of the bed and grumbled, "We'll see about that."

She didn't look very strong. Lanky. Like a teenager, though I could see she'd passed that more than a couple of decades ago. She was as pale and flimsy as thin paper. I could totally take her. I'd follow her to the door and jump her. Hot adrenaline pumped into my blood at the thought. I set my cup gently on its matching saucer. My fists clenched at my sides.

"What are you? My babysitter?"

The look that passed her face was pure pity. "No." Then she mumbled something in Irish.

"What did you say?" I asked, irritated, ready to tackle her and get the hell out of there.

She clasped her delicate hands together and took a deep preparatory breath, like she was about to deliver the Gettysburg Address, but all that came was a weak breeze of words. "We are birds in the same cage."

FORTY-THREE

"Look, lady," I said, right up in her face, close enough to maybe break through her cobwebs. "I'm *not* staying here. I have no intention of hanging around and letting these guys feed off me."

The woman laughed. In. My. Face. A fit of giggles I feared might shake loose what little glue held her sanity together.

"Where are we?"

The woman reached for a strand of her long hair, holding it between two fingers like a cigarette. She slid her fingers down to the ends, where she began plucking furiously at the tips, which were already a frayed mess. "We're in the cave of the dragon," she sang.

This woman was going to be of zero help.

"More tea," she commanded with sudden urgency, shoving the cup into my face.

I knocked it to the ground, where it splintered into pieces. "I don't want the damn tea!"

She flew frantically to a cupboard, got out another cup, and poured it full. "Drink the tea. Drink. Drink it until you can see me."

"Until I can *see* you?" I suddenly realized the absence of aura. I couldn't see her colors, which caused a surge of panic in me.

She nodded emphatically. "Tea and sleep. Sleep and tea. It's the only way to come back to life."

I eyed her warily but took the cup and ventured a sip. The tea was no longer hot, just tepid and bitter. I was so thirsty I slammed the liquid down too fast, bursting into a sputtery cough. Nothing special happened after I drank it, though. I watched the woman as she scuttled from place to place, picking up the broken glass, arranging the pieces in a pattern in the corner of the wood floor in an adjacent room. She ran to the wood-burning stove, scooped up some cold charcoal, and rushed back to her little art project. There had to be a way out of this. "What's your name?" I called to her over the clink and scrape of glass against the floor.

"Gráinne," she answered. It sounded like *grawn-ya*. After more soft clattering of glass, she came out of the other room and looked at me expectantly, wringing her bloody hands in front of her. I winced.

"What is *your* name, child?"

"Cora."

"Cora." She said my name slowly, tasting it in her mouth like it was a foreign flavor. Then she nodded and turned back to her project. I took a couple of shaky steps after her, but stopped when I saw her huddled on the floor, rocking back and forth, bloody hands around the knees of her white skirt.

I felt so sorry for her. She was a fragile stalk, blowing in an invisible wind.

"I'm going to try to get us out of here," I said. "I won't stay in here and wait to die."

She looked up at me sadly through a curtain of dark, grimy hair. "I've died a thousand deaths in here. You will, too."

I backed away, leaving her to her rocking and her ghosts. The bed was the only refuge I had. I still wasn't myself. I could tell by the heft of my limbs, by the sweat on my upper lip from moving around the room. I needed to sleep. I needed to eat something, if only to get strong enough to escape.

A hand caressed my cheek. Softly. Appreciatively. I leaned into it. "Finn," I moaned. I would open my eyes and be in my lavender room atop the lighthouse. Finn would be there to chase away my bad dreams. He'd call me his *heart* again.

"I'm sure you'll see him soon," a deep, melodic voice answered. My eyes flew open. "When he needs more of what you have to offer." Clancy Mulcarr stood over me. His hand grazed the outer curve of my breast. "I'm quite proud of him for luring you here."

I slapped his filthy hand away. "Don't touch me!" I screamed, scrambling off the other side of the bed. His aura wasn't white, had never been white since we had met. I didn't understand it. It looked normal. Peaceful, actually. Only a monster could radiate peace after what he'd done.

"Don't be thick, girl. I can take what I want without touching you. You know that."

My heart beat ebony with the poison of betrayal. My breaths came in short, strained bursts. There was not enough air in the room. Not enough space in the universe to get away from what Clancy had said. "You said Finn lured me here?" I asked, too aware of the weakness that made my voice quiver.

"Not everything went as planned in America, I must admit. Your coming to Ireland was brilliantly cooperative. Bloody unexpected, but cooperative. We'd been watching you for so long. I feel quite vindicated to know I was right about what you are. And how could Finn not lure you? It's astonishing how little you know about yourself. About Finn, for that matter. Jesus, Mary, and Joseph, if you had any sense at all, you'd never have let him near you."

The room closed in on me as Clancy and I stood there staring at each other.

"I know what you are, too, *Arrazi*," I spat. A flicker of amused astonishment showed in his face. "I have sense enough to know you're nothing but a parasite. That people like you take and kill just to make yourselves feel good!"

"Oh, pet." Clancy laughed. "It's not for pleasure. Though I admit, it's good all right, and Scintilla are especially intoxicating. If the world knew what I possessed…" His eyes narrowed. He placed his thick hands on the bed and leaned toward me. "It's a bit more serious than pleasure. We must feed off auras. To survive."

"As in, you'll *die* if you don't?"

He waved his hand in the air like my question bored him. "Yes. Arrazi require the energy of others to live. All of a regular human's life energy. A human soul is a spark from the divine fire and it feeds us. There are givers and there are takers. This is true in all of nature, Cora. The sunlight gives, the trees take, they in turn give us oxygen—"

"Thanks for the biology lesson, but what do *you* give?"

"Ah, see, the Arrazi are at the top of the human food chain. And you," he said, pointing at me, "you are our sun."

I'm sure I looked as shocked as I felt. If this was the trail of truth my mother had been following, she was right. Giovanni was right. There were different breeds of human. Mankind always had its share of predators and prey, but this was literal. This leech stood there telling me that his kind, the Arrazi, lived off other people. "You kill people! You're nothing but murderers!"

Clancy worked his way slowly around the bed as I backed into the corner. His voice was a low, menacing rumble. "Do you fault the lion for killing the gazelle?"

I didn't want to play his game. We were humans. We were equals. He had no right to kill another. And yet I knew he would if it meant his survival. "Then why haven't you killed me yet? Why am I here? Why is that poor woman here?"

"The Arrazi weren't always murderers, but our source of life has been all but depleted. Every time I take from *you*, you save a multitude of people I'd otherwise have to kill. The energy of a Scintilla is the most powerful on earth. My choice to enslave one saves many."

"How completely benevolent of you." I trembled with rage and pure fear. Both emotions gusted like the same hot wind rattling my bones.

Clancy moved closer, irritation glinting in his beady dark eyes. "If I didn't do this, I'd have to employ tacky techniques like my sister and her husband, working knee-deep around death so they can benefit from it."

Doctors. That's how they did it without being caught. No wonder they were so insistent on Finn becoming one. And I'd first met him in the hospital. Where I'd also seen Griffin for the first time. The bitter trace of tea rose up in my throat. My God, it was true, they'd been after me all along.

"Sortilege! Powers! Tell her! His soul's on a chain, it is. That is also why they covet the Scintilla," Gráinne shouted from her doorway. Now I saw her aura. The gleaming, sparkling silver of it.

He had two of us.

"Out, woman!" Clancy shouted. Gráinne jumped and shut her door. He straightened his wool sweater over his generous belly and smoothed back his hair. "She forgets herself." He took another step toward me. Then another. "She is correct, though. Another undeniable allure of a Scintilla," he said, drawing the word out in a hiss, "is that your energy awakens and fuels our powers, our sortilege. We all have latent abilities that are waiting for the spark to ignite them. Extrasensory abilities are our birthright. Through the years it's been diluted and bastardized so that some *regular* humans possess our gifts. But it's very real. Scintilla give us the only thing humans truly lust after. *Real* power. *Real* magic. Naturally, the Arrazi who controls you, controls the power."

I swallowed hard. "Biology lesson for you," I whispered. "If you stopped killing us, there'd be *more* of us."

"The Arrazi are not the only ones killing Scintilla, lass. You have great enemies in places you can't even imagine." He smiled. "Enemies who will do anything to keep the truth a secret."

"So they're your enemies, too," I ventured.

"Not quite." He looked into his palm. I saw a quick flash of a gold ring with the emblem worn on the underside of his finger rather than on top. He closed his hand around it. "I have something of an *arrangement* with them. You're a fighter. I like it," Clancy said. "I can't wait to taste your strength when your energy mixes with mine." His dark eyes roiled with hunger. His aura pushed against mine in the space between us. Insistent. Voracious.

"Please don't kill me," I whispered.

"I have no intention of killing you right now. There are far too few of you left. It's a crisis, really. I fear there may be a war for possession of the remaining Scintilla. Hell, the price for you on the black market is astounding. Having two of you makes me a very powerful man. And your friend, I'll find him, too. Three Scintilla would be the ultimate prize. I'll be unstoppable then."

Three.

Giovanni. I hoped desperately that he was far away and safe.

Clancy cornered me. I was surrounded by the bed, the wall, and the rough edge of the bedside table that dug into my thighs. His eyes bore into mine. I flinched, waiting to feel the agonizing tug on my chest. The pain of my body flying apart.

"Think of it this way. You need me to keep you safe from those who would have you dead for what you know *and* for what you are. And I need you." His whisper was hot on my face. "It's the *only* reason you're still alive."

Every hair on my body stood on end. My energy swirled and built in the middle of my chest. My fingers and feet grew numb. It was starting. "No, no, please don't," I pleaded, pushing ineffectively against Clancy Mulcarr's barrel chest. Already, my solar plexus burned where his energy concentrated. I was sliced open. "I can't handle it."

He touched my face, and the corona of his light burned brighter. I turned my head away and focused on the grain of the wood paneling on the wall. My fingers fumbled on the table next to me for anything to use against him. "Embrace your nature, Cora. This is what you were meant for. You weren't strong enough when I brought you here last night. Finn and Griffin nearly finished you off."

My hand closed around one of the small silver serving pieces from the tea set. I grasped it firmly and swung with every ounce of energy he hadn't yet taken. Sugar cubes went flying in all directions, bouncing off us. Clancy's head swung to the side, and when he looked back at me with a crescent of blood at his temple and bloodlust in his eyes, I knew I'd made it worse on myself. But there was no way I was going down without a fight.

He continued to drain me unrelentingly. I flinched when he pressed his body against mine, but I was trapped and already feeling so feathery I thought I'd lose my ability to stand at any moment. I closed my eyes as he whispered in my ear. "I have much more finesse than they do, pet, and I need you now. Though after that stunt, I'm not inclined toward finesse."

FORTY-FOUR

I blinked against the onslaught of a new day, not knowing how I wound up in bed. The last thing I remembered was having my aura raped by Clancy Mulcarr. There was a protesting grumble from my belly. I'd never been so hungry in my entire life. Yet despite my intense hunger, I didn't want to eat. I wanted to curl up and go to sleep forever. The needs of my body overruled the slaughter of my soul. I'd eat. Then maybe I could curl around myself and keep the world out.

It took everything I had to scoot up against the headboard. Gráinne sat in a chair next to the bed, eating from a plate perched on her lap. She watched me with intense and curious eyes. Nothing creepy about that. "How long have you been watching me sleep?" I asked, reaching for my plate and fork. I registered the ever-present teapot next to my bed and a generous carafe of ice water.

"You clutch your hands like you're hiding a secret in them. What are you hiding in your hands?" she asked.

I held up my hands. "A fork?" That actually brought a smile to her face. Gráinne had a pretty smile. It made her look less disturbed.

It made me want to coax another out of her.

Suddenly, the smile slid off her face. "You've been deeply hurt," she said. "I can see it."

"How can you see it?" I asked, stuffing three bites of syrup-laden pancake into my mouth. "I'm silver, like you. No colors to read."

"Your sadness rolls off of you like storms. You'll learn to read silver. It's diamonds of many facets."

I hadn't learned how to read the subtleties of silver, but I was sure she was right about my stormy sadness. Just the smell of the maple syrup had driven a spike into my heart. It was too painful to think about our first date in the forest when I was foolish and giddy and dabbing syrup behind my ears to be more irresistible to Finn. I *was* irresistible to him, but only because he was Arrazi and needed my Scintilla spark to live.

Finn had said, "*I never believed someone like you existed.*" I remembered how his aura had looked like a live thing when he played music at the coffee shop, how it blasted white before I fainted. Griffin had been there. Not a coincidence. I recalled Clancy congratulating Finn on luring me here while we ate beef stew. My mind flashed to Finn saying, "*I want to possess you. I'm with you, and everything in me wants to take.*"

To think I'd tried to protect him from the truth. He knew. He knew more about me than I did. "My heart hurts."

"As does mine."

It was the most coherent conversation we'd had yet. Would I end up like her from the constant near-death they'd inflict on me? Each minute there chafing at my sanity?

"How long have you been here?" I asked. My question shimmered like a delicate bubble in the palm of my hand. The wrong answer would pop it.

Gráinne pointed to the floor. Hundreds and hundreds of tiny moons were carved into the floorboards up and down the length of the room. So many. All the breath whooshed out of me. The bubble shattered. "Have you tried to get out?" I whispered.

"Everything. Running. Begging. Promises. Bribery. I've even tried to love him."

"How could you—"

"This…him…it's all I've had for so long. I lost everything." She picked at her food. "A heart desperately searches for something to love—"

"Mine won't." It was a stubborn vow. But I meant it. With all of my broken heart.

Gráinne shook her head emphatically. A strand of her long hair brushed through her syrup. "No, no. If you're too good at blocking the bad, then the good is sure to get caught in that net."

"Why can't we block them from taking from us? Can't we escape?"

Her eyes went up to the skylight. "I don't have the keys to the kingdom." She smacked herself in the head. Hard. "I was close." And then again. I put my plate on the table and grabbed her hands.

"Don't."

She looked up at me, startled, like she was surprised I was still in the room, surprised I had my fingers curled around her brittle wrists. "I buried everything. Stop with your questions. You *tap tap* in my head. The answers are gone."

I dropped her hands. Panic rose up in me. I had so much to say, so much to rail against, that I was speechless. My head shook back and forth, but I couldn't rattle the words loose.

I couldn't think of a worse fate than to be locked up forever.

I thought youth was the shackle. Now every freedom I would've inherited with age had been snatched from me. Look how much of Gráinne's life had been stolen. I'd end up like her, mumbling nonsense to myself, sucking maple syrup from my frayed hair, making pictures of flowers with shards of glass and blood. My life was a broken cup.

From this moment on, it would hold nothing else.

I ran to the wooden door and threw my fists into it. I kicked. I screamed at the top of my lungs. Flung my body against the wood so hard my teeth rattled. I couldn't be trapped here forever. I couldn't. Tears streamed down my cheeks. I sobbed in great gasping chokes as if fingers clutched around my neck, and I slid to the floor, my hands clawing the wood on my way down, leaving a trail of tiny splinters in my stinging palms and beneath my nails.

Suddenly, a soothing cocoon of arms wrapped around me as I sat in a spent heap on the floor. Gráinne put her hand gently on my forehead and pulled my head back to rest on her shoulder. Her legs curved with surprising strength around my thighs, supporting me. Her hand rested over my heart as her body rocked me slowly forward and back. "Shhhh, child. Shhhh. Quiet now."

I cried until I was a wrung out, a limp doll in her arms. We sat together on the floor, rocking while she hummed a quiet, soothing tune. I melted against her, giving myself over to someone who, for the moment, was stronger than me. My ragged breathing eventually became more even. My anger dissolved in a fusion of our melted silver auras. Gráinne was so brave, in her own fragile state, to run into the hurricane and hold it tight.

I looked down at her hand, warm against my heart, holding me to hers. The daintiest slice of a wedding ring shone on her ring finger. It was worn nearly smooth from being rubbed over many years. The design was still visible though: a simple and delicate silver band of clover encircling her finger. Exactly like the marking on my finger.

A wisp of breath escaped me. Every breath beyond that was painful.

I turned slowly to look at her, taking in the heart shape of her small face, the thin mouth that turned up at the corners even when she wasn't smiling. The broken windows of her eyes. Her hands smoothed my hair back from my damp skin and wiped my tears tenderly.

Motherly.

Oh God.

Please, be her. Please, do not.

He had two of us, but I didn't realize until now, he had my mother. He'd had her all this time.

My heart thrashed on the ground like an injured bird. For the second time in that place, I wanted two opposite things to be true at once. Elation and despair crowded for space in me. I'd succeeded beyond hope. I'd found my mother. Alive, but not all the way through. Something inside her had died so long ago. I saw myself in her face. It didn't comfort me. It caved me in.

She was me, in captivity, years from now.

I curled into her chest and found more tears—old tears and new. Each one a blade.

"Ah, now, dear. Hush." She lifted my face and smiled broadly. "Today we get to see the sun."

FORTY-FIVE

I wasn't sure why I didn't tell her who I was—who she was to me. Something to do with a heavy secret being on the shoulders of the one who's strong enough to carry it. Finn had said that to me. Yeah, he'd know something about secrets.

Would it mend her heart even a little to know I was with her? Or break her completely knowing I shared her fate? If I were a mother, I'd rather imagine my child growing up happy and free, even if she could never be with me. Not this fate. Never this.

I watched curiously as Gráinne ran me a hot bath scented with small lavender flowers. She told me they were from the garden and today we'd be allowed to go outside to see it. She called it "Sun" day. I suppose you find ways to amuse yourself when you're trapped in a place forever.

Tears welled up again as I shut the door to the bathroom, removed my clothes, dropped them to the floor, and slipped into the silky water. The key lay in a heavy lump against my chest, the leather string struggling to rise to the surface of the water. If I asked her about the key—what she was trying to keep secret, what it unlocked—I'd have to tell her who I was. I soaked in the water a long while, mulling it over.

Gráinne tried to offer me some of her clothes, but she was half my size. Clearly, I'd taken after my dad's empanada-eating side. I put my own dirty clothes back on and slipped into my shoes. They were mine.

Mine becomes a sacred word when everything is taken from you.

For hours, Gráinne alternated between staring into space and pacing the floor, anxiously waiting to get outside. I was as anxious as she, but only because I was fixed on the idea of escape, and getting outside put me one step closer. In the meantime, I wanted to ask so many questions but held myself back. If I blew her mind completely, she'd not be able to answer any of them. For now, I set to carving my first mark in the floorboard with the nail that Gráinne used for her moons. It was the spiral I carved. The one emblazoned across Finn's chest that had enticed me from that first moment in the hospital when I saw it peeking from under his shirt. I swallowed the fertile germ of hatred so it would grow strong and choke off the love.

Every moment with Finn had been a lie. He knew what he was and obviously knew what I was. I saw he had a secret, but I'd underestimated the significance. I'd seen little balls of secrets in nearly everyone around me. Giovanni had tried to warn me as well. But my stubborn heart had heard only one truth and clamped its ears from all others. My heart was at home with Finn. How could it be so wrong?

Pain poured into my bloodstream. I tried not to let myself feel, but I shook so violently it hollowed out my bones, leaving me empty as tears dropped onto the wood beneath me, soaking the spiral.

I clawed the itch of my rage with every scrape of the metal into the wood until the carving was complete. My first. How many more goddamn spirals would there be? My eyes scanned the floor covered in Gráinne's moons. The horror and injustice of it sickened me.

My hand found an engraving, and I lay my palm over its rugged surface, wishing I could erase it, take just one day from Gráinne's captivity and give it back to her. Red fury and sorrow mixed to form a powerful new emotion I couldn't name. I'd never felt it before. It jangled inside against the cage of me, slammed itself against my ribs, threatened to break me apart.

I was suddenly bombarded with images. They were alive. Palpable. They rose up and swirled around me, then inhabited me.

Gráinne closing her eyes, turning her head away as Clancy sucked her aura from her.

Gráinne falling to the floor, weak and desperate to be free. Slipping into unconsciousness with thoughts of my father sleeping on a couch with her baby, curved as a dewdrop, asleep on his chest, rising and falling with his slow breathing.

Tears seeping from the corners of her eyes, pooling onto the wooden floor. Her mouth uttering silent words as she carved this first moon with her fingernails. Blood soaking into the grain.

The room returned to now. My palm burned with fire. I snatched my hand away from the floor and the visions stopped, but the smoldering feeling lingered. I hissed and turned my hand over.

Centered in my palm was Gráinne's moon, churning and swirling, beating in time with my erratic pulse. Black curling lines stretched up my hand, climbing my skin like a twisted vine, stopping where the blue lines of my veins met my wrist.

There was a quick knock on the door. I stuffed my hand into my pocket, fingering the little nail nestled there. The door opened a split second later. My heart faltered when I saw the man I'd come to know as Griffin looking a bit worse for wear. A plum welt swelled fat on his upper cheek.

I scrambled to my feet, wishing the nail was a foot long so I could drive it into his beady eyes. But my visions of violence halted when I saw the large knife sheathed at his side. As if he needed a knife to keep us in check. We were his for the taking, and by the smug look on his face, he knew it.

Gráinne ran past me. More than once that day, I'd had to stop her from banging her head against the wall as she leaned on it with her knees drawn up to her chest. It would've been so easy to slip into despair myself, but she needed me to be strong for both of us. She needed me to get us out of here.

I didn't move. Griffin patted his knee like he was calling a dog. "C'mon. You wanna go for a walk?"

Bastard.

Curiosity and the desire to escape won out, so I followed Gráinne down the long, dark corridor that slanted sharply uphill as we neared a turn. I understood with sickening horror why the hallways slanted up so sharply. Our prison was underground. The skylight over the bed was at ground level. We were literally buried alive.

Griffin walked behind us. We turned left toward a glass door with sunshine streaming through it. I poised to bolt for it. But it would have done me no good. Griffin had to punch a code into a security keypad for the lock to recede and the door to slide cleanly into its groove in the wall.

"Have fun," he said, pushing me forward. The door slid closed behind us.

"He's going to let us be out here? Free?" I asked, but Gráinne was already running, her arms outstretched like a little girl's.

It didn't take long to realize why we were left to roam this garden unsupervised. Impossibly tall slabs of smooth green granite perched atop a concrete wall around the entire perimeter. The tops of trees could be seen outside the walls. It gave the illusion of a vast forest that ran on forever. Barbed wire coiled along the top of the wall. I turned away.

The garden, I had to admit, was a surprise—all bubbling fountains and lily-covered pools. One large hunk of the granite wall even had water flowing down its flat surface into a basin at the bottom filled with darting orange fish. I ran my hand over the slippery stone, letting the water flow over my newly tattooed palm and trickle to the crook of my elbow. Something about that made me want to cry.

I turned away from the weeping wall and found Gráinne in a small cutting garden, plucking stems and gathering them into a large woven basket. She must be the reason there were fresh flowers in our rooms. I wondered how much of this garden was her doing, remembering the image of her digging in the daisies at my childhood home. I left her chattering away to the flowers like they were her only friends. I supposed they had been.

I ran my hands over every corner of the granite wall, looking for a possible chink in the armor. My mind furiously scraped and scratched for solutions. There had to be a way to protect ourselves from people who wanted to take our spark. Every creature in nature had some kind of defense mechanism. Camouflage, thorns, even something as small as a horned lizard could spray blood out of its freaking eyes. What was the Scintilla's defense?

A shady place under a weeping willow in the center of the garden curtained me from the world for a moment. I leaned against the tree, gaining strength from its life force. I appreciated that we were allowed outside in such a pretty place full of the sounds and the texture of nature. But as Mami Tulke would say, "You can sprinkle glitter on a turd, *mija*, but it's still a steaming turd."

I knew then that I'd do whatever I could to get out of here. I'd barter and plead. Beg and proposition. But I'd never try to love my way out. I'd rather die than give away more pieces of myself.

"I went into town and got you some things," boomed Clancy's voice from across the wide expanse of lawn. Fear and rage spilled into my blood. I looked up but didn't move. Gráinne, however, sprinted toward him. He handed her a large green bag. She ran off to a nearby bench, sticking her scrawny arm in to the elbow to root around.

I held perfectly still, hoping he wouldn't see me, but he walked over to where I sat beneath the swaying fronds of the willow. "There's my little silver spark," he said as he parted the green curtain of leaves and held out a bag.

"You can see my aura?"

"No. Arrazi can't see auras. I can *feel* it. It's a siren calling to my blood."

I tried to remain calm in the face of his blinding white aura. Apparently, their auras looked normal until they were well fed. I shivered and crossed my arms over my chest but forced myself to hold his stare. "Unless you brought me a ticket to California, I don't want anything from you."

"May as well drop the sullen bit, pet. We'll have the rest of your life together, and I'd rather not dislike you." He tossed the bag at my feet and turned away. A bouquet of daisies flopped out. I looked up at him in shock, and Clancy smiled, satisfied, sick. "Did you like the flowers I sent to your hospital room, *Daisy*?" He turned to go, but then stopped. "Oh," he said over his shoulder. "And I've left a surprise for you on your bed."

I definitely didn't know him well enough to read the secretive smirk he cast me, but its malicious glint put me on edge.

Griffin brought us lunch in the garden: slices of tangy Irish cheddar, warm bread, and chunks of juicy melon. I ate like a prisoner of war. It wasn't hunger fueling my appetite but a desire to fortify myself for whatever lay ahead.

Shortly after lunch, we were led out of the garden to the door that would take us back inside and return us to our rooms. Gráinne was quiet but peaceful. In her arms, she carried the basket of cut flowers and both her shopping bag and mine, which she had retrieved from under the tree when she saw I'd left it lying on the grass.

Like the door that led to the garden, our inner door had a security keypad as well. Griffin punched in the code and shoved us inside, slamming the door behind us. I had watched his movements carefully, looking for habits I could exploit, lapses in attention. I had visions of snatching his knife from him. I wasn't so sure what I'd do if I got it, however. I'd have to be quicker than his ability to suck me dry.

A loud thud startled me and I spun. Gráinne's basket had dropped to the floor of our rooms, flowers strewn around it. Her hand flew to her mouth. I looked over her slim shoulder and shock and disbelief numbed my limbs so that I was unable to move for a moment, or even breathe.

Giovanni lay sprawled across my bed, bloody and very badly bruised. Dried blood caked the roots of his blond hair above his forehead, staining it a gory, rusted pink. A raspberry-colored lump marred his temple like a large marble had been wedged under his skin. His cut lips were open slightly. He was so perfectly still, so… lifeless, that the entire room seemed to hush in wait for his next breath.

I rushed to him. With shaking hands, I fumbled for a pulse on his neck because I saw no silver emanating from his body. He looked like his light had been beaten out of him. "I—I can't feel anything." My voice quaked. "I don't think he's alive." My hands were unsteady. My own pulse thudded so loud in my ears that I couldn't find any whisper of his. Seeing the lightless form of someone I knew, of someone like me, filled me with complete terror. If the Scintilla were so damn valuable, why'd they do this to him?

Gráinne came to my side. She didn't look at me. In fact, her eyes were closed. Holding her hand an inch or so above his body, she moved it in small circles over his torso. Her hand slowed and hovered above his lower abdomen. "It's there," she whispered. "He's in there. I can feel it." Her eyes opened and met mine. "But barely."

FORTY-SIX

"What do we do?" I cried. He looked so helpless, so weakened that I didn't know if he'd be able to pull himself out of it.

"I found a dead bird once," Gráinne muttered. "When I was a little girl. I tried to make it better, but it stayed dead."

"He's not dead yet. Maybe he's strong enough." I wanted to believe it. He certainly looked like he had put up quite a struggle before he lost the battle. I squeezed his fingers, proud of the fight in him. It explained Griffin's welt.

Heaviness draped over my back like a lead cloak. I sighed and curled my knees to my chest. His being here was bad news. I hadn't even realized until then that I had harbored a little bit of hope. Now all hope was gone. And Clancy had his prize, three of us. Whatever that meant.

Gráinne put her delicate hand on my shoulder as I sat on the edge of the bed with Giovanni's limp hand in mine. A warm tingle of energy infused me where her hand rested. It gave me an idea.

"Can we help him?" I asked. "Giovanni showed me we could give to people to make them feel better. Can we give him enough energy to save his life?"

"The bird stayed dead." Her hand slipped from my shoulder. "Maybe you could. I don't know. I won't. Forgive me."

"Together we might be able to help him. He's one of us. He needs us!"

She covered her heart with her hands and backed away. "Mine is mine. Mine is mine." She kept up her incantation as she stepped farther away. I stared helplessly at his still form, wanting to believe I had the capacity to give even when I'd been taken from so cruelly. If I couldn't believe in my own light, if I let the darkness win, then I might as well give up.

So instead of giving up, giving in to darkness, I thought of the old me. My old life. And the people I had loved.

My father, whose love was stifling but well intentioned. Even when I cursed him, I loved him. And now I knew why he had lied to me all those years, what he had sacrificed to protect me. His love and protection had been the most constant thing in my life.

Even if I did suspect some Arrazi in her bloodline because she exhausted me within moments of being around her, in her own frenetic way, Janelle had tried so hard to stand in as a mother. I didn't make it easy on her. She also loved my dad, despite the fact that she knew she was a stand-in for his first wife. Anyone who could love so hard from second place was deserving of my love in return.

I adored my cousin Mari with her big mouth and fierce individuality. She was like a sister to me. If I had any bravery in me, it was because she showed me how.

I felt the love I had for Dun, for his loyalty, his goofy smile, his happy light. I smiled, thinking of that little boy sitting against the tree, crying into his scrubby knees, one big toe poking out of those old moccasins, and how he had grown into an almost-man. He could always make me laugh with his stupid jokes. He was the person who taught me how to laugh at myself.

I remembered the compassion I had for little Max and all of those kids at the Boys & Girls Club who needed the world to lend them some extra love and strength until they were strong enough on their own. Giovanni had grown up under worse circumstances. Alone, with no parents at all. He was so courageous. He'd had to be.

I closed my eyes and let all the beauty rise up in me. Feeling love was risky. But instead of being weakened by it, I was surprised to realize the love strengthened me.

I held both of Giovanni's hands and thought of the powerful nature of love. How it was like water. It settled into the low, hidden places and seeped into my crevices, breaking me open. It eroded my fortresses and shaped me into something new. And even when I thought I'd had it wrung out of me, it could rain back down and satisfy a thirst I didn't know I had.

All of this, I tried to offer to him through my hands, from my body into his. It was a prayer in physical form.

Nothing. No response.

Blinking away tears, I involved my whole body, sending positive vibes through my hands, my heart, my eyes. Would any of it penetrate?

I was blowing on cold ashes, hoping for a fire.

But then his fingers moved underneath mine. The faintest groan escaped his torn, parted lips. Encouraged, I continued, imagining my aura as a rolling ball of energy washing over him, into him. I scanned his body for any sign of the shimmer that had first drawn me to him that day at the airport, but he was still snuffed out. I pressed his hand to my heart.

"Take it in," I whispered. "Come back to me. C'mon, G."

Then a small sliver of sparkling light caught my eye where Gráinne had said she felt it above his abdomen. It pulsed and grew, spreading like liquid mercury over his body. It swirled over his heart and simultaneously out toward his arms and legs. He gasped and drew in a deep, quivering breath, and his eyes flashed open.

I smiled. Joy burst out of me. He was alive! I bent and hugged him, but before I knew what was happening, his hands wound around my wrists and he flipped me over, pinning me underneath him on the bed.

I looked up into his eyes, the swirling, glassy ocean of them. He looked confused, not all there yet. His aura shone above his shoulders again, but I couldn't see it over his head. He pressed his body against mine, and I was shocked to feel his arousal. His body was completely, intensely alive, although it seemed his mind wasn't. I was about to say something, try to call him out of his stupor, when he blocked my words with a fierce kiss.

His warm mouth melted over mine. The sensation of touching my tongue to his was like licking the tip of a battery. A metallic zing of energy traveled from my mouth throughout my body. Every point of contact from my toes to my lips burned with electricity. My hands were still captured above my ears, but our fingers had interlocked. Our palms pounded with our firing pulses. We were two streams of lava, fusing together.

I kissed him back, responding. Like taking something back, reclaiming my own spark. But then I realized his was a false desire, an aura spell I had cast, that just like Finn, his want of me wasn't real but feeding off something else. And my want of him was salve on my wounded heart.

I managed to break the kiss and speak. "G—Giovanni, are you okay?"

His unfocused eyes rested on my mouth like he was trying to translate the sounds I'd made. The blood on his lip was bright and new again. I could taste it. Ever so slowly, his eyes ventured up to meet mine. There was recognition there, but confusion as well.

"Sleep now," I commanded. I sounded much more in control than I felt. I was stirred but invigorated, which seemed strange considering how much energy I had given him. His grip on my hands released as he rolled off me, burying his face into my pillow. His eyes closed, his breathing slowed, his silver aura fired to life like a match around his entire body.

I lay on the bed, staring at the canopy overhead. My chugging heart lost momentum one pounding beat at a time. I closed my eyes, lulled to sleep by the sound of Giovanni's breathing next to me. So glad he was alive. I didn't have any power in my situation, but I'd had the power to save him.

A strong arm wound over my waist, and my eyes flew open. The room had morphed into the inky blue of twilight. The only light was from the wood-burning stove glowing in the corner.

Giovanni's hand was tucked beneath my hip. With a commanding tug, he pulled my body against his. He curled around me like warm air, nestling his face into the back of my neck. I should move, I thought, lift his heavy arm from over my body and wiggle away from him. Sleep on the floor, or with Gráinne. But I didn't want to. I pressed myself for an explanation, and my internal answer, my truth, was I liked the security of his arm over me. I liked being less alone.

FORTY-SEVEN

"Cora."

A voice reached to me in my dreams, calling me out of them. It made my chest ache. I wanted to cover my ears.

"Cora," it said again, more insistent this time.

My eyes fluttered open. It was still night. An eye of inky light stared down on me through the skylight. I glanced around. Giovanni still slept against my back. Our hands were laced together, resting against my chest.

I noticed movement in the little sliding opening on the free side of the arched wooden door. I flicked on the lamp next to the bed. Finn's coppery eyes gaped at me, beautiful. Tortured.

I sat up, letting Giovanni's arm fall away. Finn and I stared at each other as I rose to my feet.

"You're sleeping together." It wasn't a question. There was hurt and accusation in his eyes.

"Sleeping. Yes," I answered in a hollow voice. "That's the first thing you have to say to me?" It killed me to see him again. My heartache and my fury coalesced into a thunderous storm. "Like you have claim? What do *you* care? I'm locked in here forever because of you! What'd you expect when you people brought him here half-dead and put him in my bed?" I hadn't realized I was moving toward him until we were face-to-face. I slapped my palms against the door. "How could you do this? How could you *be* this?"

His fingers clutched the wood around the opening, then flexed as if he were going to try to reach inside and touch my face. But, of course, Finn *could* reach me, into me, and steal my very breath. I backed quickly away, and he gave me an injured look.

"I can't help what I am. I hate what I am."

I fought the pity rising in me at the anguish hollowing his cheeks. He looked awful.

"And I didn't bring him here," he added softly with a nod toward Giovanni.

"Right. Like you didn't bring *me* here. Clancy told me all about it. What do you want, Finn?" I wanted to rip the door off its freaking hinges, pin him to the wall by his neck, and show him what it felt like to have the life squeezed out of him. I liked this anger in me. I stalked toward him again and wrapped my fingers over his on the wood, ignoring the stab of pain it caused me to touch him. "You want more of me? Hmmm?" I asked in a coquettish voice laced with spite. "Like you didn't take enough when you almost killed me?"

"Cora, you have to listen to me. I didn't know what I was doing." His head dropped. I could only see the top of his dark spiked hair as he looked down at his feet.

"Coward. Look me in the eyes!" I demanded through teary sobs. But when he looked up at me with such anguish, I regretted it. It would be so much easier to hate him if he showed the unapologetic malice that Clancy did. Finn was suffering. Maybe guilt had worn him down. I hoped so. If something ate away at his soul, maybe then he'd know how I felt.

"My parents told me they were Arrazi. They told me I'd likely come into it at any time. It was all so absurd. I was stupid to think it'd pass over me. Cora, I didn't know what you were. You were just a girl. An amazing girl. I fell in love. But I left California because I became afraid. I worried something was changing inside of me." His voice had lost its edge. It was soft. Pained. I saw dark rims around his grief-stricken eyes. Even his full lips had lost their ripeness. "I was terrified I'd hurt you."

"Convince my head, Finn. Because my heart will never believe in you again."

He took a deep, labored breath. His fingers clutched the little window as if it were a life preserver. "I didn't know what was happening that night we kissed at your house. I felt so much. Felt so good. It was the most intense sensation I've ever had in my goddamn life."

I recalled that night. I remembered sending him love, intentionally giving him my energy because he was everything in the universe at that moment. He had looked so dazed and love-stoned afterward, I'd thought he'd been drinking.

His voice was soft. "I was overwhelmed by it. I was being flooded with love…with you. You were everything in the universe at that moment."

I gasped at his choice of words.

"You were everything he needed to stay alive," Giovanni slurred from behind me. I turned to see him sitting on the bed. His eyes were half-open. His arms shook to hold himself up. "He needs you like he needs air to breathe. Food to eat. Don't confuse that with love, Cora."

Giovanni's words stung, and I hated him for saying them, even if they were the truth.

"I knew you were dangerous," Giovanni said to Finn in his thick Italian accent. "Your aura was normal, but I tuned in to energy from you that I've only felt once before." He gestured to me. "From the killer in the pub. The man with the white aura. I tried to warn you. I told you that you were not safe with him."

"You did," I whispered, looking at the floor. "I didn't want to hear."

"Don't listen to him, Cora. He can't say I'm incapable of love. You're still everything, and I will never hurt you again. I swear it." A tear dropped onto his cheek.

My own tears fell as well. "Giovanni's right. If you didn't want to hurt me, you'd have watched me walk away from the stage the other day. You couldn't help but want to be near me." I searched for the precise way to say it and found the only words that rang true. "It wasn't love."

"Of course I want to be near you, but because I love you, not because you're Scintilla. Fate put you back in my path, and I was foolish enough to believe that there was a reason for that, that it meant we were supposed to be together."

We stared at each other, broken. I'd believed that, too.

Ina's voice slipped into the room from the dark hallway. "I never should have let Finn go to America. He was too close to converting, but my brother convinced me he would be okay. Now I know he used Finn to get to you. They'd been watching you to see if you could possibly be Scintilla."

This was more smoke and mirrors. I wouldn't be played. "Your uncle said he was proud of you for luring me, Finn. Are you proud, Mrs. Doyle?"

"There's no choice for us. We were born like this. It's take from another or die," Ina answered in a weary voice. "But we're not all like my brother. I hate what we are forced to do. I didn't want Finn to change. I forbade him to date so he'd not form a strong emotional connection to someone, which often incites the change. I made him wear the crystal bracelet to block people's energy, hoping against hope to stall the inevitable. I was trying to protect him. But he met you. He fell in love with a damned Scintilla of all things! His love for you changed him."

Giovanni sighed in disgust. "Now you blame Cora for making him into the monster he was born to be? It's like blaming the sun for shining. Why have children at all if you are so concerned about what you are? Arrazi do not love Scintilla. You use them up. Destroy them."

"We didn't believe any more of you existed."

"Shut up," I said to her. "We're locked up in this prison like pets so you people can live off us. You get to keep me here forever, and I'm supposed to care that Finn's life was changed? My life is over!" I cried. Just seeing Finn had released a flood of emotions. I couldn't take being on the opposite side of this locked door, knowing he was free and I wasn't. I sat down on the bed next to Giovanni and sobbed. His arm curled around my shoulder.

The other door opened, and Gráinne peeked out cautiously like a little girl. Ina and Gráinne stared at each other a moment. Something flickered in Ina's sharp eyes. "Your biggest secret is your child," Ina whispered. I understood. Gráinne hadn't wanted them to find me. Ever. But how on earth could Ina know that?

"I have no child," Gráinne said, robotically.

Then Ina turned to Giovanni. They stared boldly at each other. She smiled with an edge to it. "And you have the nerve to accuse me of using the Scintilla," she said to him after a moment. "When are you going to tell Cora the truth?"

"What's that supposed to mean?" I looked from Ina to Giovanni, but they were locked in a silent, epic battle.

Ina's mouth opened to speak, but Finn interrupted. "I'm getting you out of here," he said with determined eyes.

It took all my courage to believe he told the truth. "What? If you can get me out of here, why the hell have we been standing here talking?"

"I needed you to hear the truth from me." A sheen of sweat

covered his brow. He touched his chest over his heart. "If you leave here with that, then maybe I can forgive myself."

"How do you know the code?" I asked. "If you didn't know I was being held prisoner, how'd you get in here?"

Finn swallowed hard before he spoke. "My ability to help you *came* from you. The Arrazi get their sortilege, their abilities, from Scintilla. It started with you."

"I know that," I snapped, remembering what Clancy had told me. "So what, now you're going to tell me you have some super-special ESP power?"

"My sortilege is…truth," Finn said. "People can't help but reveal the truth to me."

"Truth?" I asked, my voice spiked with incredulity. "That's a power?"

It wasn't leaping tall buildings, stopping bullets with bare hands, or even reading minds like I once thought he could do. I had once thought a force outside of myself was compelling me to act boldly in Finn's presence, to grab his shirt or pin him against a tree when we kissed. But it was my own force. My truth. And now I knew why. Every hit of energy I willingly gave him, or that he took, provided him the ability to coax the truth from me.

"You were able to keep one secret, though," Finn said, his tone laced with irony. "I didn't tell you the truth about me, but you didn't tell the truth about yourself, either. My *da* told me that you knew you were a Scintilla and kept it from me."

"I didn't know what I was until I came here, until I met Giovanni."

But Finn was right, I didn't tell him about seeing auras or about Griffin killing by taking auras. I'd fought hard to keep my biggest secret. "I guess neither of us trusted the other with the truth."

I said it to hurt him. I said it because it hurt that he didn't trust me. I kept my secrets to protect Finn. But I was also scared of what he'd think. Maybe I kept my secrets to protect myself, too.

Finn continued. "Clancy carried you out of the room, and when I came to my senses I wanted to talk to you, to try to explain, but you never answered your cell. I redialed Mari and Dun, and they hadn't heard from you, either. That's when we realized he never took you to the airport. We couldn't find Clancy at all, and when my uncle finally came to the house earlier tonight, I confronted him, asked him where he took you. He confessed." Finn gulped a breath, like the effort to explain had been too much for him. "My father drugged him. He's out cold right now in our wine cellar."

"What about Griffin?" I asked. "Does anyone know where he is? He could show up here any second."

Finn looked astonished. "Griffin's in on this, too?"

"Hell yes, he is. And you?" I pointed to Ina. "You took from me in my sleep. Exactly what power did *you* get out of it?"

Finn's head whipped around to face his mother. "You didn't!" he snarled.

Ina nodded, looking duly shamed. "I didn't know what Cora was, only that I was intoxicated by her energy. Now, I can see the darkest secret inside of you, inside everyone. Every time I look into someone's eyes, I fall into a hole, seeing the one thing they want most to hide at that moment. It's how I knew you had run away. It's how I knew tonight what Clancy was hiding out here in the forest. I knew it the moment I looked into my brother's eyes."

Finn's hands slipped from the door. He seemed to stumble to the ground because he disappeared from our sight. Ina shrieked and dropped down, too.

I started to jump to my feet, but Giovanni squeezed me tighter, holding me against his side. "Don't let them separate us," he whispered in my ear. "We are stronger if we are together." His blue eyes were scared and a bit wild. Trapped-animal wild. My mind flashed back to our kiss. I flushed and wondered if he remembered.

I looked from him to Gráinne, who was wringing the hem of her skirt and pacing. We were caged together. We should be free together. I squeezed his hand. "I promise I won't leave either of you here."

I ran to the door and peered through the opening. Finn lay crumpled on the floor, his arms clutched around himself, his knees up to his chin. His teeth rattled like he was freezing cold. His aura reminded me of little Max. Close to his body. Smudgy. Gray. "What's wrong with him?"

Ina crouched over Finn and smoothed his face tenderly, motherly. She looked over her shoulder at me, her face awash with tears and grief. "He refuses to nourish. Our need is much greater at first, until we learn to conserve energy—and he didn't take you to the death. The fact that you're a Scintilla is the only reason he's lasted these past couple of days. He'll die if he doesn't nourish soon."

"*Christo!*" Giovanni cursed. "You say *nourishment* like he's a baby at the breast! Who cares if he dies? It'll save hundreds of lives if he does!"

I swallowed hard. *I care. I care if he dies.* I turned to Giovanni. "If we didn't care, we'd be just like them." I pressed against the door. "Can he take from someone without killing them? Just to get his strength back? Can he take from you?" I asked Ina. "You're his mother."

"No. An Arrazi cannot take from another Arrazi. But you can save him." Her eyes pleaded.

"I'd rather die," Finn groaned. He pushed himself to a sitting position. "Open the door, Mother. Get them out of here. Now!"

Ina jumped when he rattled off a string of numbers. She went hurriedly to the wall and typed the numbers on the security keypad. My hands curled tighter with every beep, but a commotion at the end of the hallway caught her attention before she finished. Her fingers poised over the pad.

"Open it! Hurry!" Finn growled and fell back again, writhing in apparent pain.

Footsteps echoed down the hall as Ina punched in the rest of the code. I couldn't yet see who approached. Finn's eyes were glued to the hallway. I watched his face for reaction. He met my gaze. I bounced on my feet, panicked.

The door sprang open. Two men rushed through. Finn's father... and...

And mine.

I jumped into my father's arms. He held me tightly and planted kisses in my hair. Our bodies shook together with sobs. My daddy was here. He'd get me out safely. Take me home. I clung tightly to him, but someone dragged at my back, tugging me away from my rock.

"Don't touch her!" Gráinne shrieked, nearly choking me by yanking on my shirt. "Let her go!" She pulled with more strength than I thought her capable of, and out of control, like someone drowning.

Reluctantly, I let go of my father. Poor thing. I turned to explain who he was but stopped short. Gráinne's face was drained of all color, and she hadn't had much color to begin with. She wasn't looking at me but over my shoulder, at my father. Her birdlike hand covered her heart. A dried-leaf of a whisper escaped her lips. "B-Benito?"

FORTY-EIGHT

My father clutched my hand as he moved toward Gráinne. But when he reached her, his grasp slipped softly from mine. Her delicate face nestled in his hands like a heart made of snow. "Grace?"

I blinked tears. Everything fell away, leaving nothing but my parents standing in front of me, staring in awe. I was blinded by the intense light of them, the heartbreaking beauty of two lost souls finding each other again. It was like watching a supernova reassemble itself.

I wept where I stood.

Then my father reached for my hand again, reminding me that the last piece was me.

I fell into their embrace. We huddled and gripped each other tightly. Gráinne looked at me as if for the first time. Now she knew.

"We need to go," someone whispered urgently. "Quickly." We broke apart, but more whole than ever, and started for the door.

Fergus helped Giovanni up from the bed and threw his arm under his shoulders to support him. I hadn't realized Giovanni was too weak still to walk on his own. Clearly he didn't like being aided by someone he considered an enemy because he was trying in vain to pull away.

"You want to be stubborn or you want to be free?" I snapped.

The five of us spilled into the hallway where Finn still crouched on the floor against the wall. His mother had propped him up against the dark slate. His head rested on his arms over his knees. I stopped and stared, unsure what to do.

"Aren't you coming?" I asked.

Finn didn't look up. "My father will get you to a safe place," he answered with effort.

"Are you really willing to die?" I asked in a whisper.

"Go. Hurry!" he croaked.

Ina ran her hand over her forehead. "We're both doctors, and we can't save our own son." Her eyes implored, her voice barely audible, "Please, Cora."

Finn spoke through gritted teeth. "I. Will. Not."

I jogged away from him toward the rest of the anxious group waiting for me at the end of the hall. My dad stretched his hand out toward me.

I stopped.

Turned.

And ran back to Finn.

I kneeled on the floor next to his shaking body. "Do it," I said, inwardly cringing. "Take only enough to be okay," I added, uncertain whether he could control what he took from me.

"Cora!" my father yelled.

"No." Finn tried to push me away, ineffectually. "I won't hurt you again, Cora. I promise I won't. I'd rather die." His body may have been weak, but his eyes were alight with fire. He meant what he said. And he'd die keeping that promise.

One of my tears landed on his cheek. *The rain is lovely on you,* I remembered him saying.

I placed my hands on both sides of his face and lifted his chin.

He wrapped his around my forearms and tried to pull them away. "I was wrong to think I'd never hurt you. I know I need to let you go. Because I love you, I need to let you go." He dragged a ragged breath into his body. "I don't want this," he said. "I don't want to be this."

"It's who you are," I whispered. "And this is who I am."

Again, he knocked my hands away from him. I nodded, resigned. "Fine. But look at me," I said, livid because he made my heart ache fresh and raw. I wanted to stop being punched, over and over again, with the impossibility of us. For the rest of my life, would I always feel like the other half of me had been ripped away? I could barely speak through my tears. "When I kiss you good-bye for the last time, I want you to look at me."

We stared into each other, like all of those times before, dropping into a warm pool of wonder in each other's eyes. I bent and put my lips to his. I let my mind reel through our history from that first moment in the hospital, to the night he carried me out of the coffee shop, our kiss in the redwoods, being so happy to see him again in Ireland that I thought I might never go home, to the seconds before he changed, when I was willing to give him all of myself because I loved him with all my heart.

Finn might love me. I'd never know for sure. Neither would he. And that was the biggest reason I had to let him go. The doubt would always tarnish what we had together.

I hadn't needed a thing from him, and I loved him.

That was the truth. My truth.

For this one last moment, this last kiss, I set aside my confusion, my hurt, and my rage, and let my memories, my love, wash over him. Into him. Whether he liked it or not.

I willingly breathed my spark into his body.

He might die, but it wasn't going to be because I did nothing.

Finn's hands found their way to my hair. He grasped me tightly, returning my kiss. His lips grazed mine, tasted my tears, then he pulled his face away from mine. Just barely. The tempest of our quick breathing swirled over my lips.

"I hope someday you forgive me," he said, tears pooling over his warm brown eyes.

"And I hope you forgive me."

His eyes sprang wide with realization. I could already see his aura changing. A white ring of light surrounded his head. I thought he'd smile, but he didn't. "You've only delayed my death, luv." He gazed at me with an agonized face. "It's like inhaling you," he whispered. "You're part of me. You'll always be part of me." I got to my feet and motioned for him to come, but he waved me away. He glowed with white, and it terrified me to feel the pull from my heart to his.

"Go, Cora!"

I turned and ran.

FORTY-NINE

It was a strange, vulnerable sensation to exit through the final locked gate of Clancy Mulcarr's secret underground prison. The walls of the garden were so camouflaged by trees, you could barely see it if you didn't know it was there.

"Where does Clancy live? I don't see a house."

"On the opposite side of these woods. We looked there first and found nothing. But then Ina said she'd seen a forest in her vision. This is the only patch of forest on our land," Fergus explained. "It was hard to find this place, though, with it being underground. We had to look for worn paths in the trees."

With Fergus's help, we found our way through a knotted cluster of trees out of Clancy's compound. Thick fog curled and slithered around the bottoms of the trees along the path, moving like a living thing. Moisture clung to my skin. The world felt more expansive than before. Or maybe I felt smaller, more defenseless. Like evil suddenly had talons and at any moment could snap me up and plop me back into a cage.

Every footfall crunching into the gravel sounded like an army of horses in my head. I expected Clancy to pop out from behind every tree. Ahead, through the foliage, the lighthouse tower in the distance rose over the fog like a finger pointing at the moon. I couldn't believe it. "All this time, we were only a couple miles from your house?"

"Right under our noses. Bloody bastard," Fergus said with a grunt.

"How much time do we have before his drugs wear off?" my father asked, always the scientist. He had both my mother and me by the hand. He grasped a little too tightly, but I didn't mind.

"I'd guess an hour or so. It was pretty heavy stuff, but it took us a while to find you."

"It won't matter," my mother muttered. "He'll find us." She proceeded to chew nervously on the tip of her thumb. "He's a ghost. Soul on a string."

Fergus led us through another grove of trees and thick ferns. As we exited into a clearing, I saw an old shed on the edge of a dirt road. He sat Giovanni down on a large rock and fished a ring of keys from his trouser pocket. Fergus opened wide double doors to a tack shed. We followed him inside. It smelled of horsehair and dirt, and the tang of green grass crushed under a boot heel.

"We've got to find a safe place to go," I said, unable to control my restless pacing. We were standing in a shed on the same property as Clancy's house. And I wouldn't go to the manor. Drugged or not, he was there. Not nearly far enough away. Nowhere would be far enough. He'd had three Scintilla. *Three.* The magic number that kept cropping up. The number he said would make him unstoppable. And now he'd lost his prize. Would he ever stop looking for us?

"We have to call the police," my father said. "He kept a woman imprisoned for nearly thirteen years! He needs to feel what it's like to be behind bars. I don't care about any of this aura crap anymore. He can't keep another human prisoner and get away with it."

I'd never heard my father's voice so desperate or so full of bitterness.

"Aye, you can call the police. Press charges. He deserves it. But it won't make you any safer. He's but one of many Arrazi who would seize these three." Fergus clasped his hand to my father's shoulder. "Or worse. Much worse. The Scintilla had almost been relegated to myth. It's been so long since word of one had come 'round. But now…" He looked at Giovanni, Gráinne, and me with unconcealed wonder. "When people find out about you three, it will be open season." He leaned in close to my father. "If it were my family, you can bet your arse I'd hide them away. Go off the grid, my friend. Find a mountain home far away from people, and live there forever."

"That's not a life. That's another prison." My voice ricocheted off the walls. We all looked around us for a moment, but the only sound was the screech of crickets in the night and the distant static of the ocean far below.

My father put both hands on my shoulders. I knew he was about to tell me what was and what was not going to happen. "I'm not that girl anymore," I informed him. "We need to decide together."

I turned to Giovanni. His matted blond curls were the brightest thing in the room besides our silver. His face wore the bruises of his beating and his lip was still swollen. A Nordic angel after battle. He'd been staring gloomily at me since he sat down on a bale of hay underneath a row of horse halters.

"Can we go to your hotel until we figure out what we're doing?" I asked.

"We cannot go there," Giovanni said. "That is where they found me. There *is* one place we can go. I know a man in Dublin, a doctor. I told you about him. He would help us. I know he would."

"I'd rather contact the embassy," my father said. "They can keep us safe until we leave the country."

"And what are you going to say to them, Dad? Excuse me, but can you give us safe harbor because a bunch of soul-sucking lunatics are after us?" I threw my hands in the air. "They'll think we're insane." I looked at my mother curled up like a pill bug, her lips moving frantically but without any sound.

"We're not staying in this country, Cora. We've got to leave Ireland."

"We've got to find a way to end this for good. There *has* to be an answer. You heard Fergus, Dad. They're after people like us. They found us, found *me*, in Santa Cruz, California, of all places! Nowhere is safe."

That girl's not safe anywhere.

"Of all the unsafe places in the entire world, this is the *most* unsafe! You've flown right into the heart of the hornet's nest. Your mother believed this is where it all started: that the origins of Arrazi and Scintilla started here, at Newgrange. Well, I'm not having it. I'm not losing either of you again."

"I can't leave." My mother's little voice startled us all.

"Why?" I asked.

"I don't have any identification. No passport. Nothing. I don't exist. I don't exist. They erased me. They erased me, Benito."

I kneeled down and hugged her. She was so broken. I wondered if she'd ever be normal again.

"Damn. My passport. Those bastards took everything from me, too." Giovanni cursed in Italian, patting down his pants pockets. "My wallet, my cell phone. But I have a copy of all of my identification hidden in a locker at the airport. You don't travel as much as I have without learning how to protect yourself."

"I have no idea where my stuff is."

"We gave Clancy your things when he left with you," Fergus said as he went to the door.

My heart constricted painfully. "The journal." I needed a passport, yes, and cash, and clothes. But the journal was the biggest loss. The thought of that evil man with my mother's writing sent fresh hate through me.

"I'm sorry," Fergus said, seeing my distress. "We thought he would get you to the airport. Try to get comfortable in here for a bit. Rest if you can. I will hurry up to the house and get the car. When I come back, I will tap three times, like this. Then pause. And once again." He knocked the code softly on the wood.

"Why are you helping us?" Giovanni asked him, not trying at all to conceal his distrust.

"I suppose it's the drops of humanity in my blood," Fergus answered with a smirk. "Like any Arrazi, I've always been curious as hell about what my sortilege would be if I—" He looked at his feet. "But Ina feels like hers is a curse, so maybe I can live the rest of my life not knowing."

"We appreciate your help," I told him sincerely, even though his presence scared me. I could tell he didn't much like being under the weight of our suspicion, and Giovanni wasn't exactly diplomatic about it.

Fergus looked at us, one by one. "You're welcome. But don't go thinking too highly of me. It's not as though I'm not tempted. I may be human, but I'm still Arrazi."

And with that, he left.

My dad paced. A few steps, then around for a few more. "It could take weeks to get passports. Even fake ones. We need to get to Chile," he said with conviction, mostly to himself.

"You think we can hide away at Mami Tulke's?" I asked, and then suddenly remembered. "That conversation with Mami Tulke," I blurted, ignoring his startled look. "I tried to ask you about it the night we fought. You said she needed to help me again, Dad. How could she help me if I've never met her?"

A resigned sigh puffed out of him. "Until recently, she'd been able to block it."

"It? You mean stop me from seeing auras?"

My dad nodded. "That. But more importantly, to block others

from sensing yours." He rubbed his hands through his graying hair. "Until you got sick."

The air rushed out of me. "You knew what I was. You knew all this time. How does Mami Tulke know about all of this?"

"Because, sweetheart, she's one of you. *Scintilla*. We were trying to keep you safe. Protect you. Look what happened to your mother."

I wanted to argue, but I couldn't squabble anymore about his protecting me. "So that's why you were suddenly willing for me to go to Chile?" I asked, daring to hope there was a way she could help.

"I keep thinking if we can get to her, she can help all three of you. Maybe she could block it again if you were actually with her."

"How did Mami Tulke do it? I know she's some kind of medicine woman but—" I imagined potions, incense, chicken feathers…

"That's *her* sortilege," he said. "To cast a veil over a Scintilla. It's called shielding. But she was suddenly unable to do it. Something's changed."

"With her or with me?"

"With the whole damn world." Dad ran his hands through his mussed hair. He looked like he'd been through hell.

"What do you mean?"

"The world is undergoing a major, major shift. The discoveries of dark energy and then the discovery of the accelerated expansion of the universe were monumental. Science has focused its attention on the outer space of dark energy. I knew, because of my mother, your mother, you…that energy is much more personal—it affects us all—and so I began to study how dark energy might be impacting our planet and the people on it. Energy is not just something that is *out there*," Dad said, pointing toward the sky. "It's everywhere."

"We're made of it," my mother mumbled. "Star stuff."

I couldn't help thinking of Finn's starry tattoo; a family crest of sorts, he had said. Giovanni shuffled behind me. I looked over my shoulder. He tried to keep his expression neutral, but I could see his high interest in the conversation by the way his silver aura arched over my body toward my father.

My dad continued. "The increase in natural disasters was a sign that there is a serious crisis or imbalance going on in our world, but the more critical sign now is the people who are mysteriously dying."

"Please slow down," Giovanni requested. "I'm trying to understand what you are saying and what this has to do with us."

My father held up his hands. "Sorry. I'm studying the incidents of people who are dying, just…dying from no known cause, all over the world."

"It's Arrazi," I said, sure of it. "It happened right in front of our eyes at the airport in Dublin."

"That was you?" Dad gasped.

"Yes. And there was a man with a white aura across the street— Arrazi."

"No, no, no," my dad interrupted. "The blood of the people who are dying shows a cellular abnormality. Violent expansions, if you will. Cellular activity is accelerating and expanding at such a rate that, well, I believe that dark energy is killing them, not the Arrazi."

"And?" I asked. "What if you're wrong?" If it wasn't the Arrazi killing those people, then I didn't see what this had to do with Scintilla and Arrazi at all. How could he possibly connect ancient breeds of humans to this theory about dark energy?

I still believed it was the desperate Arrazi doing what they were born to do, but I was trying to be open. I had a new respect for my father. His interest wasn't just in trying to save the Scintilla he loved. He wanted to save the world.

"And your blood, Cora, it has the same abnormality. Only—"

"When those people died of our sickness, I lived."

My father smiled as he did when I was little and had finally grasped a complex math problem he'd been trying to explain. "I know I sound crazy. But somehow, I think you, the Scintilla, are the key to the energetic imbalance. You lived! It somehow has to do with your life-giving, positive energy. I believe that. I proved it in the lab when I combined your cells with the cells of one of the victims. The expansion slowed, was brought back into balance."

"You're trying to tell me a few Scintilla are supposed to save the world? Oh, a simple little thing like that?" My voice sounded shrill, near panic at the enormity of what my father proposed.

"We can hardly save ourselves," Giovanni pointed out rather unhelpfully. He reminded me of Mari that way.

"In so many cases, simple doesn't mean easy, sweetheart." He stepped close and put his arm around my shoulders. "People are going to keep dying. Catastrophes are going to keep occurring. The Arrazi are going to keep killing innocent humans. And if they find you, they'll kill you, too."

"Or enslave us," I said with a nod to my mother.

Giovanni placed a hand on my shoulder. "Unless we correct the imbalance by killing all the Arrazi."

My father and I both flicked our gazes to Giovanni. To kill for our own survival was as callous as what the Arrazi had been doing all along. Could I kill Finn, or his parents, who appeared decent at heart despite what they were? There had to be another way.

My mother reached out. "Sit with me, Benito." It hurt the most when she sounded normal because I knew it wouldn't last. He looked at her like she was new. Again.

My heart broke for the sorrow in their faces. Lost years. Promises broken in order to keep promises. Sorry was greenish-yellow, cloudy fingers grasping from Dad's heart outward. I peered at my mother's silver aura and could swear the silver softened, liquefied, in front of her heart as if her aura was fractured there.

My dad kneeled down next to her and placed his hands on both sides of her face. "I want to get you out of here, Grace. Make sure you're safe. I used to look for you. I used to go with Cora to the redwoods, hoping you'd come." He hung his head. "Eventually, I gave up hope."

Then my dad cried, openly and without shame. He let go of her and buried his face in his hands. A big, sucking sob came out of him. She pulled his hands from his face. He looked at my mother with such regret. "I'm so, so sorry."

I covered my heart. Tears streamed down my face to see my father's sorrow. He hadn't wanted to leave her. He was lashing himself with blame.

A bit of clarity surfaced in my mother's eyes. "I was stubborn," she whispered. "I wanted to know the truth so badly." She looked at me from across the shack and pressed her lips together. "I thought I could find a way to end the danger somehow. That I could keep her safe. All of us safe. Oh, my love," she touched his face. Then she looked back to me. "My little dark Daisy."

All three of us were sobbing then. This tempestuous ocean of life tumbled us around and around and spit us back on shore together, forever changed. I backed away from my parents' embrace. They deserved their time together.

Giovanni pulled down a horse blanket from a high shelf and spread it on the floor. He motioned for me to sit down next to him. I did. Mostly because I wanted to be next to someone but felt selfish to intrude on the intimate whisperings of my parents' reunion. I was cold, too. Probably in shock. I wiped my tears and leaned into him.

"You did something to me," Giovanni said low. "I am altered, not entirely myself."

"I gave you some of my energy. You were nearly dead. I didn't know what else to do."

"It's a fairy tale, no? Being brought back to life by a kiss? You've done it for two men now."

I set him straight. "I didn't bring you to life with a kiss. You revived and"—I blushed deeply with the memory—"you kissed me." I avoided his stare. "You were pretty out of it. I didn't think you'd even remember."

He looked at me for a long moment and said, "I'll not forget."

When I didn't answer, he added, "And I didn't like to see you kiss that Arrazi boy."

"Finn," I said, irritated. Though I wasn't sure why I felt the need to elevate him from "that boy." I didn't simply kiss a boy. I kissed *my* boy. I kissed my boy good-bye.

A spike wedged deeper in the middle of my chest. Not only was Finn a danger to me physically, he was dangerous to my heart. And now I had a new worry: how many innocent people did I condemn to death because I saved his life? Or did he really mean what he said?

Had I only prolonged his life until he died by his choice?

"What's this?" Giovanni asked, tracing the inky swirls above my wrist and opening my palm where the moon blazed. "I didn't notice you had a tattoo on your hand before."

I yanked my hand from his, leaned away from his warm body, and curled on my side on the smelly horse blanket. I watched dust motes bounce on the shafts of light from the lone bulb overhead. A few moments later I shoved myself up to my knees. My hands on my hips. "Tell me the secret Ina mentioned. I can't have any more secrets. What's the darkest hole in your heart?"

Giovanni stared into my eyes. For the first time, I saw uncertainty there.

Outside, I heard the low purr of a car engine approaching. My parents must have heard it, too, because the low murmur of their conversation fell silent. We all looked at one another. My mother's and Giovanni's silver auras pulsed in frightened unison with mine. The vehicle stopped right outside the shed. We listened as the car door opened and closed. Footsteps.

A hand rapped three times on the door. A pause. Then once more.

"Fergus," I said with a sigh and stood.

My father stepped forward and unlocked the door.

Clancy and Griffin blocked the open doorway.

FIFTY

Griffin's knife glinted in his hand. Clancy wasn't holding a weapon, but then he didn't need one. Neither of them did.

Giovanni struggled to his feet and gripped my arm.

"Who are you?" my father demanded.

Gráinne whimpered, crawling away to the corner of the shed. Her fingers clutched at the wooden slats as if she could tear them away and run. My dad's eyes followed her, and then he looked at me. I nodded slightly, and I knew he knew. I saw pure fear and rage in my father's eyes and in his aura. And I saw the moment a decision clicked in place for him.

The whole world suspended, hung in its big black night, and waited.

Dad rushed Griffin, whose knife was held ready. Their bodies clashed for the briefest moment, no more than the time it takes for a bird to land on a branch and then flit away. In the space between breaths, their movement stopped. Then Dad's hands grasped at Griffin's arms and slipped down them as he fell to his knees. Blood dripped from the tip of the knife.

"No!" I screamed. The spark of Giovanni's hand fell from my arm as I ran toward my father, but before I reached him, Clancy swung full out, his fist slamming straight into the side of my temple. The pocked wood of the ceiling rafters slid around dizzily, and I dropped to the rough floor of the shed. My vision blurred.

"Sometimes I think you possess no sense of self-preservation at all, girl," Clancy spat.

Griffin's knife was at my throat before I could move again. My father's blood trickled across my neck. Or was it my own? Instinctively, I reached up to push the knife away, but the second my hand landed on the woven leather handle, visions bombarded my mind.

Clancy and Giovanni speeding through Dublin in a car. Giovanni lying unconscious, bloody, and beaten in the backseat. Griffin caressed the knife, unsheathed on his thigh. Clancy's resonant voice:

He'd better live, Griffin. There's an army of people who would kill for just one. But three…it changes everything. I can't believe our fortune. The Society can't know about this.

He's nearly dead. We should finish him. How long since someone claimed to have taken a Scintilla to death? Don't you want to know what will happen?

No, idiot. You're shortsighted. Too many impatient people have done that, killed when they could have collected. You went too far with the boy. I said to bring him in no matter what, not kill him. Daft bastard. We need him. The only thing we can do now is put him in with the women and see if they can save him.

But, Mulcarr, keep three together? Isn't that dangerous?

Trust me. It's more dangerous to let him die.

I screamed when a sharp, searing pain burned between my shoulder blades, bringing me back to the present. My hand was still on the knife at my throat so it couldn't be that. I arched my back and cried out again as a hot iron branded my skin. That was a familiar pain.

Giovanni ran forward but stopped short when Clancy yelled, "Don't be a fool. Do you want her to die right here, right now?"

My father coughed and clutched his side. I pulled my gaze from Giovanni's extreme blue stare and silver energy reaching for me like arms and shifted my head slightly to look at my dad. The blade bit into my neck as I turned. Dad's hands were bright red. He hadn't moved from his knees. But he hadn't fallen, either. That was good, right? There was a lot of blood, though, dampening his shirt. Gráinne sucked in her breath and began to cry.

"How did you find us?" Giovanni asked. "Fergus said he drugged you."

"Soul on a string. Soul on a string," Gráinne chanted from the back of the room. She had obviously returned to Crazy Land, and I wasn't sure I could blame her. This was too small a taste of freedom to have it end so soon.

"Hush now, pet," Clancy crooned to my mother. "I have you to thank for my ability, Gráinne. Astral projection is a handy power. Luckily, I was able to slip into it when my brother-in-law drugged me. You were still at my place when I went under, still within my reach. I followed you here, astrally." He smiled, sinister. "I can follow you anywhere, pet." He leaned down over me. His hand ran across my throbbing cheek. "A very affecting good-bye you gave my nephew. Near broke my heart."

I gritted my teeth and swatted his hand away. "If you had one."

Griffin pushed the knife harder against my throat. It punctured my skin, slicing a gash in my neck. Something hard settled into my collarbone. Disoriented, I reached for it, expecting to feel a piece of my white bone protruding from my skin. But my fingers instantly recognized the shape of the key.

"Don't hurt her," my father choked, the blood under his rib cage spreading into an alarming scarlet blot. "Please. I'm begging you."

Clancy stood, put his hands on his hips, and surveyed the room as if deciding what to do with all of us. Giovanni's fingers twitched against his jeans like a gunslinger.

"That's a right nasty wound you've got there," Clancy commented to my dad.

My dad's brows furrowed deeply as he worked through possible arguments, trying desperately to find a crack in Clancy he could exploit. "Money," my father gasped. "How much will it take to let us go?"

Clancy laughed. "There is no price large enough, chap. I cannot buy what a Scintilla can give me. But you *do* have something I can use."

My dad heaved forward like he'd been yanked by a giant, invisible hand. I realized then that he had. Clancy had reached inside him and dragged his colors, his beautiful colors, right out of his body in a slow, steady stream, drawing them into his own.

I struggled to free myself, but Griffin slid his knees over my shoulders, pinning me to the floor. The jagged edge of the knife pressed deeper into my throat. "Stop! Please stop," I cried. "You don't need him right now."

"No, pet. This is purely for pleasure."

My dad had that same bewildered look that Mrs. Oberman had. That the lady in the park had. Like they couldn't understand why their energy was plummeting with every weakened beat of their heart, why their vision had narrowed to a scary point of light intent on consuming them. I now knew it was like drowning slowly.

Watching it killed me. Tears as hot as the blood on my neck slid down my temples. "Please…," I sobbed. "I love you, Daddy."

"Take me!" Gráinne suddenly screamed. "Take all of me. To the death. You know what might happen, Clancy. Do it!"

"Rumors," Clancy scoffed. "Legends. And you're far more valuable to me alive than dead." Clancy grabbed a clump of my father's hair. "He's worth nothing, however. There are millions like him all over the world."

"No, no, Benito," she cried. Gráinne wept in a ball. I struggled harder against Griffin, felt another sharp nick in my skin, a stinging line of fire across my neck. And I didn't care. I needed to get to my father. I thrashed, kicked, bucked my body up against him, used every ounce of strength I had to get to my dad, all while the knife bit repeatedly into my neck. But it was useless. Griffin was too strong.

My father reached out to me. Clancy's aura exploded into white as my daddy's aura broke from his body. He fell over in a pool of his own blood. His warm body, his crimson blood, his dark eyes open, fixed on a horizon I couldn't see. The essence of him, stolen.

Gone.

"Noooo!" The word bounced around the little wooden shack. I stared up at the rafters as the screams echoed around me. My father was dead. I was numb with shock, overtaken by a pain too great to accept. The air touching my skin, the air I sucked into my lungs— every cell in my body was saturated with an all-encompassing pain. I wanted to close my eyes and sink into myself. I almost did, but the knife suddenly released from my neck, the flash of steel sailing over top of me toward Giovanni.

I expected to see the knife impale Giovanni, but the handle flew right into his outstretched hand. I tilted my head back to see Griffin standing, staring in dazed shock. I swung my legs around, heaving a kick right into his crotch, doubling him over. Giovanni lunged past me, flying through the air, sweeping down to drive the knife into Griffin's body.

I scrambled to my feet. As soon as I stood, I was paralyzed by the familiar tug on my aura. Clancy's eyes were fixed on me. His greedy white aura took up the small room. It reached for me, stronger than before. Pulled me out of myself. No matter how hard I tried, I couldn't stop it. I couldn't reel myself back in, couldn't tuck my soul away from harm.

Giovanni leaped in front of him, releasing me from the manacles of Clancy's energy. I gasped to catch my breath. Without pause or mercy, Clancy began taking from Giovanni's silver spark. He meant to weaken us all so we couldn't fight. Giovanni's body shuddered. He was already weak; he couldn't take this assault. His head slumped forward, and he fell like a crumbling wall, folding at the neck, the waist, the knees, until finally, he landed in a heap at our feet.

I raised my arm to hurl the only weapon I had, chucking the key as hard as I could.

It landed square in the middle of Clancy's forehead and bounced to the floor. He blinked, startled, and stumbled forward a bit, fingering his forehead for blood. The key lay on the floor between us. I took a quick step forward and scooped it up.

"Don't move," Clancy said, holding his hand up, palm facing me. I saw his ring. Embossed within the smooth, gold oval winked an emblem. Two pyramids, joined at their apices. The same insignia that was engraved on the key in my fist stared at me from his outstretched hand.

"Where did you get that key?" he demanded.

It had to be important. My mother had made sure this key and its secrets were buried. Until I dug them up. I glanced at her, hoping she could help me with answers, but she was still sobbing on the floor. I needed to touch Clancy's ring. I needed to know what secrets it held and if it would show me anything I might use against him. I struggled to recall the vision from the knife.

"You're afraid," I ventured. "I can see it in your aura." It was a lie. I could see nothing but white. I took another step forward. If I was going to bluff, I was going all in. "I know what you're scared of."

"Little lass, there is nothing I fear from you."

I grasped for the fragments of memory the knife contained. "You're afraid for them to know what you possess."

Clancy's eyes widened a fraction. I stepped forward again.

"I. Will. Kill. You." Clancy's lethal words puffed out in a cloud of curling black, and I knew.

I forced a smug smile onto my face. "No. You won't. And it's why Griffin didn't kill me before. You have three of us, just like you need." His eyes flew open in surprise. I could see his mind scrambling. I took another step toward his palm and the eye. One more step. It was my only hope. I was so close now. Inches.

Clancy closed his fingers over the ring and lowered his clenched fist to his side. A sigh rushed from me. What could I possibly do or say to get us out? "They're on their way here now," I spit out, desperate.

He grabbed me by the neck and squeezed. Silver sparks of energy flew off my body toward him. He sipped slowly from my aura. A cold, pressing ache radiated from my chest outward. I scrambled for the word he'd used in my vision, hoping it was the right one. "The—the *Society*." I gasped. "I contacted them. Why do you think I have this key?"

His hand dropped from my neck, and he stepped backward. His white aura retreated into his skin like a frightened animal. I didn't know who or what *the Society* was, but Clancy Mulcarr was obviously very afraid of them showing up. "They wouldn't like to find you here with three Scintilla."

Clancy surveyed the shack with a frantic look. My mother, rocking in the corner, crooning to herself; Giovanni, barely conscious but stirring; and me, strangling him with his own words. Using his secrets and his lies against him.

"I will never stop until I find you," he said as he stepped to the door. "And when I do, you three will die."

No smoky words in that statement.

And then he fled into the heavy mist.

Giovanni struggled to sit upright. I took his shoulders and blew my energy into him. Fast and frantic, I gave him whatever he needed to be a help and not a hindrance. We had to get out of here fast. I didn't fully trust that Clancy would let his prize go so easily.

"What? No kiss?" Giovanni said as he wobbled to his feet. He reached for Gráinne's hand, but she sat frozen in fear, covering her head with her arms. He picked her up and slung her over his broad shoulder, his knees buckling a moment before he steadied himself. "Come!" he shouted to me on his way toward the door with my mother flapping against his back and reaching out for my father.

I couldn't leave my dad in this place. I tugged on his arm, but he was so heavy. Too heavy. "Help me!" I screamed to Giovanni.

Fergus fell through the doorway of the shed with car keys in his hand. "I'm so sorry," he said, surveying the scene with shock. He dropped to my father's side and felt futilely for his pulse. Sympathetic eyes met mine. "I'm sorry. I went to check on Clancy. I didn't expect he'd be alert. And I didn't expect his friend to show up."

Clearly, they had fought. Fergus's cheekbone swelled and blood clung to the corners of his mouth.

Giovanni rushed back in. "We must go, Cora. Don't make me carry you out of here as well, because I will." He savagely ripped the knife from Griffin's body and wiped it clean on his pants leg.

"I can't leave him here."

"You must!"

I fell to my knees over my dad's body, adrenaline and sorrow hitting me all at once. I bowed my body over him, his blood soaking my knees. His colors gone forever.

Somewhere in my mind I heard Griffin groan on the floor. Arms gripped my waist, but I didn't fight them. I let Giovanni and Fergus pull me up. They poured me into Fergus's car, and we screeched away from the shed and down the dirt road leading toward Rising Sun Manor.

"You'll have to ditch this car very soon," Fergus said. "I'll retrieve it when it's found. There are some supplies in the trunk, and cash." We drove up to the manor, and Giovanni slid into the driver's seat when

Fergus jumped out, waving us on. "Godspeed!"

I leaned my head into the cold glass of the window and glanced over my shoulder at Gráinne, who had curled into a fetal position in the backseat. It wasn't going to be easy to be covert with her, and we needed to find a place to regroup. To recover our stolen strength. To mourn. To figure out where we could possibly go from here.

Giovanni placed his hand tenderly on my leg. "I'm so sorry, Cora."

I bit my lip and turned my head away. But something niggled at my brain. "The knife," I said. "I don't know how, but it looked like you took it from Griffin. Did he throw it at you?"

"No. He didn't throw it." I glanced at Giovanni and could see by his eyes and the way he worked his mouth that he struggled with his words. "I didn't tell you everything. It's like with the book at the library... I *pulled* it to me." When he saw me trying to understand, he added, "The Arrazi are not the only ones with special abilities. I've used mine to steal. Many times. I'm sorry I didn't tell you."

"It's okay," I whispered, glancing at the tattoo on my hand, reliving the memories that had assaulted me when I touched certain objects. I hadn't been able to look, but I knew there was a knife etched on my back. How poetic. I didn't understand why I had to be marked by the objects, but for once I was glad I had the ability to retrieve memories. That, and being able to detect the lie in Clancy's aura. It had saved our lives. This time.

"Take me home," Gráinne moaned from the back. For a second, I wondered if she meant the home she'd had for the last thirteen years or *our* home, the one that lived on in her mind all the time she'd been a prisoner. Did she imagine in her wrecked head that we could stroll through its daisy gate and red door once again? Live happily ever after?

How I wished to be home, too. Sitting on my bed, with Mari, with Dun, spread out on the floor, all of us listening to music, trashing the VIPs, complaining about Dad's strict ways. Dad...

That was another life.

This new life demanded more, so much more. If my father was right, it demanded we somehow find a way to stop the Arrazi and balance the energy in the world. Do that, all while staying out of the Arrazi's clutches and avoiding a hidden Society that even Clancy had feared. I nearly laughed to myself. One girl, one boy, and a crazy woman were supposed to fix the universe's energy? We either attempt the impossible or we spend our lives running. Hiding. More people die. And the world goes down with our cowardice.

Rain pelted the windows as we bumped down the narrow drive toward the iron gate.

"Home," Gráinne moaned again.

I swiped at a tear snaking down my face, and a new determination etched into my soul. "We don't have a home," I said. "Until this is over, there is no home for us. There is no home for the hunted."

I looked back at my mother mumbling in the backseat.

No wondrous thing was ever discovered were it not for someone brave enough to seek it.

Those words weren't just Mom's legacy. They were my father's as well. And now, mine. I wasn't done seeking answers. I refused to live my whole life running. I would not let my father die in vain. Scintilla were something beautiful in a sometimes ugly world. We were givers of light in the darkness.

I would not let the light go out on my watch.

ACKNOWLEDGMENTS

This dream would not have come true were it not for my brilliant and colorful children who made me promise to never give up. They motivate me every day to prove by example that anything is possible if you know who you are, know your truth, and dedicate yourself entirely. Sydney and Cooper, I love you. Promise me you'll do the same.

Dear Patrick, I thank you from the bottom of my heart. Our paths will always run parallel. I love you and am grateful for all you've given.

My mother, Yvon, who always encouraged me to be colorful and strong, and to use my voice. This business requires all three, and I'm so appreciative.

The Tribe—Monica (Jo) Bogue, Mary Claire Bouchér, and Lucy Hunter. In one form or another, you three are in *all* my pages. I love you, sisters of my heart. And to my dear Tribettes—Samantha, Sierra, Makenzie, Sydney, Sage, and wee one—you are who I write for. I hope you feel understood.

My wise and wonderful agent, Michael Bourret, who believed even before I truly did. And my editor, Karen Grove, whose words

"This book haunts me" will go down as one of my all-time favorite compliments. Huge thanks to the entire Entangled team for bringing my books to life.

Deep, everlasting gratitude to Ellen Hopkins and Susan Hart Lindquist, who've been unwavering mentors and friends, for believing in me, pushing me, and guiding me. Thank you for always saying, "Not if, but *when*." You've helped me grow in so many ways. I adore you.

I received invaluable editorial insight from dear colleagues and friends, Lorin Oberweger, Jackie Garlick, Eric Elfman, and Lia Keyes. Each of you, in your own ways, helped me to see a better way to tell a story and that knowledge will carry forward forever. Thank you.

I owe so much to SCBWI and to my Nevada SCBWI family. I'm certain this would have taken years longer without your support and friendship. The Criterati emerged from this clan! For years of critiques, beta reads, and sanity maintenance, my sincere thanks to Heather Petty, Chris Ledbetter, and Julie Dillard. You've taught me so much. I am indebted to so many people who've read my words and have shared their words with me over the years. Too many to name, but each written on my heart.

A special thanks to Tony Bates who handed me the right books at the right time.

Jason Roer, my cohort and conspirator. Thank you for your boundless enthusiasm for my work and for your constant love and support. You see, really see, my true colors. And I see yours. It's beautiful. 333.

Finally, to the writers, published and unpublished, who inspire me with their creativity and passion. You light my way.